C. L. DONLEY

Finding Camille

an historical bwwm romance

Contents

Winter, 1943

My dearest Carl:

You must humor me, my dear. By now, I have learned that you are unable to write me back now. That I will never receive another letter from you. Not by your own will, but by that of God, since he has seen fit to take you home instead of reuniting us. Nevertheless, I have to do the only thing that is in my power to do, the one thing I have done for these many months, and that is to write.

And so, my lovely handsome Carl, I will take it upon myself to say goodbye. I pray that your death was clean and swift, and gave you a sense of peace and purpose. It was a hope and a joy to have known you. Had I known that our love wasn't meant to blossom, the first time I laid eyes on you at my lovely Donna's wedding, I want you to know that I would not have done anything differently. I am glad that you parted the crowd to dance with little old me. You gave me the hope that a handsome soldier would be my future. And most of all, I am glad that I could be the one you carried in your heart while you were over there in the dirt. Thank you, my dear. The gratitude I feel is beyond belief.

Yours,
Camille

To the fianceé of Carl Downey, Camille Winters:

My company just received a letter that was meant for
Lance Corporal Carl Downey. The captain thought it fit to
pass the letter along to me, as I was Carl's closest friend
and colleague.

It's unlikely that you know me, but my name is 1st Lt.
Stanley Whitman. I spent many a night in the trenches
with your fiancé stationed here in the Pacific. We bonded
side by side in battle, before we knew a thing about each
other. In the quiet lulls, which weren't scarce, we laughed
and told hometown stories and made future plans out
of desperate hope. He was the brightest light in our
company, full of life and passion. As much as Carl's death
is a loss for you, it is an even greater loss for us, who relied
on Carl's effervescence to get us through this horrible war,
and his humanity to remind us what we fight for.

I felt compelled to write to you and tell you that I am
the one who opened your letter, and I'm not ashamed
to say that it made me weep openly. Not only because
of your expression of love and loss, but of strength and
gratitude. You must understand that as much as Carl
was the engine that propelled our company each and
every day for thirteen months, you were the engine that
propelled Carl. When one of your letters arrived, he greatly
cherished them. He was distressed when your picture
went missing while we were stationed on the Augusta.

When you managed to send him a replacement he was right as rain, and transformed into our fearless comrade.

And so, I would like to thank you, Ms. Winters, for loving our Lance Corporal. After suffering heavy losses that I will not bother you with, your letter arrived as though nothing had happened. And when opened it had the same heartrending affect on all of us. You are the secret to his legacy and bravery.

With respect,

Lt. Stanley Whitman.

March 4, 1943

Dear Lt. Whitman,

I can't tell you how much it meant to receive your letter. Thank you so much for your kind words. When the Marines informed me that Carl was killed in battle I felt as if I had suddenly been severed from the ground and floated away like a balloon in the wind. It dawned on me that I did not prepare myself as well as some of the other mothers and sisters and wives who are also waiting for their beloveds to return. Perhaps because ours was such a new and fanciful love. We met right before he left for the Pacific and he urged me to write to him.

I wasn't entirely certain he was even real for half of our relationship. He'd had to convince me of his adoration through letters, and of his desire to receive mine. Even still I remained paranoid that it was the drama of war that compelled him to remember me as more than I was.

So I found special comfort in the portion of your letter where you mentioned his reaction to receiving my picture. He told me as much, but it has been my brief experience with Carl that he tended to warm everyone in his path with light as though he were the sun. I am happy to know that his adoration of me was apparent to those around him, even while the confirmation also rouses my unspeakable sadness and self-pity. I continue to pray that his company returns home safe and unharmed, and full of stories of their beloved fallen friend.

Sincerely,
Camille

April 4, 1943

Dearest Camille,

I've included some personal effects of Carl and thought you might like to have them. They are trivial things here amid a war, so they will not last long: a hairbrush, razor, his grandfather's timepiece, his favorite magazines. Our squad leader frowns upon carrying excess weight, but I did not see fit to throw them away.

With love,
Stanley W.

April 20, 1943

Dearest Stanley,

You are adorable! I hesitate to tell you that most of what you sent me is considered trivial for civilians as well. I'm sorry that they won't allow you to carry remnants of your friends, but since I am not a man in war, I cannot judge the appropriateness. I was glad to receive the timepiece that seems to be a precious heirloom. I will return it to his *family. I'm sure they would be glad to have it.*

P.S. In the time it has taken me to mail this letter, I've visited Carl's family. I told them that I would pass on their gratitude for thoughtfully returning the family heirloom, even though it garnered many tears and anguish at the sight of it returning to them without its former owner. They urged me to have it, but the notion was so off-putting since I hardly knew Carl in the manner that everyone around me had, including you. It all reminds me of how fleeting life is and even moreso our love was. The letters were a promise of love, ultimately miscarried. It's as though I am forced to birth a child dead in its womb, and care for it until the grief of everyone around me has subsided. As it is, I feel like a charlatan, having taken such a place in his life in his passing. Still, I am grateful that everyone has humored me and recited the fantastic plans he made on our behalf and circulated beyond me. I hope that whatever else you find of Carl's, you feel entitled to keep and that it brings you the solace needed to see this war to its hopefully swift end.

Your friend,
Camille

May 20, 1943

My friend Camille,
It was serendipitous timing that I received your letter when I did, because I have to admit that there was one thing I did not include in Carl's belongings, and that was the cache of letters that he kept of yours. I hesitated because I wondered whether someone would want their

own words returned to them. Some of them I practically know by heart because Carl liked to often re-read them, as he was taken with your poetic way with words. They had a peculiar calming effect on him, especially amidst the bloody horrors that turn men cold and apathetic of everything. He lamented that he didn't have the breadth of attention to take the time to sit down, gather his thoughts and thoughtfully write to you as often as you did to him, but he was grateful.

It was your sweet soul, your idealistic hope of your eventual reunion that inspired him, and so it pains me to hear you speak of yourself the way you do, as if it were foolish to expect the future to deliver the things it promised. It's not you who are foolish but the world, that sees fit to deprive young men of the delight of companionship and the contentment that comes with a life well-built. Even now, it's hard to imagine that Carl will become the memories and myths of others. I predicted plain as day that he would be an old man surrounded by his children.

Forgive me for the dismal subject matter. You may have the impression that I have an unhealthy fixation on these topics, but I assure you that nostalgia has no place in our daily lives. We rarely have the chance to contemplate the men whose tags we recover. As I have no one in my life who would miss me if I was dead, it is a kindness from God to have received these few correspondences.

I ask you to indulge me taking those hopes that you so eloquently referred to in your letter to heart, by not taking offense to my keeping your letters. And that you would allow me to hope to one day return the letters to you in person. Ideally, you will have caught the eye of some other great man who adores you by then, and the memory of Carl will be a fond recollection that you freely share with joy. In that hopeful day both of us will be whole, and letters between two mutual acquaintances will have returned to its rightfully trivial place in the world.

Sincerely,
Stanley

June 6th, 1943

Stanley,
It seems I am not the only one who has a way with words. I hope someone has told you that you certainly have a long career ahead of you as a writer. By all means, if my letters can continue to carry purpose and meaning for someone else, then please keep them. I would also like to meet the recipient of such a hope, but I must tell you that the thought of receiving yet another correspondence, potentially about your death, gives me an irrational sense of caution! What if I find my letters are simply bad luck?

Camille

June 22, 1943

Camille,
Your letters could never be bad luck. I watched them first hand bring faith and verve to a hopeless situation. If Carl's death were destined, he simply had no idea of it and I am convinced that is because of you. As it is, there is no one to receive word of my time here, and after reading your fears, I don't think I would have the heart to have someone send word of my untimely death. But if

by chance I make it home safely, do I have permission to pass on the happy news to someone who would receive it?

   Stanley

July 8th, 1943

   Stanley,

   It would give me a great thrill to know that out of all of the dismal outcomes of this war that you have made it home safe, wherever that is, so please inform me when that happens. Also, I hope it is not too forward to suggest that in the meantime, it would be no inconvenience for you to receive letters of your own, you need only to ask. If one wants to receive a letter, one must simply write!

   Camille

1

Present Day, 1954

Camille Winters looked in the bathroom mirror of her Brooklyn brownstone, her evening routine abuzz with the excitement of the day to come. She always got excited the night before a new assignment, but that was because she was a bit of a square.

This wasn't just any secretary's job, however. This was Madison Avenue.

Working for Hargrove & Chase was the most exciting assignment she'd gotten in many years. And apparently, she'd been requested.

She wasn't told by whom, which was uncommon. She supposed she could ask, but she didn't get paid to ask. She got paid to do what she was told and do it well.

She'd been working off of recommendations for the past five years, so that was nothing new. But this was the first time she'd been pulled off of one job to work another. Which meant the person who requested her was fairly high up on the totem pole.

But the buzz was even more than that, though she fought to ignore it. In her mind she was successful. But her body couldn't

1

lie.

She had a feeling that she had been requested by Kenneth Hargrove himself.

Bzzz bzzzz....

For one, it was the only explanation. He was the only person she'd met from Hargrove & Chase after all, briefly while on assignment at a car dealership where Mr. Hargrove had come in to buy a car for the family.

He had been warm and doting to his children, a boy, and girl, each in their Sunday best. The wife seemed terribly frosty— odd but not surprising.

She'd been used to seeing prominent people at the Cadillac dealership, so she noted him and his family the same way she would any VIP. He'd acknowledged her with a simple head nod and a faint grin when she seated them.

It wasn't much, but it was by far her clearest and strongest connection to the company. Camille smiled in the mirror, re-acquainting herself with the story.

Bzz bzzzzzzzz...

The buzz was in no way sexual, but it may as well have been. In an industry full of sharks, commendation on her quality of work was the only kind she was permitted to enjoy.

Few men had given her something close to that type of buzz in her personal life. One even became her steady. Jeremy. And he was sufficient enough. But he'd objected to her working life, especially for that of white people, and that was that.

Once she became consumed with her work, she was surrounded by industry titans in tailored suits day and night, which gave her less and less time to go out and find the buzz of that other kind.

In the beginning, a few of her bosses complimented her looks in passing. An attempt at open rapport, she assumed. Young women like to hear such things, was probably their reasoning. She always smiled politely, but it had the unfortunate effect of either getting her yelled at by her female bosses or re-assigned.

It took her a while to catch on. Being still unmarried in her late 20's, she'd had to learn these female patterns the hard way.

She had to assume they felt threatened in some fashion, which she tried not to dwell on. Catching the eye of some drunken white man with a sudden urge to experiment was her ultimate nightmare, not a dream come true.

So she trained herself to stop smiling at such compliments. For years she walked a fine line of looking plain but not unattractive. Unassuming but representative of the company. Placid but approachable.

Now she was nearly 30. In her old age, she'd become less of a threat to the younger white women at her assignments, and more impatient with incompetence on all levels. Yet to her shock, this seemed to cause her working relationships to flourish. She was good at her job, and people noticed.

For her first day at Hargrove & Chase, she wanted to exude professionalism, rather than power. Her simple black fit and flair Dior dress with matching purse and gloves would do the trick. It was pressed and already hanging on the open closet door of her bedroom.

She placed the last of the rollers in her freshly pressed hair and laid gingerly on her pillow that night. It was only 7:30, but she knew she would toss and turn, and she needed her rest if she was going to be fresh tomorrow.

She waited patiently outside the offices the next morning, 30 minutes before her first day of work was to begin. She scanned the wall of artwork hanging in the lobby. Artwork that was

3

their previous campaigns, numerous and instantly recognizable. Name brands of household items, clothing, and hotel chains.

Just then a young woman approached the receptionist's desk. She looked over at Camille sitting patiently in the lobby.

"Miss Winters?" she asked, sounding surprised.

"Miss Caldwell," Camille assumed in a mature voice, a deep velvety contrast to Christy's cheerful squeak. She stood, ready to meet her open hand.

Christy Caldwell was to be her supervisor on this job. She was short and compact, blonde and blue-eyed. Her eyes perfectly matched her peacock blue dress, her blonde hair like a perfect pastry sitting atop her shoulders.

"Please, call me Christy," she smiled. "You're early!" she added, verbatim of every first meeting she'd ever had.

"If you're on time, you're late, Miss Caldwell," Camille said without a smile. It was customary for Camille to comply with a supervisor's request to use her first name only after the third ask and not before.

Camille followed Christy through the glass doors of the office and past the receptionist, who she could see out of the corner of her eye following their every move. The front lobby at Hargrove and Chase hid from view the largest open office space she'd ever been in. The entire floor was theirs, an endless rectangle of corners and office doors.

"I trust you understand that this will be a temporary placement? Until the work is done?"

"Temporary placements are the only kind I take, Miss Caldwell."

"Perfect. Let me show you to your office," Christy said politely.

Office?

4

"I presume you mean my desk, Miss Caldwell."

"Christy, please," she blushed. "You've been at this longer than I have. I was told you have managerial experience. And some accounting."

"Of course, but I'm used to proving myself. I'm certainly not here to replace anyone."

"Nonsense, this is advertising," Christy scoffed. "Everyone loves the madness, but no one's competing to make sense of it. You won't be in anyone's way, I assure you."

They followed one of two carpeted walkways down the middle of the lobby where there was an ocean of desks, mostly occupied. Nearly everyone stopped to look at the pair of them as though she were a well-dressed giraffe.

Nothing Camille hadn't dealt with before. Her honey-toned skin in the context of white society created a mental puzzle that had to be solved right away. She pretended not to notice as she followed closely behind Christy until they got to a narrow hallway that diverted into three other directions. Christy brought her to an abandoned windowless room with papers stacked to the ceiling on top of two desks shaped like an L.

A typewriter with its cover collected dust in the corner. There were two doors on either side to make it accessible from two separate hallways.

Her very own office?? What was going on.

"What's this?"

"This... is what we like to call A-L. Job bags, logo files, film, and negatives from all of our campaigns from 1935 to the present, up to L. And occasionally the supply closet for those secretaries too lazy to go beyond the front lobby.

"I see."

"We waste hundreds of billable hours simply looking for

5

previous work. Creative calls it the landfill. I endure it. I've even started to learn my way around."

"And you need someone to organize it."

"More than that. We need a liaison. Someone between Creative and Accounts to keep it all straight. So that all I have to worry about is Mr. Hargrove."

"You're Mr. Hargrove's girl?"

"Correct. I report directly to him and you'll report directly to me. Ideally, all the girls will come to you for all their daily needs, eventually. So? What do you think?"

"Well, Miss Caldwell..."

"Christy."

"Well, Christy... I must tell you I can't wait to get started."

"Perfect. Your references were outstanding. They tell me you work just as hard as the boys."

"Harder, I assure you."

"Very well," Christy laughed. "I usually take my lunch at my desk, so ring me anytime if you need me."

"I take it Mr. Hargrove is rarely seen in the office?"

"Only for quarterly meetings or if he's bringing clients to the conference room, of course. Rarely on this side of the building. Nothing you'll need to be worried about. You'll have a good view on the way to the Creative Director's office, but other than that, no."

Christy sighed, adopting an air of confidence. "You've been at this for some time, Camille, I'm sure I don't need to tell you. Only speak when spoken to and all that. And that includes clientele. Refer guests to one of the girls and come directly to me with questions. The girls are easy to overwhelm."

"Of course."

"Also, I have to say you're a bit overdressed. Surely they didn't put *you* out front at Cadillac?"

Camille brushed off the backward-facing insult. She wasn't sure, but she was confident Christy was referring to her being colored.

"The men were a bit more out front than the girls were, I'm afraid. They liked to see a potential sale before the door chimed."

"I see. Well here, there's no need to worry about... first impressions," Christy smiled. "I'd feel awfully guilty if something happened to that beautiful dress, where on Earth did you get it?"

"Dior. One of my bosses' wives handed it down to me," Camille lied. "You needn't worry about me, Miss Caldwell. As you said, I've been at this some time. I know how to blend in."

"Thank goodness," Christy sighed. "I've never had to have such a conversation before. I must say, I was dreading it. I had no idea how this was going to go. We don't get a lot of negroes on the 16th floor who aren't working the elevator."

Camille let out a breath unconsciously when her suspicions were openly confirmed.

"I can imagine. But I've been doing temp work in the city for five years. I know how to be seen little and heard even less."

Christy put out her hand for Camille to shake, equal parts guilt and respect.

"Welcome to Hargrove and Chase, Miss Winters."

"Thank you, Christy."

* * *

"You look stunning."

"Thank you," Camille smiled. Her hair was more professional than flirty in a pulled-back curly pompadour from her earlier

7

interview.

Her Dior could easily go from day to night. She barely needed the heavy coat on this oddly warm November evening.

"So do you," Camille dared to add. Lawrence gave her a surprised chuckle.

Lawrence was tall, dark, and handsome just as her sister had promised, and had that bizarre problem attractive men sometimes have where they end up bachelors for far too long, paralyzed by their choices.

It was her first blind date in years but she was pleasantly optimistic. She was a little older now and knew what she wanted. Or rather, what she didn't want. She kept her expectations at bay.

"Did you have any trouble finding the place?" he asked.

"Not at all."

"You should've let me pick you up."

Camille smiled. "Nonsense, I was already downtown. Why put you out?"

Lawrence was Donna's idea, one of her three sisters.

Donna was a toffee color, the darkest of all the girls, with reddish-brown hair that the rest of them envied. She got looks from every type of man there was and looked good in every shade of lipstick.

She'd only been married a few years to her husband Anthony. Lawrence was Anthony's co-worker at St. Mary's Catholic Hospital.

"So, how did the interview go?" Lawrence urged her.

"You know about that?"

"Your sister tells Anthony everything. And Anthony tells me everything."

"I see," she smiled. "It went about how I expected. I got the job."

"Good for you. Whereabouts?"

"Madison Avenue. An advertising firm called Hargrove and Chase."

"I'm scared a' you," Lawrence crooned. Camille cracked a smile then shrugged.

"Just a secretary job, you know. Nothing they wouldn't have another colored girl doing. Although I may be the first there, who knows."

"Pay's good?"

"Better than my last one."

Lawrence leaned in a bit playfully. "Then that's all that matters."

"I'll drink to that."

"What are you having?"

"I'll have a gimlet."

He summoned over the waiter with a long arm and the nudge of his immaculate jaw, in an elegant fashion that made Camille re-evaluate him. He'd ordered for the two of them, which she hadn't seen a man do ever. She didn't know how she felt about it.

"Apologies if I rushed the order, but I came straight from the hospital and I'm famished."

"So how do you work with Lawrence again?" she small-talked.

"I don't actually work with Lawrence in a traditional sense. I'm not a medical technician."

Camille turned her neck a bit in curiosity. "No?"

"No. I'm a doctor. A surgeon, to be precise."

"Really?" Camille stopped mid-sip, intrigued.

She should've been smitten at that very moment. Should've

been flattered.

A whole black doctor had agreed to go on a date with little old her? Plenty of beautiful girls fresh out of high school who would gladly pop out his babies out of sheer adoration.

Unfortunately, all she could think about was how much he probably worked and how he would eventually want her to quit working. They always do.

"Steak tips and chicken kiev for the lady?" they were suddenly interrupted.

"My, that was fast."

"Looks good," Lawrence dug in.

"Careful, it's hot," the old black waiter warned, careful not to stain his spotless white gloves.

"You seem shocked," he noted.

"I'm sure you're used to it," Camille replied.

Lawrence gave her a gleaming smile as he used his steak knife. "I am. I must admit I was shocked when Anthony said his sister-in-law was not yet married."

"I know spinsters have been in short supply after the war."

He laughed through his bite and then retrieved a napkin. "I would have liked to find a wife while I was in my residency but the hours were grueling. Plenty of my class found wives but I found it cruel. You can't even provide for the poor girl yet, let alone be awake at the same time. As it was, she never materialized so I had nothing to worry about."

"You're very candid, Lawrence."

He finished a sip of his coffee. "You don't like it?"

"No, I love it," she smiled to herself. He observed it across the table, harboring one of his own.

"I think when you get to be our age, you owe it to the world to be candid."

10

"*Our* age?" Camille raised an eyebrow as she performed her own surgery on her kiev.

"I told you Anthony tells me everything," he muttered with a charming look.

Camille sighed in familial exasperation, rolling her eyes. Lawrence laughed.

"I would've found out eventually," he assured her.

"You're saying I look my age?"

"Not at all. Are you saying I look mine?"

Camille's food was finally arranged well enough to dig in. She took a carefully coordinated bite of chicken, broccoli, and buttered rice.

"Everyone knows it doesn't work like that on men. Of course, you must look your age, you've earned every ounce of it."

"Men may be allowed to age more gracefully at first but in the end, the old woman takes the lead," he argued.

"You think so?"

"Absolutely. The old woman rules us all."

Camille's prep had paid off. Within a few bites they were caught up. She piled the latest one on her fork.

"Only if she has children. Otherwise, her life is seen as a burdensome waste," she opined.

"Well. I wouldn't go so far as that. But I do admit it is a sight to see. An old woman, coming into this world as one. Now is three, seven. Twelve or more. My great grandmother has thirty-four grandchildren if you can imagine it."

"Mine only has five, poor thing."

"You don't see yourself as burdensome, do you?" he asked, curious.

She tried not to focus on the way he held his utensils, which also happened to be steady and regal. She knew surgery and

11

eating steak were not the same. And yet.

"No. Not yet, anyway. I've always liked to earn my way. Perhaps by some miracle that will always be possible in some fashion. My mother thinks I'm mad, of course. She raised us all to be wives and mothers."

"Anthony tells me you were once engaged. To an army man," he casually interjected.

Camille chewed while she thought of the best way to broach the subject. "A Marine to be precise. Honestly, I don't know what to call it. He proposed, that's true. But we barely knew each other. I was certainly taken with him. We wrote letters. But he died about six months in."

"I was drafted but they rejected me because I had flat feet. I felt like I'd gotten a second chance at life."

Lawrence suddenly stopped cutting his meat as if he realized what he'd just said.

"...I'm so sorry."

Camille gave him a shrug of absolution. "You weren't wrong. At the time, we all expected it to be over within months."

"It really was a massacre, wasn't it?" he openly opined.

Camille's gaze drifted to the candlelight dancing in the centerpiece. "Sometimes I can't bear to think of all the brave men that war has yanked out of this world."

"Not to mention an economic depression."

"Was it bad where you were?" she asked.

"I was here. My father left us. To find work. It was a dark time. You?"

"My father has a lucrative job with the government. Land surveying, specifically. Work slowed down but he had a nest egg. We tightened our belts, of course, like everyone else but still. Had to hide how well we were doing compared."

"One of the lucky ones."

"Indeed. When my fiancee was killed it felt... morbidly over-due. So much tragedy."

"All in a little over fifty years. Our century is doomed."

Camille tilted her head. "A bit cynical for a surgeon."

He huffed. "All of us are cynical. It's General Medicine who are the optimists."

"I suppose holding people's organs in your hands can get a little dull," she replied.

Lawrence looked up to see her diligently hacking at her kiev and couldn't tell if it was sarcasm or not. After a bit of silence, he had to laugh.

"This date isn't going very well is it?"

Camille smiled but didn't directly answer.

"I honestly don't know what people expect from coordinating a date for two people that didn't have a hand in it."

"To married people, everyone is one-half of a perfect match."

"They didn't do a poor job, to be fair. You're probably the most handsome man I've ever been on a date with. And who wouldn't want a surgeon in the family?"

"And you're as beautiful as they said. More beautiful. Clever. Mature. Would you like another?"

Camille shook her head as she sipped her watered-down drink. "It wasn't going as bad as you thought it was," she quietly mused.

"But you admit it was indeed going badly," Lawrence grinned.

"No, you're lovely," she smiled. "But I don't think I have the heart to give you what you want. Nor do you for me."

"You assume that you know what I want," he said with a flirtatious stare.

Camille felt heat between her thighs as she reached into her

13

cigarette case. More than she'd felt in ages. "Got a light?"

"I don't smoke."

She retrieved her lighter and used it with a sophisticated air. It gave her time to properly assess him. She blew a cloud of smoke away from the booth before she began:

"You want to be a husband, as soon as possible. A father. You want to empty your bank account and buy her a house big enough that she can tend it by herself, maybe afford her a little help. You'll come home late, and sporadically, but you will always come home. And she'll always be there waiting. Grateful. Smiling."

He sat back and wiped his mouth with his napkin, watching her take another drag of her cigarette. A nasty habit, but nothing looked sexier.

"You think it's obscene," he deduced.

"No no, I think it's perfectly reasonable. If I were you, I'd want the very same."

"I hope whoever she is, she's built like you."

Camille gave him an amused look as her cigarette tip glowed orange in her mouth. "My model is still being made faithfully. You must be looking in the wrong places."

"P.S. 13?"

Camille laughed, tastefully balancing her drink and her cigarette in hand.

"You're bad," she teased.

"She even comes with a sense of humor," he grinned. Somewhat mournfully. If she wasn't how she was, he might've proposed this very night.

"You never got engaged again? After?"

"I'm both light-skinned and uppity, Lawrence. I'm only going to get so many takers, especially in the city."

"Light-skinned and uppity are the same thing, Camille," he replied with a deadpan expression.

Camille's smile curled unconsciously. She took another drag. "Where do you live? I'm not going to marry you but I would still like to continue this date."

"Bronx. I'm not going to marry you, but I'd like to smear that lipstick a little."

Camille felt a little shock to her middle, glad to be smoking right now. "I don't know about that."

"What would it take?" he asked in a low rumble.

Camille finished her drink in one gulp. "You'd have to do everything completely right from this moment forward. I don't think you could manage."

Lawrence gave her the intense gaze of a learned man with steady hands and concentration that lasts for hours.

He leaned back and said: "Let me at least try. Waiter? Two more please."

2

Summer, 1943

July 24, 1943

Lovely Camille,

By your permission, I will endeavor to kick off our first official correspondence as friends. My name is Stanley Whitman. I was born an only child in Mobile, AL in 1920, a fantastic year to be born by all accounts. The Depression was unkind to our family, as it was to many. I watched my father build our lives back one brick at a time by the sweat of his brow in an industry that was alien to him. I have heard word since my time here in the Pacific that he has died.

Death does a funny thing to the mind. The admiration that I feel for him now that his life is finished is crippling. I can't say that I ever loved my father. Like most fathers, he was a cold planet. And my mother was the sun. My heart hurts for her more than anything. I fear that the older I get, the more I will live life, contemplate my father, and ultimately love him. And then I will be sad, and long for his companionship the way that I came into this world longing for it. And that would be unbearable.

But I've drifted into dismal territory again, haven't I? I must confess, writing aligns my thoughts and emotions in a way that I have come to look forward to while I also dread. And yet, once exorcised, the monotony and uselessness of duty dull the senses like an anesthetic. I would send you the compensation due a head-shrinker if I had money.

At any rate, before I enlisted I was a man with no purpose or honor. Or friends. I now have all of these things at heavy cost. Though death can easily sweep away all of my gains as it has already begun to.

I don't know whether it is better to hang onto gratitude or apathy. I don't know whether or not I should tell you that I have the reputation of being good-looking. It's something I heard a lot in my house and among my parents' friends but now I'm convinced of the truth in it.

The men in my regiment have never been outside of the U.S., and find the reception they get from women of all nationalities a shocking and intriguing thing. I seem to have taken Carl's place as the handsome chap responsible for acquiring girls for the rest of the regiment once we go on leave in Australia in two weeks. But I must tell you that my heart is not in it. It's a shame, because I know in two weeks no one will be in the mood for my complaints. Carl was blessed with a gregarious manner that I couldn't begin to emulate. I have no idea how to be myself.

I'm as dreadful at describing myself as I am living it. I'd much rather hear about you, though I must confess that I come into this communication knowing a great deal more about you through your letters to Carl. If there is something you'd like to know I will gladly divulge. I eagerly anticipate whatever details about yourself you wish to include. I hope you are well.

Stanley

August 12, 1943

Dear Stanley,

If you have been reading my letters to Carl, then you know a bit about my life already. I finally graduated from secretary school in Brooklyn and I have taken an assignment at the high school where I just recently gradu-ated. I know everyone there of course and the atmosphere is pleasant. A few of them also knew Carl and what happened to him. The pity in their eyes has finally subsided but now I'm afraid that they have signed me up for endless blind dates. I tell them that I simply am not ready to move on at this time and they are respectful. When in truth, I simply have no interest in most men. They all seem silly and disingenuous. With the exception of perhaps my father and of course, Carl. Carl was an exception because he was exceptional, as you know.

I have to tell you, that the part in your letter where you have finally discovered your good looks makes me laugh over and over. I don't think I've ever heard of a person who didn't know they were handsome, even after being told. It makes me want to request a picture just to be in on the joke, but I know you have no way of providing that without great strenuousness to you so I won't. I am happy to imagine.

I have to say that for me it has been the opposite. I've

always been quite fond of my reflection, but was taught early on that I had no right to be so. Then as I grew older it seemed more and more that people started to take my side again. It taught me a lesson that people can't always be trusted to see what you see. And how not to doubt myself ever again.

I hope for the sake of your men that you do your duty to boost their morale. You should make love as much as you can and help others to as well. You must leave the real world behind while it is in your power. Do it for Carl and for me.

All the best,
Camille

September 22, 1943

Camille,
It does my heart good all the way from here to know that I have made you laugh over and over. I don't know why, but it surprised me to hear you speak the way you spoke about shore leave in your last letter. You will be pleased to discover that I did exactly that, as we were in good spirits for those two weeks which were far too brief.

There was no need for me to rely on my good looks, in case you were wondering. When we arrived we were given a massive reception that we did not expect. We had been marooned on a God-forsaken beach in the middle of the ocean for months and assumed we were alone in the world. But it turned out that everyone there had heard of our exploits. We got to see that the outside world is attentive and full of patriotism, which did wonders for our spirits that had been sorely tested in the last campaign.

We ate and drank and had our fair share of women. Many of them had never seen black men before, and coupled with the fact that the Australian army have been occupied in Africa, the women eagerly welcomed our attention, much to the dismay of the MP's and kiwi soldiers there that attempted to keep their eye on us. But that hardly stopped the women from finding us wherever we were. They were lovely, and more welcoming in general than America in certain places. One of us has even gotten engaged, though I do feel pity for the young lady that will now pray every day for his safe return. She reminded me much of you.

As indelicate as it sounds, I was hoping to find a girl that resembled you. But I could find no smiles to equal yours. Australia doesn't have much in the way of variety, as you might expect. I did find an Italian woman whose family had moved to Australia when their home was destroyed under Mussolini. And she was lovely and promised to write to me. But there were no colored women there, which I would have preferred.

As sweet as it was, the knowledge that war was waiting for us was ever-present, and eventually we preferred to go back where things were certain. When your letter came, I took it as a great sign that arrived just in time. There was a tragedy that took place that very day that I won't go into now, or ever. Just know that it has taken many weeks for me to put into words what I felt the moment I received your letter, which was gratitude. It was a much-needed levity.

I can think of nothing else to say. Do write me again.
Yours,

Stanley

November 21, 1943

Stanley,

So strange to think of life as a series of Thanksgivings. Two Thanksgivings ago I was alone, and one Thanksgiving ago I had the romantic promise of true love, a promise of joining a large and loving family, like in one of those TV shows. A black version. And now I'm worse off than I was two Thanksgivings ago.

My mother prepares the works. Her mother immigrated to New York from Guyana so we always have an international spread after a fashion. Roti and cook-up rice and lamb. Pepper pot. My father's from Alabama too, I meant to tell you. I don't know how, but he manages to find a whole hog to roast. We have ham hocks for the entire holiday season, all the way until black-eyed peas for New Year's. It's enough to make me feel bad for every Jew in a ten-mile radius.

I've picked this letter up after a few days and I now think maybe it's cruel to make you hungry like this. But then I thought, if you don't get any letters from home, it would be a nice thing to hear about regular life. Do they celebrate Thanksgiving there in the Pacific? Carl never sent me the details on being stationed in "the Pacific" if that even still meant the U.S. I couldn't tell if it was for the sake of secrecy or to keep me from worrying that he was in the thick of it. From your description of the valiant reception you received in Australia, I assume you were speaking of Guadalcanal.

I pray for your safety every day and that no letter gets

sent off to you in vain.
   Camille

                                    December 15, 1943

   Dear Camille,
   *Your letter made me smile. It made me think of you
alone at a crowded family Thanksgiving table. Surrounded by friends and family but still lonely. Not that
your loneliness makes me smile but it puts me in your
shoes which are somewhere other than here.*

   *I shouldn't complain so much. It is dreadful here, but I
cannot honestly say that I am depressed. I am surrounded
by nothing but family now, for instance. Though I once
felt the way you must feel now. And did not think there
was ever a place for me in this world.*

   *Your food descriptions were pure torture. I read them
every day. I don't know what pepper pot is, but it sounds
like something English that involves gelatin and potted
meat juice. And of course, pepper. I would love to eat that
about now.*

   *I don't know what cook-up rice is, and even though
I've had my fill of rice to last a lifetime I have to admit
that I am fixated on it. I imagine that it is rice mixed will
all manner of things, not just protein. Maybe vegetables.
Or something else exotic like fruit or nuts or capers or any
number of things I haven't seen in months.*

   *I thought we would be going back to Australia for
respite but they shipped us off right away to another
island, this one more miserable than the last, which I did
not think possible. It is as though the Japs have stopped
fighting us directly and have sent their natural climate*

to do their bidding. It has not stopped raining. There are rats everywhere. Crabs making their homes in all of your holes. The mud rots our shoes and toenails away. It is more trying than seeing your comrades littered all over the beach. While I am not so depressed I am part of a minority. Some of us have become completely vacant, simply waiting for death and with no care for life.

I am thankful that I have your letters to feed me, while other men have no such thing. It puts a smile on my face to think of you longing for your deceased love, morbid as it may sound. You are just so lovely in every way. Even the way that you mourn for him. Filled with such dignity.

If it hasn't become apparent by now, I have a very real crush on you. I know some man will one day wipe your tears and it both comforts me and tears me apart. It makes me want to survive this war and come to you. It makes me want to face the blackest of despairs with hope and use whatever is lying around to spear through the heart of every enemy that prolongs my time here. I promise that whatever happens if God sees fit to spare my life, I will come find the benevolent writer of these life-saving letters and ask her to dance with me.

To answer your question, we are stationed in a part of the Pacific outside of U.S. territories. Some of the married men in the regimen have come up with their own special code to send their wives the details of our missions but it seems the military has caught on. But if I were to guess, I'd say Carl was simply trying to spare you the worry. From the little I have gathered from your letters, it seems to me his fears were unfounded. You don't seem like a girl given to hysterics. Though sometimes a man likes to imagine

23

such things, so that he can be the one to give comfort.

Affectionately,

Stanley

December 23, 1943

Stanley,

It will be long past Christmas unfortunately before you get my package, but please know I tried everything to get this to you in time, though I admit the idea came to me too late. I hope you enjoy the molasses cookies my mother included, which should keep well enough in transit. I don't have the patience to wait for a response so I will send you another letter in the meantime.

Lo and behold, once I began this letter, a new one freshly arrived. It must be fate! It baffles me that in the conditions you describe that you would even have the presence of mind to write letters, let alone the resources. I have nothing to say in response to your current conditions because I simply can't conceive of it, even with your vivid description. And I think it would be disgraceful to say that I could. Instead, I will stick to the things that I can conceive of, which is my tedious life.

In regards to your invitation to one day dance together, would like that very much. Your idolization makes me uncomfortable, as Carl's once did. But since you are a virtual stranger, I feel an odd lack of inhibition to simply tell you as much. But I understand that these times have turned young men intense, and as uncomfortable as it is, I can't say that I hate it. Only that it is different.

I have a bit of a strange mind, you may as well know. Sometimes I wonder if I am somehow manifesting these *letters to myself. Or if some strange neighbor with morbid fantasies is merely toying with me in his spare time. It amuses me to think that you could not be real. It is oddly... titillating to entertain that you are real. I too hope that you will come to me and that our lives can find a context outside of this war. I cannot promise more because I don't know you beyond the tone of your letters. So I will not promise more. Except that if my solitary life brings you joy, then consider yourself the patron of a great many more raptures to come.*

Thank you for saying that I don't seem hysterical.

All the best,

Camille

3

Chapter 3

Camille had stumbled on a great discovery in her weeks at Hargrove and Chase.

The copywriters were the first to pioneer it, as usual. And then later their secretaries. But she noticed that she could say the truth directly to white people's faces there, as long as she knew their names. They all found it hilarious and not insulting.

Nothing rude, of course. They simply typecast her as the stern schoolmarm of the office and that became her shtick. Although now that they were beginning to remember her name, these brief office cordialities were starting to draw out and become more frequent, much to Camille's dismay.

More than her lack of feeling over being liked, her white colleagues seemed to enjoy her aggressive professionalism. The men found her stoic taunting hilarious. The women found her non-threatening, as she'd removed herself from any possible male competition with her bullish demeanor.

She wore bright red lipstick whenever she wanted. When she started wearing pants to work, no one complained.

It turned out the act of giving her an office so soon was not benevolence. She gathered as much within the first week and the first fifty times someone opened one of the doors at either end and apologized as they saw themselves back out.

It had become something of a highway while it was unused. The girls at the switchboard cut through it to get to the break room— or at least, that was the excuse they used.

The copywriters used it to kill time when they had a "creative block." In other words, they used it for the exact same reason. It'd become a bit of a hotspot for loitering. Putting a colored girl smack in the middle of the office was the easiest way to put a stop to that.

Now she understood. The bit had been done so many times that by the end of the week, she was sure that the others in the office who'd made the mistake first were putting others up to it as a prank.

Camille never thought of her beige skin as an impediment to all tomfoolery until she started working with white people. But she was glad of it. Men's pants and women's blouses stayed buttoned in her presence and that's the way she liked it.

She honestly didn't know how white women could stand working in places like this. If she were white, she would be basically functioning as something between a mother and a waitress, rather than an actual employee.

She understood the allure of a potential matchmaking fairy-tale, but it was ultimately as rare as becoming the princess of Monaco. A minute or two of attention from a [usually married] man you might actually like didn't seem to be worth all the rest of it.

"Have you been down to casting yet?" Camille overheard.

"Not yet," Max grinned, a heavyset copywriter with thick glasses and curly black hair. She could hear the scheme in his voice.

Now that the loitering secretaries had cleared, the men of the office had subconsciously claimed the space like it was the wild west.

Her office was between Josh Manning and Max Steuben, two of the copywriters that worked on nearly every campaign. Chet was the other. A junior copywriter that they liked to haze by pretending he wasn't there.

Camille suspected they were just jealous because he was handsome and young and rode a motorcycle. Chet always took it on the chin, finding his way into one of their offices and into their conversation.

"Cigarettes or pantyhose?" Max asked.

"Neither. *Chewing gum*," Josh jogged his memory.

Josh was reasonably attractive but had a smug, weasely demeanor and voice.

"Holy moly, how could I forget?"

"Are they *all* identical?"

"They're certainly dressed like it. I've never seen that many pearl necklaces," Josh continued to ringlead. They all snickered like schoolboys.

"It's like some forbidden, desert sultan's exotic zoo down there," Josh bragged.

"So Hargrove's place?"

"You know he prefers brunettes," Chet finally got one in. They ignored him.

"Wait, what are we talking about?"

"Blondes."

As if whatever Production was doing had activated every testosterone-laden human to his office, she noticed Mr. Shaw and Mr. Daniels from Accounts mosey past her door as if they had nothing better to do and didn't have wives. All the seats must've been well taken because Mr. Cohen was practically hanging out of the hallway.

"Not that God-awful Wrigley's twins ad," he gasped.

"We were *joking* about that," Max recounted, with a wide-eyed snicker.

"Well, I hear the client fell head over heels for it," Josh defended his juvenile creation.

"The client or Production?"

"Both," Mr. Shaw confirmed.

"They're dying to catch up to Hershey's. They'll do anything," Cohen filled in.

"Drew's had his pick already, I'm sure," Chet tried his hand at being the office gossip.

"You're in denial if you think McCain catches the worm simply because he's early," Josh cut him down.

"You don't think he'll actually take *two*, do you?" Max mused, only mildly offended.

"Why not? This is America isn't it?"

"Hargrove will take the other."

"Have you even been listening?" scoffed Josh.

"Who doesn't love Marylin Monroe?" Chet asked in wonder to no one in particular.

"Maybe blonde pubes remind him too much of the Battle of the Bulge."

"He wasn't in Germany, you boob," Cohen rolled his eyes.

"Just don't get too many drinks in him. He starts shaking and ranting about how we gotta watch the Soviet Union."

"You've never had a drink with Kenneth Hargrove in your life," Mr. Shaw ragged on Josh. Everyone laughed except Josh, who was not-so-secretly sore about it. He was senior copywriter, after all.

Camille finally braved the hallway to make her way to the sandwich cart.

Only the most studious or brown-nosing ate their lunch at the office. Creative simply procrastinated through the day and starved, or decided to order in when nearly every establishment was closing its doors.

Camille walked past the makeshift locker room that had formed in the hallway and all was deathly quiet, either out of guilt or something less appropriate. Camille had long been immune to such speculation. She was well-trained in the art of minding her business.

"Camille!" Max exclaimed.

"Mr. Steuben," Camille acknowledged him.

The copywriters liked to hear Camille address them formally. She was the only one that did. Though she ran the risk of inflating their importance, it was worth the risk.

"Why don't you ever smile, Camille?" Josh teased as she walked by.

"Because I don't like being bothered, Mr. Manning," Camille tersely answered. She heard the room titter, followed by a terse silence.

The more she fraternized the more opportunities there were to mess up or go too far. The only thing she knew about white society was what she had learned so far in ten years of working.

She was bound to let some etiquette slip, evidenced by one of their elongated silences. And then there would be no more said about it until she was one day escorted out. She couldn't afford to ever get fired so she would need to be careful. Which didn't help her demeanor.

After a month Mrs. Hargrove came into the office, dressed

elegantly in a matching plaid coat and dress, coordinated with satiny lavender gloves.

She couldn't have been much older than Camille and yet she looked it. Having two children who looked to be around teenage was probably the culprit. She was blonde and blue-eyed like Christy, wearing her hair in a mature updo, accented everywhere with tasteful pearls and gems.

She had her daughter with her who Camille had met at the dealership. Christy made a show of keeping them busy until Mr. Hargrove arrived.

Camille was committed to staying in her office until they'd gone. She wished she could shrug off her brief icy encounter at Cadillac but she couldn't. Her best bet at remaining professional was to avoid interaction altogether.

But it turned out to be unavoidable. She heard the women approaching and the slowing footfall in front of her office. The daughter appeared first in the doorway, followed by Christy and Mrs. Hargrove.

"Do you remember me?" the girl beamed.

"I do," Camille smiled. "Katie, isn't it?"

"That's right. You work here now?"

"I do," Camille repeated, feeling suddenly awkward.

A horrible picture entered her mind, as she realized what this must look like to a paranoid white wife who didn't have the greatest impression of her to begin with. Thankfully, Katie ran interference.

"Mom's taking me shopping. Then I'm to get my hair done and Dad's taking us to dinner."

"I used to love going into the city with my parents," Camille shared fondly.

"Katie, go wait in your father's office."

"Bye, Camille."

"Bye," Camille smiled. The women were stoically silent.

"Did you need me, Miss Caldwell?"

"Find Mrs. Hargrove an appointment for this afternoon, Camille."

"Certainly. What time is dinner, Mrs. Hargrove?"

"No need to address Mrs. Hargrove. Dinner's at 5," Christy barked.

"Of course," Camille replied, reaching for the directory in the bottom drawer of her filing cabinet. She tried to ignore the ringing in her ears and refused to look up until the two women had gone.

What the hell did she know about white women getting their hair done in the city? And why would she come all the way out here without an appointment?

It must be a test of some kind. Or a prank. Or a show of power for some reason. At any rate, she knew she had to come up with the proper appointment, for the perfect place, at the perfect time.

She'd had supervisors do similar things in the past, but Camille hadn't had any problems with Christy so far to make her act that way in just over a month. She had to assume it was the wife's influence.

Camille made her way to Christy's office, appointment sheet in hand, just in time to catch Mrs. Hargrove chatting up the creative director. Clearly, Mrs. Hargrove was royalty and everyone was bending over backward to keep her occupied until Mr. Hargrove arrived.

Camille worried they'd be waiting forever, as she hadn't laid eyes on Mr. Hargrove since she started. For some reason, she had a strange feeling that he would be right behind her when she turned around. It was an unbearable thought and she was glad when it turned out to be sheer paranoia.

It was enough to make Camille take an early lunch. She would've left the building if she wasn't frightened that she might run into him on the way out. She couldn't bear another introduction today.

She ate lunch huddled in the break room, praying no one would come looking for her. Thirty minutes seemed long enough to make sure the coast was clear.

Strangely, Christy's hostility seemed to subside after their encounter. But it did tend to resurface at odd times, and always in flashes.

It was a few weeks later when she was introduced to Holly Chase, Lyndon Chase's widow and now a stakeholder in the company. She was older and elegant with a shock of orange hair. She always had a long cigarette in her fingers and as far as Camille could tell, she did no work. But she sometimes came to the budget meetings.

It was an open secret that she slept with the creative director whenever she wanted and that he more or less wasn't allowed to object. Not that he would. Camille spotted Mrs. Chase in the hallway with Christy in tow.

"Was there something you needed, Camille?" Christy was quick to ask.

"I was headed your way, actually, Miss Caldwell. I couldn't get you on the phone."

"No, of course not, Camille. I'm in the hallway," Christy defended herself tersely.

"Is this the new girl you were telling me about?" Holly interrupted.

"Camille, this is Mrs. Chase, senior partner, and wife of the late Lyndon Chase."

"You're Camille?"

"Yes, Mrs. Chase."

Mrs. Chase gasped and grabbed Camille delicately by the chin and turned her face this way and that. "Uncanny."

"What'd I tell you? Wouldn't you *kill* to tan like that?"

"If you were any lighter you'd look... Italian or something," Mrs. Chase said, sounding alarmed.

"My youngest sister often gets spoken to in all kinds of languages. My father is very light-skinned."

"Christy tells me you're a sorceress with shorthand."

"No sorcery, just secretary school. Thank goodness, or I'd never make it here."

"Nonsense," Christy scoffed. "We put Camille in A-L and look, it's nearly cleared."

"Congratulations, Camille. Barely a month and you already have the third biggest office on this floor."

"I'm happy to move," Camille offered, sensing a conflict.

"No no. It's perfect. Timely, really. Have you been keeping up with the boycotts, Camille? In Alabama?"

"...Of course, Mrs. Chase."

"It's good that you lot are finally standing up to those brutes in the South. I personally refuse to set foot any place lower than Washington D.C. Positively inbred, the lot of them."

"My father hails from Alabama," Camille divulged in a rare moment of conversation. "He'll never say it, but I know he hates the city. But he refuses to go back there."

"Camille's here before everyone," Christy forced the non-sequitur. "I put her in charge of the time cards. No one even dares to give me grief about it now."

"Ugh, you're *delicious*," Holly declared rapturously.

Camille remained modest and unaffected. "I'm happy to take some of the workload. Once A-L is cleared I'll likely need something else."

"We'll cross that bridge when we get to it, Camille," Christy discouraged her.

"No one's tried to sleep with you, have they?"

Camille furrowed her brow, but only slightly. "Certainly not, Mrs. Chase," she said. She didn't want to appear naive. Or accusatory. White people hated that.

"I'm very old, Camille. I've seen many things. But I've never seen a prick that wasn't progressive," Holly Chase shamelessly asserted.

"Perhaps. But with all due respect Mrs. Chase, I'm here to work," Camille replied, instantly wanting to retract her statement. That definitely sounded accusatory. She really wished she didn't know about Holly and the creative director now.

Mrs. Chase kept her eyes on Camille as she addressed Christy. "Has she met Kenneth yet?"

"Mr. Hargrove is the one who scalped Camille from Wayne Dileo over at Cadillac," Christy filled her in.

"Oh, we should send him something. He must be livid," Holly mused with an odd glee.

"He wrote me a glowing recommendation," Camille assured them.

"I'm sure he did dear," she said.

Great, now Mrs. Chase thinks she's a moron. Camille supposed that was inevitable.

Holly then drew conspiratorily close.

"If someone ever tries to give you a problem here, I want you to call me right away. We can't lose you over some account man with loose morals."

Okay, so maybe 'moron' wasn't a bad space to be with this lady. Otherwise, Camille might be made to suffer her confidence.

"Surely accounts are more important than me, Mrs. Chase," Camille grinned respectfully. Naively.

"*Women* are more important, Camille," Mrs. Chase nodded with a confident tilt of her head. "Don't forget that."

Camille returned her nod of female solidarity. "Indeed. Thank you, Mrs. Chase."

4

Chapter 4

Camille distantly perceived the phone ringing in her kitchen in the middle of the night on a random Tuesday. She'd just begun a dream when the ring suddenly cut through the surreal scenery she could no longer remember, only feel.

She rushed like a dutiful zombie to where the phone was hanging, worrying about consciousness for when the ringing stopped.

"Hello?"

"I can't stop thinking about you."

Camille forced the cobwebs off, flexing her eyes in the dark.

"Lawrence?"

"I can't stop thinking about you," he said again after a moment. A jolt to her heart propped her faculties up like a car battery.

She gave him a thoughtful sigh, touched. "Well, you have to."

"Why?"

"Because last weekend has to be a one-time affair."

Things had progressed between her and Lawrence. Maybe it

was the fact that they were wrong for each other and they knew it. Maybe because they were two attractive 30-something professionals in the city. But Camille had completely disregarded all the lessons she'd grown up learning. It's as though the moment she turned 30 all bets were off.

She'd long given up on love and marriage. But Lawrence understood her. Or at least, pretended to.

Last week they'd gone to a show in the city and taken a carriage ride in the park. They looked so perfect together and they each knew it.

"Meet me somewhere," he said.

"It's nearly midnight."

"Then I'll come there."

"You're on until 2am."

"Wait for me in the lobby. I'll ring you again when I'm on my way."

Camille hesitated, but she knew she was too lonely to refuse.

"I won't be trapped, Lawrence. And you cannot fall in love with me."

"I won't. I promise."

"You already have."

"I haven't," insisted Lawrence. "I just want you. And if I don't have you I'll never get you out of my system."

Camille pinched the bridge of her nose with a sigh. "I should've never let you smear my lipstick."

"Don't say that."

She lay awake until 2am like an idiot. She told herself that it was because she was worried about the upstairs tenants being disturbed. The moment the phone rang she was able to pick up.

"You're awake."

"I could barely sleep thinking about you waking the entire

38

building."

"Your voice is exquisite. Has anyone ever told you that?" he flirted.

"I think you meant to say mannish," she squelched him.

"You should take a job in radio."

"It's just because I'm tired and it's late."

"I'm on my way."

Camille waited in the dark of her living room, watching the night owl stragglers walking to the train by the light of the street lamps, usually on their way to or from Harlem.

Finally, she recognized Lawrence's purposed gait directly outside her bay window.

She hopped off the couch and out her apartment door to let him in the lobby before he buzzed the building.

He looked dashing in his coat and hat, and had the desperate look of a man starved for her, a look that haunted her fantasies, a look that she tirelessly craved.

He wasn't the man she wanted. Still wanted, to this day.

But the shocks between her thighs and the beating of her heart told her he was close enough.

When he grabbed her right then and there and began to kiss her, she knew that whatever happened next would be out of her control.

He groped her everywhere right there in the foyer, slivers of moonlight shone right above their heads from the transom window above the door and the slender panels of glass on each side. Their breath filled the hallway.

She noticed that he was a good kisser but that was about it. She wanted to feel his passion but she was trapped just outside of it as she looked into his eyes.

He was a liar. He was falling in love with her. He wanted to

39

FINDING CAMILLE

come inside her place, she sensed. But she didn't want that and didn't want to hurt his feelings.

The moment wasn't ecstasy but hardly the worst way she'd spent a Tuesday night.

She opened her satin robe, exposing her pale pink frilly nightgown made of a see-through blend. He put one of her clothed nipples in his mouth straight away and she gasped, trying to use the warmth of his tongue, the foreign sting to her nerves, the vulnerability of the public space to heighten her ecstasy.

But it was just a blur of muddled sensations. Honestly, what was wrong with her? She knew she wasn't a lesbian.

Was a handful of letters exchanged as a teenager really enough to dwarf the feel of a real man? That wanted her?

"Let me see you," he whispered. She wasn't entirely sure what he meant until he'd gotten on his knees in front of her and lifted her knee-length nighty to expose her satin underwear.

He was the first man to put his dark hands on her naked skin down below and it felt... foreign. It was all happening too fast, and she could sense that he was pretending not to know better.

But there was neither guilt nor shame. It simply was.

She thought he would try to pull them down but he only lowered them a bit, until her rubbed skin from her panty line showed and the coarse dark hairs of her sex threatened to peak out. She was glad that she wasn't attracted to Lawrence enough to be self-conscious.

He seemed to watch her with a reverent hunger that made her jut her hips forward. She heard the sound of a man unbuckling his belt, a sound typically associated with her father... until now.

She shivered at the faint sound of people drawing close and then further away on the sidewalks, confident that no one would be approaching the door at this hour, let alone discern what was happening in the dark hallway. If the upstairs tenants were awake it wouldn't be a secret to anyone.

Suddenly Lawrence sprung to his feet, still wearing his coat and hat. Shielding the sight of her with his big body, his arm bent up above her and down below, nothing but his erect member exposed.

She knew her eyes were wide, her breath arrested. A desperate gasp from him let her know he was pleased by her surprised reaction. She knew he was watching her face.

She licked her lips and her body warmed and cooled. Her hands didn't quite know what to do as the sight of him etched itself on her mind.

Like an old injury, she dragged Stanley to the front of her reality.

She remembered what he only sometimes came close to describing in his letters to her. He would've been darker than Carl, she somehow knew from his description. Perhaps not unlike Lawrence.

Was this what it looked like when he thought of her the way he described? When he carved out a space on that crowded island just for her letters? For her picture?

Her body began to tighten and become sensitive everywhere. She rubbed her own thighs and brought her hands inward until she was touching It.

She didn't typically like to use her hands. She liked to writhe on the sheets, or a pillow, or cross her legs on her lengthy train rides into town when she worked in Jersey.

The one and only time she did it that way she was sitting upright in a chair, and her orgasm was so arresting and her eyes rolled uncontrollably like a button had been pressed on her brain. Just as her sister was headed down the end of the hallway to her room and she narrowly escaped humiliation. She never did it that way again.

"That's it, Camille," Lawrence breathed, "let yourself go..."

She tried to block it out. It wasn't something Stanley would say. Certainly not what Carl would. Carl was a saint.

She tried to focus on the sight of him barely touching her skin as if she were behind glass. The fury of his pace. She rubbed across the fabric of her underwear and shivered at the sensation. His groans made her sex quiver and she pet it with her fingertips.

"That's it, make me come all over you," he said aggressively, powerfully, as if he'd gathered up all his loosening control, ready to relinquish it in one final breath. She moaned, her voice quivering with the breath she'd held on for too long.

Suddenly there was a soundless twitch from him and she was being doused in liquid from his dick. Gobs of it that seemed to never be quite finished.

She was at the height of her arousal, but the unexpected interruption seized what was left of her functioning mind.

Spunk. So that's what it looked like. It was warm enough to match her body temperature so that she didn't notice where it was on her wrist. She wondered what it felt like. Inside.

It cooled on the fabric of her gown almost instantly.

"I've never done anything like that before," he panted, dabbing himself a bit on her nighty before returning his member back to its place in his pants. So wildly convenient.

"Neither have I," she quickly confessed. She was so calm that she worried that it might seem like a lie. It wasn't. She doubted a man would lie about such a thing either.

"Can I stay?"

Camille hesitated.

"Nothing scandalous. It's just that I'm tired. I'll be good now, I promise."

"I'll be leaving for work at 7:30. You can take the couch. It pulls out."

"Oh. Of course."

"I think that's best. Don't you? As it is, I might be up the rest of the night trying to get this to wash out," she teased with a smile, hoping to appeal to his guilt.

He seemed hurt, but she couldn't imagine how he had the right to make her aware of it. She knew she was being used, so why didn't he?

Her apartment door was still open and he followed her inside. She replaced the deadbolt and they stared at each other in the dark until he finally spoke.

"I really... thank you, Camille. I didn't know I needed this."

She received his slow peck on her lips as he stroked her cheek. "Neither did I," she lied.

* * *

After three months Camille still hadn't run into Mr. Hargrove again since they met at her previous job.

She sometimes heard him around the office giving Christy orders, or respectfully addressing the other girls as they walked by. He was usually walking into his office with clients, or out with them from the conference room.

Camille observed him differently now. At Cadillac, he was imposing and important. At Hargrove and Chase it was the same, but only internally.

To the outside world, he made himself into whatever he needed to be at the moment. If he was with boozy clients he made himself into a lush. When clients came in from out of town, he knew all the places to take them. With chauvinists, he was a womanizer. With the cosmopolitan, he was a renaissance man.

She seldom laid eyes on him. When she did, it always sent her a rush. Right before she turned and went the other way.

He was the highest-profile boss she'd ever passively worked for. A giant in the industry, picking up where his legendary father had left off after 25 years in the business.

He stayed at arm's length with most of the office, a slight exception for the department that was the most responsible for keeping the lights on: Creative. Even then, sharing the same space with them was reserved for account business or some morale-building attempt to get the copywriters to bust their balls without thinking to ask for a raise.

So far, he hadn't addressed her. If for some reason he managed to be in the same part of the building at the same time, Camille found another route. If she couldn't do that, she kept her head down and refused to be seen.

She wasn't actively trying to avoid him, but some part of her felt slighted. She assumed that he'd procured her from her previous assignment because he'd been jealous for her to do some similar work for him.

Though she was grateful for the challenge, her current assignment resembled the one at Cadillac very little. So she was at a loss. It seemed as though he'd taken her away from a far more lively environment to stow her away in one of his closets.

She'd was starting to doubt the fate that even brought her. It was as though she'd imagined ever meeting him. She was beginning to hatch a plot to somehow sneak into personnel and see what she could find out for herself.

Until the day she felt his tall lingering presence darken her doorway.

Slow and deliberate he moved across the hall, like a Thanksgiving parade balloon patiently headed down Broadway. The smell of wealth wafted closely behind and her brain was in the midst of knowing as soon as her gaze had too quickly raised to automatically meet his.

She didn't remember him being so towering the first time she saw him on a lazy Sunday with his family. Or so young. He practically took up the entire door frame. And it dawned on her that it was strange for him to already be the head of such a company when he wasn't much older than her.

She had no time to take in the immaculate cut of his brown tweed suit and vest, a hand pulling back one edge of his suit coat like a curtain as he reached slowly into his pocket.

Her eyes shot down as she rose slowly out of her chair, as slow as she could manage. She'd done everything but curtsy.

"Mr. Hargrove."

"The infamous Miss Winters, I presume."

Presume? Did he not remember her?

"If you're looking for Miss Caldwell, I believe she's having lunch at Katz's this afternoon."

"Actually, I was looking for you, Miss Winters."

She raised her eyes and nodded casually. "Of course."

He gave her a tentative, diplomatic smile.

"Forgive my rudeness, taking so long to finally greet you formally. How are you liking it here?"

"Very much, sir."

"Everyone treating you well?"

"Of course, Mr. Hargrove."

"I'm asking sincerely," he said in a secretive way. Intimate.

Beyond the implications of her race or gender, as though she were an old friend.

No wonder his only job was to tell clients how brilliant they are for bringing their business here.

"Everyone has been stellar, sir. Thank you."

"That's good. I want you to let me know personally if anyone is giving you trouble here, Miss Winters, is that understood?"

"Mrs. Chase told me the same."

"Did she now?" he replied, amused.

"Almost verbatim, sir."

"Well. I will let you choose your own allies, Miss Winters."

"I'd prefer to come to you, sir. If it's all the same," Camille grinned.

Another eternity stretched between them and Mr. Hargrove took a breath. "Good. Miss Caldwell has been singing your praises since you started, and she's not alone. Keep up the good work."

She held back another smile. "Thank you. Mr. Hargrove."

He was about to walk away when she caught his attention. "Sir..."

He addressed her, somewhat startled. His crystal blue eyes were attentive, every dark brown hair perfectly in place. She swallowed.

"Forgive me, I couldn't help but wonder... how you and the family are enjoying the Cadillac. Sir."

"Very much," he chuckled.

"I'll have to pass it on to my former colleagues."

"No need. Wayne is a friend of mine."

"Of course."

Luckily anyone who could've been watching had been doing so from the other side of the door. But it wouldn't have mattered anyway. She never noticed Mr. Hargrove stop at anyone's door in the short months she'd been there, and it must've been just as rare to the office.

Casual conversation with Camille Winters all but stopped after that day. She could guess the nature of the sudden change in regard, but she supposed it was inevitable. It was the way of every office she'd ever worked in. And inwardly she was glad of it.

5

Spring, 1944

Camille,

I don't know what prompted you to send me another picture, but I am glad of it. I must confess that I do prefer to see your eyes close up in the one that you sent to Lance Cpl. Downey, though I'm happy to have the chance to admire you from head to toe.

You are beautiful indeed! I wish I hadn't told you to move on to some other young man over there so hastily. I'm joking, of course. But truly, your eyes alone take me aback, let alone the rest of you. I hope you don't mind that I showed your picture to the rest of the unit. When the letter came the entire unit fell upon it like a pack of jackals and it couldn't be helped. In fact, that has been the routine of all your letters. It felt a little inappropriate to horde the thing and to not keep them abreast when you have taken the time to keep in touch.

Stan

April 21, 1944

Stanley,

I am glad that you received my letter safely along with the picture I sent. I'm a little embarrassed to tell you that I put on my best dress and had my good friend take it in front of her house. You see, after hearing the effect that the first picture had on morale, it made me feel quite guilty because the picture was what I had at the time— hardly one of my best. I hated feeling so vain by wanting to send another one— especially since its original recipient is no longer here. And yet, you deserve your own memories, I think. At the very least. Not the remains meant for someone else.

Knowing that you've shown the picture to the rest of the unit as well makes me feel a little strange, but I understand. I never meant to put you in an awkward position. If you'd like, I can send them a bit of something as well. Or maybe I can ask a few friends and see if they would be interested in starting some kind of pen pal group, if you want to pass along their information.

May 2, 1944

Camille,

It seems my communication skills aren't the best. I won't make you feel awkward for sending me letters again. And I will keep our correspondence between us from now on. Thank you again for the picture. I keep it with me everywhere. I study your eyes and try to read them.

If I may be so bold, I couldn't help but notice that your letters have all but dried up. If the picture was consolation

49

for your dwindling attention, I would forego them entirely to continue receiving your correspondence. If you have found someone that has taken all your attention, please tell me so. You don't have to worry about wounding me.

But it seems I was naive in taking on a relationship of any kind with a human on the outside. Yesterday I witnessed the exploded head of a man from the path of a fighter jet, and the reaction of the men who were the recipient of its contents. And yet nothing has put me in more of a state of limbo than the indifferent passing of the courier through our barracks without a word or piece of mail.

I would also accept any communication along the lines of me being an insufferable baby no longer worthy of your envelopes. When my father was away in World War I, my mother had sent him a letter along those lines. I understand the parallel universe that war causes makes it unrelatable to the slowness of civilian affairs.

Regards,
Stanley

May 18, 1944

Stanley,
Forgive me for becoming slack in my letter writing. Please believe me when I say it is never an inconvenience. I've come to look forward to your doting and colorful letters and grown accustomed to them, I'm afraid. But I have been busy. You can relax knowing that I have caught no one else's eye in the weeks that I haven't written, nor has anyone caught mine. But it was equally as exciting in my estimation.

I came across the opportunity to become a stewardess for Cunard, and the training was quite intense. But there appeared to be some sort of mixup, because the upper management apparently did not know that I was colored. Though I made sure to emphasize it over and over, and they assured me that they would be considering certain candidates for their transatlantic voyages.

As it was, it turned out to be a mutual parting. I admit I was inspired by you and Carl's letters. The more he talked about all these different places, the more it made me realize that they were really out there. I thought I should go see them, to honor his memory. But I simply don't have the courage. So when my application was denied it was somewhat of a relief, though I could hear the guilt in their voice that they had to turn me down.

I sometimes wonder if my lighter color is hindering my progress or helping it. It would definitely help me know better what white people thought they were seeing. Perhaps if I were darker I would stand out, be more of an anomaly. Would I gain more respect? From some, perhaps. And in turn, more abuse from others. I've never been dark-skinned of course, but I can only assume, observing a few instances among friends and family.

I know they assume that I have an easier time fitting in simply because of my visual proximity to whiteness. But acceptance is just as capricious for me as it is for them, and sometimes even more unpredictable.

I hope it doesn't sound strange to say that I have assumed that you are dark-skinned through the way that you talk, or write that is. I know I said that I can manage without knowing what you look like, but it's hard. Not because I am shallow, but because I've never been in this position before of writing someone I've never once met or seen. I will have to trust that you are handsome by your own account.

Camille

June 2, 1944

Camille,

I'm sorry to hear that you won't be traveling the world. As selfish as I am to think of you leading a safe and chaste life at home, I admit it would be a joy to hear about the wide world coming through your eyes.

I sense you are more crushed than you are letting on. But don't despair. I have seen too many of our particular race give up over so little. If they did seem disappointed, I would encourage you to keep in touch and do your best to gain a rapport with whoever is there. Perhaps when they are ready, they will likely call you first. And trust me, if they kept you on at all, they are closer than not to being ready.

Things will not always be the way they are. It sounds naive coming from an Alabama son, but it's true. Before I came here, I was involved a great deal in my father's business. Many doors slammed, but never for long. Eventually, quality work wins out, and the doors fly open. But sinful men cannot stand in the way of righteousness forever. It eats away at their bones and tears their fortunes down until it is wrenched free from their grasping hands. Were it not for the greedy and the bigoted conspiring together, change would have come a thousand times over, as it has attempted to sprout many times.

52

You are not shallow to want to know what I look like. To answer your query from an earlier letter, I am indeed very real. I have sent you a drawing of my likeness. I hope it will suffice.

Stan

June 16, 1944

Stanley,

My word, you are an artist on top of it all? It does suffice. Thank you.

Thank you for your... pious words of encouragement. I sent the lovely secretary a bouquet of flowers in congratu-lations of her new engagement, which I was able to catch wind of while I was there. She sent me an invitation, but I will not do her the disservice of actually attending. I sent a timely RSVP instead.

I've recently acquired work at a temp agency and it is teaching me more of the ins and outs of the white working world. It is very ordered and meticulous, which is challenging. But also appeals to my strengths which are anticipating every terrible thing that could possibly happen, and also obsessing over the balance of budgets. Numbers in general. Not that I haven't found any white counterparts with this type of neurosis, but I find that it is noticed and valued. A peculiar feeling.

I seem to be the object of gossip with some of the other older secretaries but they will not let me come near it. But I do notice how conversation ceases when I am present, and seems to thrive in dark rooms and corners. Since I am now on my second decade of life I feel confident guessing that it has to do with my being colored first, and young and unmarried second. It affects me little since I live to mind my own business and despise the frivolous pecking of hens.

Sometimes I wonder if I was truly born a woman. Besides the occasional indulgence in a dress of bright colors, I have no other conventional feminine interests. And I don't understand the lot of them, nor they me. My mother lives to worry me about everything, and I can't imagine doing the same to someone else, not even an enemy. Yet she and my aunts can spend the afternoon exchanging worries of all kinds, until they are worn down to almost nothing and no solutions are ever found.

Though I admit I have never found any camaraderie around men, who seem to be bereft of all verbal communication after some time. They are quite simple to work for, I will admit. Everything that appeases them is concrete and real. But I noticed that other men seem to be uneasy in each other's presence at work, and many more words are exchanged. I can only assume it is because these men are not friends. And in fact, may even hate each other.

I seem to be the only one who likes everyone equally. But that is only because I've been taught since childhood to think little of white people and expect even less. I can only guess what their opinion of me is. But my father who is very light, and has suffered abuses that he refuses to do anything but hint at, always says, "give them no reason to hate you, and give them even less of a reason to like you." I didn't understand him for the longest time, but now I think I do. As long as I am not seen as a threat to them, things so far have been just fine.

Camille

54

July 1, 1944

Dear Camille,

Your meaty letter has made me smile all day. Your observations of men are quite astute, and I hope you don't think it's childish of me to admit my pure jealousy at not being one of those men under your very keen eye.

Humbly I will add my assurances that you are every inch the woman, no matter what your interests are. Your insights into the working world are interesting and I loved hearing about your brain and how it works. Now that I have practically memorized the lines of your face and the contours of your frame it is nice to know something new that I could not have guessed.

I don't know much about how white people behave in an office but it sounds like you will do fine. I worked as a porter in Philadelphia for a time and if it's one thing white people appreciate from colored people, it's politeness. You seem to understand the importance of polite gestures and decorum, and that will take you very far. It is true that women do gossip, and in that department, I am as little help as you must be.

Just keep an eye on those white men who talk too much. In my experience, they have never been good news.

Stanley

6

Chapter 6

I t was the beginning of the fall quarter and time for another account meeting. Camille had earned herself an ambiguous role.

Christy's attempts to turn her into the headmistress of the secretaries fell apart. Essentially what she had done with A-L she was now doing with the current campaigns, taking some of Mr. Hargrove's workload.

Reaction at first was mixed— behind the scenes, of course. She was essentially doing the job of a high-level executive.

But after a few months of Camille checking on the progress of every active client in the company of the account execs, it seemed to them it was a job more suited to a secretary anyway.

The men in the office suspected that Mr. Hargrove had a bit of a fetish for Camille, especially when they all learned of how she was hired in the first place.

Everyone could see she was competent, mindful of her place nearly to a fault. But Mr. Hargrove was simply using his name to break rules for a colored girl, and they couldn't understand why a man would bother breaking rules that didn't even apply to him.

After the creative department was finished prattling on about their weekends, Mr. Hargrove called the conference room to order.

"Miss Winters, the room is yours."

"Let's start with Colgate. Mr. Daniels?"

"Production needs half upfront, and we're waiting on a check."

"And when will you be calling the client about that?" Camille plainly asked.

Mr. Daniels shifted in his chair. "Well, I spoke with him before Labor Day."

Camille gave him a stern look.

"I'll be checking with him again this afternoon."

"Very good. Remington?" Camille turned to Mr. Cohen who was in charge of the account.

"The ad that we ran in the Saturday Evening Post did so well they want to resize the ad to run in TV Digest."

"Big ad," Mr. Hargrove gave an imperceptible nod of encouragement.

"Tiny magazine," Mr. Daniels pointed out. Mr. Cohen gave him a look.

"Art department's problem," Mr. McCain, the creative director said with a wave of a hand.

"Pabst."

"Mr. Shaw?"

"Sales are great. Art and copy's great. Client's happy," Mr. Shaw rattled off.

"Marketing begs to differ," Camille retorted.

"Pardon me?"

"I spoke with Mr. Harris' secretary recently and according

to her, they haven't been satisfied with the numbers since last quarter."

Mr. Shaw gave her a terse, paralyzed look, during which Camille was undeterred.

"Camille, I know you've gotten promoted from the field to the house in just a year but you're not an account man, alright?"

"Jesus, Al. Relax," Mr. Daniels rebuked him meekly.

"I'm sorry, Phil, but your girl is out of line."

"I'm not anyone's girl, Mr. Shaw," Camille calmly answered him.

"Of course you are," Mr. Shaw sneered.

"Then I am this entire agency's girl. Which is why you should heed what I was trying discreetly to tell you."

"I should *heed* it?" Mr. Shaw scoffed, taking a drink. The room had become hostile and not in his favor. "I tell you, this is what happens when you give them a little power. Every time."

"You're a fine one to say that, Mr. Shaw," Camille retorted before someone could chime in on her behalf.

"...Excuse me?"

"I'm agreeing with you, Mr. Shaw. I did get promoted from the field to the house in just a year or two. And yet... here you are. Being lectured. By me. Now, I've never had a problem getting promoted so I don't know what that's like, but I imagine if you don't like your circumstances, Mr. Shaw, you should find some way to change them."

Mr. Hargrove bellowed with some authority, interrupting before Alan could do something to get himself an involuntary vacation.

"Phil, why don't you and Mr. Shaw catch an early lunch."

"You put that thing on a leash, Ken," Mr. Shaw emphasized with his pointer finger, "or this place will become a zoo."

"Get him outta here. *Now*," Mr. McCain clamored, irritated that no one had yet begun moving.

Everyone was hesitant to walk out on a meeting with the bosses, but Mr. Daniels led the charge, after which Mr. Shaw reluctantly showed himself out as if voluntarily deciding to leave.

They left the door wide open and Christy got up from her desk, sensing the commotion.

"Everything okay in here?"

"Get us some coffee, Christy."

"Right away."

From his seat next to her, Mr. Hargrove could see the way Camille hid her trembling hand behind her yellow pad.

"Miss Winters, do we need to cut this meeting short?"

"Absolutely not."

A minute later, Josh was back with Max, his primary writing partner. He sat in Mr. Shaw's empty chair.

"Max, you worked on Pabst, didn't you?" Camille politely asked.

"Yes, ma'am."

"They're not happy. Give me 20 taglines before Friday," Mr. McCain gave him his marching orders.

"Son of a bitch," he muttered.

"Anyone else have any incompetencies they would like to disguise as racial epithets?" Mr. Hargrove asked.

"Ezra's a filthy Jew," Mr. Daniels offered. The room broke up instantly.

"I've been wanting to say that for years," Josh continued. More laughter.

Camille could only manage a slow disapproving shake of her head, her signature sign of amused disapproval at their impenetrable boys' club that she mostly loved but sometimes hated.

The table interpreted it as a sign of absolution. Everyone except Mr. Hargrove, who caught Camille using the room's laughter as an opportunity to relinquish a heavy sigh.

* * *

"What do women want, Miss Winters?"

Andrew McCain, the creative director stood in the doorway of her windowless office, an hour before quitting time.

"Mr. McCain," Camille greeted him. He had two tumblers in his hand with a small helping of something brown. He handed her one. She politely took it without taking a sip.

"You're asking me?"

"You are a woman, aren't you?" he innocently confirmed.

You tell me, she nearly answered.

Mr. McCain was trouble. Always setting her up. Pretending he didn't know what he was doing. Nothing mattered to him. He could never get fired.

"Is this for a campaign?"

"The boss and I will be meeting with a client this evening. Do you have plans?"

Camille hesitated, not quite sure where this was going.

"I... yes."

"Cancel them."

"Mr. McCain, I don't understand. Why do you need me?"

"If I tell you that, you'll try to back out."

"If it's in any way immoral Mr. McCain..." Camille gave him a disapproving look of suspicion.

He smiled.

Andrew McCain was criminally attractive. Like a figment of one of Hargrove and Chase's own ad campaigns to sell cigarettes. Watches. Cologne *and* perfume. Vacations. Anything.

Whereas Ken Hargrove was criminally cute. He had a small chin and gave you no indication that he would ever intend to break your heart should he set his mind to wooing you.

And yet, the pair of them left a notorious trail of devastation in their wake. Unbeknownst to their wives at home in the suburbs. Or maybe with their full permission. But that was none of her business.

"6 pm, The Rainbow Room."

"Don't be silly, me in a place like that. I have no time to change."

"What you're wearing is fine, Miss Winters. Don't be late."

Lucky for her she kept a dress hanging up behind her file cabinet. These white folk would just love to catch her slipping.

She didn't worry so much about Mr. McCain and Mr. Hargrove being cruel. Or untoward. But after the day she had, it felt better to be ahead of the curve.

She finished work early to get to the restaurant in her black Dior dress and white gloves on time.

When she got there the two men were still entertaining a client. The hostess was expecting her and escorted her to their large booth.

"Don't you look smart," Mr. McCain smiled as she approached.

"Camille, this is Mr. Paxton from Palmolive. Will, meet Camille Winters."

"We've spoken. A pleasure to meet you, Mr. Paxton," Camille politely smiled.

"My goodness. What are you, dear? Cuban?"

"Lower. My mother hails from Guyana. In South America."

"And your father?"

"Alabama."

"So you're a mulatto."

"If you prefer," Camille chose to say. A space of confusion passed.

"We wanted you to be surprised," Mr. McCain interjected.

"What he means to say is that our very capable accounts coordinator is here to talk business. And early as usual," Mr. Hargrove teased as he got up to escort his clients out.

"If you're on time you're late, Mr. Hargrove," Camille dutifully teased back as the men got up from their chairs.

"Ken, have your girl see us out."

Mr. McCain stopped and looked at Mr. Hargrove, who was formulating a delicate letdown he wasn't sure would work. Mr. Paxton had already had a few and had misconstrued the focus of the night.

"Actually, I was on my way to the ladies' room. Has everyone ordered?" Camille saved them.

"We haven't," Mr. McCain smiled.

"A shame."

"Surprise us, Camille," Mr. Hargrove nodded. He gave Mr. Paxton a slap on the shoulder. "Where are you staying, Will?"

* * *

Camille surveyed the elegant ballroom in the round, surrounded by booths and tables of the restaurant like a permanent wedding reception. The live band was off today, thank goodness.

"You never answered my earlier question," Mr. McCain startled her as he sat back down in the large Chesterfield leather booth.

"Which question was that, Mr. McCain?"

"What do women want?" he repeated, offering a cigarette with his case open. She refused. Mr. McCain smoked menthols.

"Difficult to say. Not all of us want the same things."

"Of course you do."

"Oh, I see. You already know the answer, is that it?"

Mr. Hargrove re-joined them in the booth.

"You want more. More of everything. And all without feeling guilty."

"Miss Winter's isn't your typical housewife, Drew," Mr. Hargrove insisted, reaching for his own cigarette.

"I think surveying a colored woman about this may skew your research," Camille said, still dutifully holding onto the purse in her lap.

Mr. McCain tilted his head as he took a drag, intrigued. He decided he was in the mood to learn something.

"You're saying colored women don't want more?"

"Colored women are still trying to get the full portion of whatever it is white women want more of. And you'd be hard-pressed to make us feel guilt about any of it."

"Colored women have families, keep houses," he argued.

"They also keep other families and houses."

"Is that what your mother did?"

"Not a day in her life. She met my father practically the minute she set foot in America and that was that."

Mr. McCain blew out a cloud of smoke. "So it's really your mother I should be talking to."

"Perhaps. But my mother has plenty and doesn't want anymore."

"She envies *you*, I bet."

"She doesn't understand the impulse to work. Because my grandmother worked in the rice fields in Guyana and raised her to make marriage her only goal, which she did. My grandmother hates the fact that I work. I'm the only one of my sisters not married. She says my mother didn't marry a light-skinned man just to see her daughter not snag a husband."

Dinner arrived all soups and salads. Upon realizing she hadn't ordered like a person with money, she felt a bit embarrassed.

"Well, you may have dodged a bullet, Miss Winters. The data is in. Housewives are bored. Unfulfilled. Their work is monotonous."

"Most hard work is. The only reason modern women love the workplace over the home is the reward system goes from long term to short term. With motherhood, the only job well done is the 20-year fruit of a functioning adult, added to society. Between the money, promotions, pats on the back, a job is a constant validation drip compared to keeping a house."

"Holy shit. Ken, you writing this down?"

"I'm paying you for the ideas, Mr. McCain."

"You're saying colored women don't have this same desire for constant validation?"

"No. I'm saying the grass is always greener. Find me a time period, Mr. McCain, where colored women *weren't* acquainted with work."

"But how long have they been *paid* for said work?" he pointed with his cigarette between his fingers.

"Jesus, Drew," Mr. Hargrove cringed.

"It's a valid notion," Mr. McCain defended.

"Be that as it may, the working world is not some promised land to us. Nor is the need to be taken seriously, to be honest. We know what it is, and we know what it isn't. Middle-class white women, less so. Our priorities are exactly opposite, nor will they ever be the same."

"Your theory is good," Mr. McCain exhaled a cloud of smoke, grinding his cigarette into the crystal ashtray, "but it certainly doesn't explain you."

Camille took another measured spoonful of soup to her mouth. "No, I suppose it doesn't," she agreed.

Chapter 7

"So, Miss Winters," Mr. Hargrove finally began.

"Mr. Hargrove."

Camille had only sat with Mr. Hargrove a few times, and never across from him at a restaurant. He was so guarded and yet the most unbelievable vulnerabilities flowed out of his mouth. As though he had total command of himself.

You both wanted to get to know him and knew that was impossible all at once. You settled for him knowing you.

"I suppose you're wondering why you're here."

Once Camille noticed she was the only one eating she put down her soup spoon and wiped her face with a napkin. "Not at all, Mr. Hargrove."

"No?"

"...I simply mean that I'm at your disposal. Naturally, Mr. Hargrove."

"I see," he smirked nervously. "Well. About this morning."

"No need to mention it."

"Nonsense. I want you to know that I'm mortified completely."

"Don't be."

"When I told you to tell me if anyone was giving you trouble here, I meant that. I never imagined that I'd be a witness to it. Or be the one to put you in that position."

Camille absolved him. "You weren't. You didn't. I chose to push someone that no one else seemed to have the guts or the desire to. I knew there was a chance to get the reaction I got."

"You're under the impression that it's your job to do so?" Mr. Hargrove presumed with a raised brow. Both men gave her the smolder across the table as Mr. McCain lit another cigarette.

Camille felt comfortable answering truthfully. "To be honest, yes. I know the impression that I have in the office as a bit of a hardass."

Mr. McCain smiled through his puff of smoke, clearly enjoying Camille's frank way of talking. Mr. Hargrove's steely gaze hadn't changed.

"You enjoy this reputation?" he asked.

"I'd rather be known as a hardass than a pushover. There are certain tasks that the other women— and some men— in the office find unpleasant to undertake that simply bother me less."

Finally, Mr. Hargrove was inspired to retrieve a cigarette of his own. He tapped the tobacco-filled end on his embossed silver case. "I'm afraid I have relied on that courtesy for too long."

Uh oh. Was she being fired?

"If I've been overzealous on behalf of the company, then I apologize," Camille began seriously. She pushed her soup bowl fully to the side. "Perhaps Mr. Shaw had a point."

"Jesus. What an awful sentence," Mr. McCain scoffed into his drink.

Mr. Hargrove lit his cigarette with a deft finger on his equally beautiful lighter. He put it away and took a drag. "You are now

Head of Personnel, Miss Winters," he announced.

Camille looked cautiously stunned. "You mean... you're hiring me on permanently?"

"I think it's about time, don't you?"

"I see. Does... management know about this promotion, sir?"

"They will." Mr. Hargrove held his cigarette between his fingers gently as he puffed. "Continue to do what you did in today's meeting, in every meeting, without impediment."

"Yes, Mr. Hargrove."

"You're not in the house Camille, you're the overseer," Mr. McCain smirked through a drag of his own cigarette. "How's it feel?"

"Like I need to watch my back."

The smoke came out with a smiling billow. "Smart girl," he said.

"A strange sympathy I've never wanted to feel," Camille added. The two men laughed.

"Another round," Mr. McCain gestured to a hovering waiter. Camille had been miming sips of her cocktail for nearly an hour and soon the jig would be up if it wasn't already. She should've known the "dinner" was gonna be all liquid.

"So does this increased level of risk come with a raise of some kind?" Camille asked.

Mr. McCain looked at her like a proud parent.

"It's really a shame that no negro gentleman snatched you up in time," he said for no reason.

Camille didn't know if that meant there wouldn't be a raise or what. She didn't know how to answer, but she suspected that saying "thank you" would only encourage him in a way that would cause her to lose her respect for him.

She decided to use the truth, knowing they wouldn't be

scandalized.

"I would agree with you Mr. McCain, but in my limited experience, I would imagine the two of us would only ever make each other miserable."

"Limited? So there was some attempt?"

Oh geez. She hated being right about Mr. McCain.

"Drew..." Mr. Hargrove warned.

"I'm sorry, I don't mean to pry. But I'm genuinely fascinated."

Fascinated. Camille was in no real danger, then.

Mr. McCain was a World War II vet like Mr. Hargrove. Through that slick exterior, they were crippled. Hardened. Every woman who was old enough to observe the pre and post-war male recognized it.

War seemed to have the habit of making these men fascinated by few things, and fascinating things didn't turn them on or into animals. Not anymore.

It was only the underlings she had to worry about, mere babes when war broke out. Besides, with Mr. Hargrove there, Camille felt safer.

"Some. There was a negro doctor not long ago. A surgeon, to be exact."

Mr. McCain lifted his eyebrows in approval. "He must've been a sight."

Camille felt an odd pride as her own eyebrows lifted. "He was."

"What happened?"

"Married. Several months ago."

"To a younger, less ambitious woman I imagine."

"I'm hardly ambitious, Mr. McCain. Merely competent."

"And before him?"

Camille couldn't help but snicker at his frankness. "I can't imagine why the mating habits of negroes should interest either of you in the slightest," she teased.

Mr. Hargrove relinquished a rare grin through the puff of his cigarette. Mr. McCain cackled.

"My God, Camille," he shook his head. "You sure you don't wanna write copy?"

"Positive," she curtly answered.

"Come on, Camille. You're not on the clock. Give us something salacious," McCain urged, obviously the bad influence of the twosome.

Camille reached in her clutch for a cigarette. Instead of using the table's lit candle in the centerpiece, Mr. Hargrove politely offered her a light with a shaky hand. She took it.

It gave her the time she needed to think of the most outlandish thing she could possibly say that they would never expect out of her mouth. When she had it, she waited until Mr. McCain's drink was nearest to his lips to engage him in a rare bout of teasing.

"I keep a peckerwood gimp tied up at home in my basement."

Mr. McCain was immediately in shambles, his drink having gone down the wrong way.

Mr. Hargrove merely chuckled as though he heard that sort of thing all the time. Hardened.

He smiled big and watched as Andrew tried to recover. Camille took her time taking her next drag.

"He's gonna be sore after the day I've had," Camille continued with a blow of smoke, her deadpan expression immovable.

"We're fine, thank you," Mr. Hargrove assured the waiter as Andrew's choking attracted onlookers. Ken gave him a few healthy pats on the back.

"Are you alright, chap?"

"I think she might be serious, Kenny," Mr. McCain burped.

"What Miss Winters does in her private time is none of our business."

"The truth is terribly boring I'm afraid," Camille confessed. "I've always been the way I am. I'm very clean but I only cook a little. And I work the most. Very little to interest most men, as you can imagine."

"You should've gone into modeling. If you won't let a man enjoy that face of yours then you should let the whole world. It pays, you know," he said as he sat back, wiping his chin with a napkin.

...Okay, so Mr. McCain would definitely have sex with her. She walked a fine line of politeness with her answer. Cold candor seemed to be having the opposite effect she wanted.

"And where should a colored girl go to model, Mr. McCain?" she smiled.

He shrugged as if there were black modeling agencies on every corner. "This is Madison Avenue. Colored women buy dresses to my knowledge. Nylons."

"She'd have no trouble overseas," Mr. Hargrove offered to the table as he blew his cigarette smoke out of his nose and mouth. His arm extended slightly behind Mr. McCain casually in the booth. Andrew pointed his finger at him in agreement but stayed otherwise silent, as if in awkwardness.

"Never too old for voice work," Mr. Hargrove pointed out.

"That voice alone could sell a million automobiles."

Camille didn't know where this was going anymore so she rushed to fill the silence with small talk of things she already knew.

"You were in the Marines, weren't you Mr. Hargrove?"

Mr. Hargrove stiffly eyed the table and Camille wondered if

she'd overstepped. But there was a lot of that going around.

"I was," he confirmed, taking a drag.

"Did you know of any colored regiments where you were?"

Mr. Hargrove's eyes narrowed for a moment. He shook his head. "Not in Asia, no."

"Eureka," Mr. McCain smiled. "You had a beau who was in the war."

Camille gave them an enigmatic smile through a puff of her cigarette.

The sips had become too large, she deduced, even though they were mimed. She was such a lightweight compared to these guys.

"You must've been young," Mr. McCain opined, almost salivating.

Camille hesitated, leveling her cup of information before she continued. "I was barely eighteen. We hardly knew each other, but he proposed before he left."

"He must've been smitten, poor chap," Mr. Hargrove unexpectedly volunteered.

Camille acknowledged him with a polite grin. "I suppose."

"I take it he never made it home," he continued.

Camille shook her head. "He did not."

"And the young Camille never recovered," Mr. McCain couldn't help narrating.

"Something like that," Camille nodded with a terse grin, her shoulder in a knot.

She walked right into that one, she supposed. It didn't take many details to put it together.

"I'd tell you to go out there and try again, but we just landed Brooks Brothers and I'm far too selfish," Mr. Hargrove muttered.

Camille's eyebrows did an elegant hop. "Congratulations."

"For your ears only, for now, Miss Winters."

"Of course."

"See? I told you this was a business dinner," McCain gave her another one of his sly smiles.

"Indeed. Well, I hope you don't mind, I did have a prior engagement."

"Thank you for indulging us, Miss Winters."

"Of course," she said, gathering herself out of the booth.

She bid them good evening before turning back toward the table after a five-second count.

"Forgive me, but we never discussed the pay in detail, Mr. Hargrove," Camille firmly reminded him.

Mr. Hargrove smiled. "Of course. Name your price, Miss Winters," he replied.

Camille's stern demeanor returned, as if wary to trust the goodwill. "I'd be more comfortable with a solid figure."

Mr. Hargrove was undeterred. "Take a day. Think about it."

"Go home and run it by the gimp," Mr. McCain smiled.

"Get a good night's sleep, come in with a figure, Miss Winters."

"Very well. Enjoy the rest of your evening gentleman."

* * *

Camille came home to the downstairs room in her Brooklyn apartment and collapsed on the couch. Having lost the buzz from her drink she wasn't quite ready to climb into bed just yet.

She found some leftover wine in the icebox and poured herself a glass. She took a deep breath, trying not to relive the last hour and a half every few seconds to no avail.

She should be happy. Triumphant. Stripping down naked and looking at herself in the mirror with a mischievous look in her eye.

A permanent hire. Not only that, a promotion.

But the moment was sogged, overpowered by the stench of the old stale past, let out in front of perfect strangers.

She couldn't believe that she'd brought up the war to her veteran boss. An embarrassing social faux pas.

Sure, they'd committed their own, but that was unavoidable. She supposed they gave her no choice.

She *really* couldn't believe she'd brought up Carl to them. She hadn't even thought about or mentioned him in ages, and now she'd babbled on about him to at least three other people in just over a year.

In her mind now her once dreamy fiance was a child. He'd been 21 when he died but only 19 when she'd last saw him.

She'd written Stanley, his commanding officer, more times than she'd written him. And yet even though she'd never properly laid eyes on him, he loomed largest in her mind. A fact that bore her tremendous guilt.

Had her lofty plans ever panned out, perhaps she wouldn't feel guilty. Had Stanley made it home in Carl's stead, come to her as promised, and made her an honest woman, she could forgive throwing herself at the next available soldier with the elegant hand.

Carl would've understood. Perhaps approved.

She stumbled over to the closet and retrieved the hatbox at the back of her top shelf.

She put on a record, sat in her fancy dress, untied the bundles, and poured over the letters she hadn't looked at in years as she sipped the last of the wine.

"*I don't know why/but I'm feeling so sad...*" the record player crooned. "*I long to try something I've never had...*"

Stanley. So smart and eloquent. Creative. So dead. That singular brain dashed to the waves.

She dug until she found the one where he'd sent her a self-portrait. He couldn't send her a picture, so he'd drawn one of his own.

He was an immaculate artist. She dared to run her fingers across the image, unafraid to smear it.

Dark. Chiseled jaw, thick lips, dark hair, and eyes that were stern and gaunt cheeks. Clean-shaven. Not as naturally handsome as Carl was, but mature and mysterious.

In his drawing was honesty so stoic and objective that it was dripping with emotion. He could've been exaggerating himself, but she didn't get that impression.

"*Loverman, oh where can you be... the night is so cold/and I'm so all alone...*"

All her favorite ones she knew by the dates. She found the one about him discovering he was handsome while on shore leave.

She imagined him in his uniform, surrounded by foreign white women. Fucking and kissing and enamored with each other while the end of the world was hidden by the evening.

But it was her he'd dreamt of, some little girl in Brooklyn with sad, naive eyes and a stern full mouth. Even while her betrothed didn't know it.

He was so melancholy and introspective. She longed to comfort him. And he clearly longed to be comforted by her.

Ten years ago she couldn't imagine anything more blissful. But alas, it would never be. She stuffed down how much she used to romanticize war when she was young.

How had ten years gone by? At 18 years old, ten years alone

seemed to go by between letters. Especially the last one. She dug at the crusty wound, thinking of her ignorant bliss.

"I've heard it said that the thrill of romance/Can be like a heavenly dream..."

She'd trained herself so well to be patient. Thought herself disciplined. Until her oxygen began to really run out and her lungs ached and she realized she was in real trouble.

When the talks of surrender began she was still under the illusion that a letter was finally on the way. That Stanley had only been busy before now. The fighting had intensified. Maybe he was undercover. Maybe he was injured.

She tried not to kick herself for being so cryptic with him. Did she have to be so shy, even in letters? He needed the will to fight, and now he had none because she refused to bare her soul.

She vowed that if he made it home she would not make the same mistake. If he turned out to be alive she would laugh and scream and bare her breasts and tell him never to leave her.

Once the end was in sight, she took solace in knowing she would be the first person he couldn't wait to tell. Perhaps he would come to her ahead of his last letter.

Then the surrender came, and it was the only thing that came. The moment the war was over there was celebrating and ticker tape and soldiers in the street. But she couldn't hear it or see it. She may as well have been deaf and blind.

"I go to bed with a prayer that you'll make love to me/strange as it seems..."

She put the fingers that touched the lips of the drawing to her own lips.

Loved from afar by two men. Once a promising future, now a dreadful black omen. Even at 18, she knew that love stories shaped the way her and Carl's was didn't come around more than once.

She kicked herself when she thought back to her youthful mindset. The way she let him say goodbye. The way she told him it was better to wait until he was back home. What on Earth had she been thinking?

Then again, if she had succumbed she might be left alone with a child that would've wondered every day why they were brought here. No, her heart was destined to die on a foreign field somewhere. Wandering.

"Someday we'll meet... and you'll dry all my tears/ And whisper sweet little things in my ear..."

Organizing other people's affairs kept her busy. She could get lost in the details for hours. Maybe she wasn't good at her job, just desperate for a distraction.

She dove into the deep end of white men's chaos, again and again, taming balance sheets and busy schedules and attic spaces full of dubious records. It was tiring and insurmountable and consuming, to the point of regret.

But eventually, order would prevail again. And she would be left in the quiet. Alone. With herself.

She finished her drink and let herself cry for the first time in a long time. Only because she was too inebriated to be afraid that she wouldn't stop. She was so utterly lonely.

But she did stop, falling asleep sideways on the bed and over the covers in her now wrinkled cocktail dress, memories left sprawled around her like barbed wire.

"Oh what we've been missin' loverman... oh where can you be..."

8

Summer, 1944

July 25, 1944

Camille,

I should probably be ashamed to tell you that I medi-tated on your face all day like you were the holy virgin. And that I longed to touch you. But I'm not ashamed. Nothing happened today. Nothing at all. The stars were close enough to touch, but I could no longer make out your sweet sad eyes by the light of them, so they were of no use to me. On days like these, I wonder why I simply cannot just be "home."

Some civilized part of me is horrified by even thinking of sending this to you. But I admit I've felt that way from the very first letter. Who am I to you but a stranger? And what right do I have to be saying any of this? Not a beau or a lover or an intended one. You can't even see me. But I am on the very precipice of civilization. Trying to keep its fringes from unraveling. And it causes a man's mind to go raw.

The island we are at now has no water. The little water we could find the Japs had poisoned and made undrinkable. Beyond Captain's orders, our communication has become rhythmic grunting or nothing at all. The stench is incredible. We are thirsty. And yet, never have any of us come this close to glory as we have during this, close enough many times to reach out and grab it. I think many of us contemplate it. Many of us know we are going to die on one of these days. For six months or so it becomes a state of torture. After another six it merely becomes inevitable. And then you are free. Maybe it is these circumstances that have made me so bold.

I have to be mindful that you are not experiencing such things at home. And yet I cannot help myself. I will probably send this letter off into the wind.

Yours,
Stanley

August 10, 1944

Stanley,

I'm glad that you changed your mind and decided to send this letter to me. I've read it several times and am still contemplating it. The way that you say things. The first time I read it I felt sure enough that if I turned around I would see you standing there. It felt as though you were just near me. I can't explain it. It made me pray for water, rain, anything that could alleviate your suffering. I feel powerless. And yet, I am moved that you would write to me about these things. I know that there are Marine's wives receiving misleading letters of general substance or no letters at all, only condolences.

Don't ever feel ashamed to want something so simple as human affection. I would love to be there to see those stars. I've never left this stoop in Brooklyn and I think I should like to see any stars, especially those close enough to touch. I am not ashamed to say that your letter made me want to rip myself from this skin and tear across the other side of the world to let you. I feel terrible pity and a strong intuition to comfort you and bring you relief.

Your letters seem sad in a way. Full of angst. As much as Carl made me feel loved and seen, you make me feel... wanted. More than simply wanted. Like some man's oasis. There's something irresistible in it. You've been a great comfort to me in Carl's absence. When I sent that last letter to him, it was with the last of my hope of ever being loved. But you have shown me there's more. You have shown me want. And for that, I am grateful enough to let you have me.

Camille

August 25, 1944

Camille,

And I would have you. Over and over.

Write me now. Tell me your true thoughts. You are kind, but I feel as though I am simply a tolerance to you. Meanwhile, I am positively bursting. I should've been more honest with you from the beginning. It's what I get for being deceptive and cunning. I thought getting one letter from you would be enough. But it was not. In fact, I am more in love with you now than ever. I cannot keep you at arm's length as you have done with me. I know I am crazy, so please don't mention it. I know you think *that it's brought about by loneliness but it isn't. I have seen a million girls. You are simply different. You are simply what makes me happy. Tell me never to write you again and I won't.*

September 9, 1944

Stanley,

I can't say that I'm in love with you. How can I? I would complain that I've never met you but we are in the same boat. Still, you know a bit more about me. And I dare say that men need very little to fall in love, from what I have observed.

I don't think you're crazy. Put yourself in my place. I'm an unpopular girl from Brooklyn, getting letters from a dashing colored soldier in the Pacific. Well, I have added the dashing part, haven't I? I know personally what you are enduring. And I will not punish you for that.

But I won't tell you never to write to me. I won't turn you away. I'd like to know more about what you meant by the first thing you said. What did you mean by it? Do you mean to tell me that you have been in love with me from the first?

September 23, 1944

Camille,

The moment Carl first handed me your picture, devastation overtook me in waves. If the experience hadn't been so demanding on me physically I would have laughed it off. I know it makes no sense. Feel free to make fun of

81

me. But I do intend to one day lay eyes on you, if only to put this obsession of mine to rest. And to put in your hand the letters that Carl himself regarded as his prized possessions. I know you said to keep them, but they are not mine, and I'd rather honor my friend's memory by returning your love to you. If I didn't think he was in a better place, focused on better matters, I know he would be concerned with your happiness and peace more than any other thing. And he would regret leaving you alone, as any man should.

I imagine it every day. I know that you live in that sprawling concrete jungle up north but in my mind, I can't picture it. In my mind, there is grass and a fence. And a bus stop right in front of your small country house that doesn't exist. And I get off the bus to see you standing there, minding your business, doing chores. And then, even though I am a stranger, whom you've never seen, our eyes meet and nothing more needs to be said. And then you run to me. We lay together in the grass and I tell you all the stories that can fit in my head about how much you meant. To us both.

The vision changes a little each day, in what ways I will not divulge. But it is the vision that I run to. The one that brings me peace when I look into the eyes of another enemy soldier hurdling towards me, more determined than I could ever manage.

October 7, 1944

Stanley,
I had a rough day and then I came home and this letter

was waiting for me. I cried because I realized that it was all so trivial. I don't know what I want more, for you to be here or me to be there. Your vision sounds beautiful enough to hold you to your promise.

Do not judge me by my tepid demeanor. I am simply a bit more hardened after the unexpected loss of a previous soldier. Not that I was all that unguarded to begin with.

I'm afraid I may not be as sanguine as I look in my picture. Which is why I lamented catching the eye of a man like Carl, whom I was desperate to impress and keep entertained. Please don't interpret my prudence as disinterest.

The best way I can describe it is to say that I am open to you. And you have become as synonymous with anticipation as food or a holiday. Please keep writing to me and I will keep writing to you. Please don't feel guilty for what you've told me either. I'm glad to inspire a man to write such fanciful things. It makes me feel that all these titillating feelings you bring up inside of me are some kind of charity to boot.

If you must look into the face of hell for the time being, by all means, allow me to be your muse. I will lay here in the moonlight, feeling the blissful agony of the bedsheets against my skin, until you send word to me that you made it through once again. Think of me and be strong. I feel in my heart that we are nearly at the end. Do your best to find me and I will be here.

Camille

Chapter 9

Mr. Hargrove's office was an ominous door at the end of the hall, in a furthermost corner of the office floor. Christy enjoyed a much larger desk in front of his much larger office, indicating her status among the other girls.

She was a Buckingham palace guard in muted pastels and among mid-century furniture. Even Mr. McCain had to show sufficient reason to be let in before barging through. Though he never waited for Christy to usher him in.

But even when Camille was far off, and heading closer and closer in the direction of the only office left at the end of the hallway, Christy would let her through without a conference. Whatever it was that Camille couldn't handle on her own, Christy wanted no parts of. Camille suspected that Christy getting up out of her chair to usher Camille anywhere was simply beneath her.

"Mr. Hargrove, Camille is here to see you," Christy buzzed.

"Send her in," came Mr. Hargrove's reply without hesitation.

"Go right in, Camille."

"Thank you," Camille politely replied. After some hesitation, she decided on leaving the door cracked behind her.

Mr. Hargrove's office was as big as her living room and with a considerably nicer view, obscured by orange-ish colored tweed curtains. A small, rolling liquor cart was stationed in the corner, presumably for clients. Or sometimes for the accounts department, should one of them need firing.

In front of that was a modest sitting area of a couch, coffee table, and two chairs at each end. Well, modest for a large house, perhaps. For an office, it boasted who had the most seniority of them all.

To his left was a less modest shelf of various personal memorabilia. Family portraits and trinkets from war, including a large worn army green satchel that hung on a coat rack behind him, with several medals pinned to it.

Camille had only been in his office one other time, and it shocked her to see such an open shrine to his service, in comparison to how little it seemed to be part of his identity.

She had to conclude that even this too was in service to clientele. If nothing else, to guilt them into joining and then again into never leaving.

"I spoke to accounting and they seemed a little lost on the details of my new position. You could just have Christy talk to them," Camille suggested, standing instead of sitting as Mr. Hargrove perused the paper.

"I will handle that. Did you think of a figure?"

"I would like a lock on my office door."

"You can have a new office," he offered, as though trying to get her to think bigger. "With a window."

"If you don't mind, Mr. Hargrove I think it's best that my

office remain centralized."

He gave her a terse nod, conceding. "Whatever you think is best, Miss Winters."

"And I think ten cents more an hour is sufficient."

"You will be salaried, Miss Winters."

"I see..."

"This is not a raise, Miss Winters. It is a promotion."

"Of course," she breathed as though frustrated. Asking for ten cents was hard enough.

"Your deceased young Beau. The one you mentioned over dinner," Mr. Hargrove suddenly brought up, folding his paper to address her.

"Yes?"

"I've been thinking a lot about that. Since we spoke. Was he part of the colored regiment that was stationed in the Pacific?"

Her heartbeat quickened, the room closed in a bit.

"He was."

"I thought so. I have a few connections in the service. I'll see what I can find out for you." He returned to his paper unceremoniously. Camille hadn't moved.

"That's very generous, Mr. Hargrove, but I know the details of his death."

Mr. Hargrove seemed startled as if surprised by her answer. "You do?"

"Yes. A friend of his was kind enough to write me after the fact. On his behalf."

"A friend?"

"His commanding officer. Apparently, they were close and my... he spoke of me often. To him. He was kind enough to reach out to me after he died."

"I see. Well, that was good of him," Mr. Hargrove said but

didn't mean. He seemed to be crushed that someone had beaten him to the punch.

"Yes. It was," was Camille's cryptic response.

"The family of the young man, do you keep up with them at all?"

"I do. I did. Not so much anymore."

"Is there anything they might want to—"

"I do hate to interrupt you, Mr. Hargrove, but I'm afraid I can't imagine anything else to do beyond what you've already done," Camille politely absolved him.

Mr. Hargrove surveyed her as if she'd just unknowingly given him a challenge. He quickly averted his eyes.

"Yes, of course. Forgive me, I suppose I'm feeling a bit helpless," he said, sitting up straight. "The war is somewhat of... a bittersweet subject for me. As I'm sure you've gathered. But I'd like to be able to do what I can for you in this regard. I feel I owe you that which is in my power to do."

"May I ask why, Mr. Hargrove?"

Mr. Hargrove let out an uncharacteristically long sigh. "I suppose Mr. Shaw's behavior from the boardroom yesterday still haunts me. Unfortunately, Mrs. Chase would never stand to let me fire her son."

"I would never expect that, Mr. Hargrove."

"I know that you wouldn't."

"And as Head of Personnel, I'm humble enough to admit he's a decent enough account man besides. Lazy, but that's hardly deadly. Or permanent. As he is, he's too expensive to replace."

Mr. Hargrove regarded her again as if in thought.

"At least let me find this good Samaritan for you. The commanding officer that informed you of your intended's untimely death."

87

"Mr. Hargrove—"

"Please."

Camille sighed. "I hate to seem so elusive, but I truly don't want it done."

"It's morbid, I understand. But I've been a soldier. If he took the time to reach out to you then, I assure you, he hasn't forgotten you. It wouldn't be nothing to him, if that's why you're worried. Did he reach out to you more than once?"

He's dead. Leave it.

She supposed she could've said that. But she'd made him out to be nothing at all. A needle in a haystack. And it would only encourage him even more.

Camille sighed with a dismissive laugh. "Mr. Hargrove. Please. This is inappropriate."

Mr. Hargrove didn't seem amused at first, but finally relented.

"You're right, Miss Winters. Forgive me. Tell Christy to ring me on the way out."

"Of course. Thank you, Mr. Hargrove."

"Shut the door behind you, Miss Winters."

Camille's insides swirled with dread as she headed back to her desk. She had a horrible feeling that Mr. Hargrove, instead of honoring her wishes, was planning a surprise.

Not that she thought this trivial endeavor had any chance of bringing about a result. Stanley was dead. Carl was dead.

Only, there was a terrific, uncharacteristic seed of hope formulating underneath the stale stack of stifling letters in her mind. The horrific notion that he might unearth some official record that put the whole matter ruthlessly to rest.

No more would they just be invisible, weightless, and floating. They'd be long decayed and defeated by death. Some brutal statistic that blotted her from their histories.

But the alternative was also no better. If the search came up as fruitless as she also sensed it would be, what's to stop him from upping the ante to some other pursuit until his conscience could be properly eased?

"Camille... Camille?"

Someone called her name but she didn't hear or see who it was. It wasn't like her to just ignore it.

She was starting to seethe something. Resentment? Rage?

She hated that she could not control him and make him do what she wished. Couldn't Mr. Hargrove see what was happening?

A silly question. They never could. But once she reflected on the entire matter being her own fault, she could feel the anger lifting off like the lid to a pot, revealing boiling regret and fear.

She should've never brought up the war. Now that they had this in common, the fondness between them that was creeping beyond respect had picked up speed.

And now he had given Camille more work to do. She could understand such a favor being born of a sense of guilt, but any more and she would owe him.

With any luck, he would consider himself absolved after this. She respected Mr. Hargrove, but she didn't want to constantly have to navigate her way around his gestures. A man like that will eventually be offended at a colored girl constantly fending off his kindness.

"Camille, can I speak to you a moment?" her intercom buzzed. It was Christy.

"Of course, Miss Caldwell."

A moment later, Christy came in and shut the door.

"I didn't mean to pry, but I couldn't help but overhear you in the office with Mr. Hargrove."

Shit.

Camille never felt comfortable shutting the door behind her when going into any office. So she expected there to be some fallout from that little decision.

"You had a husband in the war, Camille?"

"Not really my husband. I hardly knew him, he was... we were... engaged."

"It makes so much sense now."

Camille could be offended by whatever that meant, but Christy was probably right. War had given her such a complex.

Not to mention every living man seemed to pale in comparison to that brave soldier who survived artillery fire just to get a scented picture of her.

"Did I hear right, or was there another soldier? The one who wrote to you?"

Geez, this tramp heard everything. Which means she heard the part about Mr. Shaw. About her being head of personnel.

She wasn't in the wrong, but Camille was a black woman. She was gonna have to campaign to these hens if she wanted them on her side. She was going to have to let these white people know her business.

Oh well. It was between this or going in to the office of the boss, locking the door, and coming out with a mysterious promotion.

Camille dug deep and put on a personal performance for Christy. If the story was going to circulate the office, it may as well have the added detail of Camille literally breaking down in front of her. No one would believe it. And yet, they would have to.

Camille reached for tissues in front of a shocked Christy. She dabbed at her minimal mascara.

"He's dead too. Stanley, was his name. Whitman. His

commanding officer," Camille said as she dabbed her eyes. "Stanley tried to send me some of his belongings but I didn't feel right having them. We barely knew each other when he proposed. He was practically a stranger to me."

"Wait, which one? What was your fiance's name?"

Camille grit her teeth unconsciously, her jaw tight.

She was going to have to tell her everything?

Her lips trembled themselves into a frown and she thought she might actually blow up and start throwing things everywhere.

"Carl," she said in a whisper. Tears suddenly warmed her cheeks. At some point, the performance had become real.

"You poor thing," Christy clutched her chest, having grabbed a tissue of her own. "What happened to the one who wrote to you?"

"I have no idea. We kept in touch until the war was over. Or at least, almost over. I never received another letter after Spring of '45 so I have to assume it's because he's dead."

"He never wrote to you again?"

"Not that I know of."

"So he could still be out there," Christy swooned.

"I don't think so."

"How do you know?"

"I don't," admitted Camille. "But he'd made a promise to me once. He used it as motivation to get through. At least, that's what he told me. And perhaps I'm being naive, but I have to believe that he's dead. If not then.... well, he's dead to me anyway."

Christy's look turned even more gossipy. "I see. Did things ever turn... romantic? Between you and the commanding officer?" she asked in a low voice.

Camille sighed. "...Letters turn everything romantic," she

summarized.

Christy held the balled-up tissue to her chest and sighed as if in ecstasy. Camille giggled. Okay, so maybe this wasn't so bad.

"You have to keep this to yourself, Christy. I can't have anyone around here thinking that I'm a big softie."

"Of course, Camille, I just... oh my heart just breaks for you."

"I'm okay, Christy. Really. It's been ten years. Everything happens for a reason."

* * *

From that moment in Mr. Hargrove's office, it only took two weeks for Camille's life to change.

After that day she'd all but forgotten about it. Even when she heard the mailcart squeaking down the hallway and her heart gave her a little jolt. The squeaking only reminded her of one thing.

Today was payday. Her first paycheck as a salaried employee. A whopping $100 dollars. She could barely breathe.

She could start looking for a place in the city. She was finally going to let herself splurge on something. New clothes. Pampering. The movies. Fine dining. Perhaps all of them in one day.

"Mail for you, Miss Camille."

"Thank you, Winston," Camille smiled. Winston was an older black man that'd been delivering the mail since before Mr. Hargrove's father had died.

"There was a letter too," Winston added. "It was sent to an old address. Seems it went all over the place before it ended up here."

Camille took one look at the letter and nearly fainted from

shock.

"You alright, Miss Camille?"

"Yes, Winston. Is that it?"

"That's it, ma'am."

"See you tomorrow," she sent out the door as he continued down the hallway. She couldn't seem to remove the letter from her field of vision.

She looked at her name in the impersonal type. Coupled with the impossible name in the upper left corner. The anachronistic rubber stamp of a stateside letter.

Stanley S. Whitman. From a Pennsylvania address.

She dropped the letter as though it were toxic. It simply couldn't be. It wasn't possible.

She shouldn't open it. She couldn't.

She checked the postdate. September 24th. Only a few days after she'd spoken to Mr. Hargrove.

But he'd never brought the subject up to her again. She hadn't even given him a name. How can they find a soldier without a name?

There was only one person outside of her that knew the name. Christy. And she couldn't believe she could've ever been so stupid.

Hadn't she told Christy about Stanley the very same day? Did she go against her wishes and tell Mr. Hargrove anyway?

Had Mr. Hargrove... *sent* her??

* * *

"Mr. Hargrove, Camille Winters is here to see you," Christy came over the intercom.

"Send her in."

This time Camille closed the door. She wasn't worried. It wouldn't take long.

"Yes, Miss Winters?"

"Mr. Hargrove, did you... I received a letter today."

"Is that so?"

"From the lieutenant I told you about?"

"Of course," Mr. Hargrove nodded with faint recognition. "Looks like my request found its way to the proper department."

"Apparently so."

"And was I right? The young man was still alive?" he eagerly asked, his blue eyes clear and inquisitive.

Camille tried not to be smitten. Tried not to let him off the hook, but she was at his mercy. Professionally and otherwise.

"You really should not have gone through the trouble," she said, sounding defeated.

"It was no trouble," he said dismissively. "But you should know that I would have done the same even if it had been."

"Mr. Hargrove—"

"I won't hear another word about it, Miss Winters."

"How did you know?" she challenged him.

Mr. Hargrove looked puzzled. "Know what, Miss Winters?"

"His name."

He all but shrugged. "I didn't. I told my contact your name and nothing else."

Camille scoffed in disbelief. "How on Earth..."

"Military letters are not sent directly. They are printed and screened. On microfilm and then sent. Originals are kept in storage by the U.S. government," he filled in.

"I see. Your contact must be very high up," Camille presumed, impressed.

"I don't know if he is, but I am," he replied with a layer of annoyance.

"Of course, Mr. Hargrove," Camille nodded, annoyed with his annoyance. Should she be *honored* that he overstepped his bounds??

"Is there anything else?" he asked.

"No sir," she answered tersely, turning toward the door. "Thank you."

"Very well. Oh, and Miss Winters."

"Yes?"

"Was I right?"

Camille turned toward him with a furrowed brow, her hand on the knob. "About?"

"The lieutenant. He remembered you?"

"Yes, sir," she lied. "He was very glad to hear from me. You were right."

She hadn't opened the letter and didn't know that she ever would.

"Very well, then," Mr. Hargrove said with a dismissive return to his work.

"Open or closed?" Camille asked on her way out.

Mr. Hargrove had forgotten to hide his satisfied smirk. Luckily Camille hadn't seen it.

"Open."

* * *

"Bullshit," Camille uttered to herself.

The letter was so light, so slight that it may have even been empty. That meant no picture. So this was a waste of time.

If whoever this was thought she would want to pick things back up after ten years with a disembodied voice then he was out of his mind. She wasn't 18 anymore.

She put the letter in her purse. Until her purse became too distracting in its place on her desk so she set it down at her feet.

She couldn't open it but she couldn't throw it away either. Finally, on her lunch break, she put a sheet of paper into her typewriter. She began to type:

> *To whom it concerns,*
>
> *I feel obligated to let you know that I did receive your letter. However, I have no intentions of opening it. I don't know who you are, who put you up to this, or what you want from me. But what you are doing is cruel, so please stop. If by some miracle the person writing me is indeed Stanley Whitman, please know that I have moved on as I well know that you have. Whatever caused you to break your promise to me is forgotten. I have forgiven you.*

When she got to the last line she had to quiet her sobs behind her hand.

> *You have lived your life without me these eleven years. Please continue to do so.*
>
> *With respect,*
> *Camille*

She placed the letter in an envelope, copied the return address, and added it to Winston's outgoing mailcart at the end of the day.

Mail service had greatly improved since the war, it seemed. Though it probably helped that they were both stateside. By the end of that week, there was a reply. Not a letter, a postcard.

"Greetings from Philly" boasted the front in big box letters. She couldn't resist turning it over and reading what was on it. He likely knew that.

> Camille,
>
> It is me. I am alive. I imagined this day many times. I will write you again to explain. When it arrives, please open it. Please.
>
> Stanley

Camille stared and stared at the bitterly familiar script, just as elegant as it ever was. She retreated again to her typewriter and didn't even think. Her fingers just moved.

> Stanley,
>
> You once said that you wished that one day the memory of Carl would become a fond recollection that I freely share with joy. And that both of us would be whole, and that letters between two mutual acquaintances would return to its rightfully trivial place in the world.
>
> Well, it never happened. And that is all because of you. Knowing that you are truly alive only fills me with pity and disdain. I hate you Stanley. I have forgiven you, but

still, I do hate you. As of September 24th, 1956 I do. And I will never open another letter from you again.

That should do it. Sick bastard. She dropped the letter in Winston's mailcart like a match into a wastebasket.

There was a reply in record time. Two days later. If it wasn't post-marked, she would've assumed it was hand-delivered. Another postcard:

Camille,
    Well, that is a shame. Because I love you. Still. And will never stop.

10

Present Day, 1956

September 24, 1956

To whom it concerns:

I confirm that my name is Captain Stanley Whitman of the H company 1st colored division of the U.S. Marine Corps. I was stationed in the Pacific for 30 months as the commanding officer for the deceased marine in question, LCpl. Carl Downey. I did contact Camille Winters on his behalf and would be more than happy to provide my contact information and receive hers in turn. Please pass this on or contact me again regarding this matter.

Yours,
Cpt. Stanley Whitman
58743 Wapokaneta Ln.
Lansing, PA 12345

October 8th, 1956

My dearest Camille,
It breaks my heart to hear you say what you said. Not

because you are angry with me, but it sounds as though you mean to tell me that you never found that great love of your life, or any love, which eats away at my very insides. I can't think of anything more cruel if that is the case. I know that it is common for a man to go through his life unfulfilled, but if a woman does so too then what good is it?

I wish I had a good reason for allowing you to think I was dead, which I do readily admit. At some point, I did nearly die, and yours was the only face that could calm me down as I felt myself slip away. Miraculously, I somehow survived and awoke in the hospital unit. I missed Iwo Jima. I had to leave my men behind without saying goodbye. I was close enough to the surrender to be ashamed of myself. Only to return home defeated, and broken everywhere but on the outside. But no one seemed to see or understand that.

I should never have survived, my sweet Camille. I somehow earned a medal of honor for not dying and attempting to keep my brothers from dying with all my might, even though I largely failed. I was inundated with celebration. No one knew me at all. I should have died. Many times. Everyone tells me never to say that but it is true. I know that I can tell you, and that you would not patronize me. You weren't the only part of that war that I abandoned. I tried to forget my men. The rest of whom died in Okinawa. I tried to forget it all.

I started to think maybe I imagined you. That it was the war that made you into what you were to me. I'm ashamed to say that I even made a habit of writing a lady I had my eye on, and she was charmed by it. But it wasn't the same. She wasn't you. I would say that I missed you but that doesn't nearly say it.

I send this in hopes that you will decide to break your promise and actually open one of my letters. I myself am done breaking promises to you. I will write you as long as I am able. Forever. And perhaps one day you will allow me to return the letters from your intended that I have carried faithfully to this day.

As for any response, I will have to live with the strange agony of never hearing from you again. I must tell you, even though your first letter in ten years was designed to rip me open as well, it was a sweet blissful ignorance seeing that familiar script of yours in my mailbox.

I don't mind admitting to you that it made me cry, and I nearly smelled the smells and heard the sounds and felt the sun baking my back, taking my time with the seal. I'd hoped there'd be another picture in it, smelling of you, but it was nothing so sweet as that.

You are etched in my memory forever, sweet Camille.
Stanley

October 11, 1956

Camille,
In my earlier letter I assumed that you never found the great love of your life, and upon further rumination I do want to apologize if that was too presumptuous. I know you are a complicated woman. I assumed your passionate feelings came from resentment and emptiness, not realizing that it doesn't matter how successful or full of diversion your life has become, you have the right to rake me over the coals.

101

I truly can't tell how wrathful you are. Part of me wants to see. I dreaded the thought for many years but now that it is here it is not enough. My greatest fear perhaps, were I to contact you, was that you simply would not remember. Or that you would be as cold to me as you could possibly stand, because you did remember. It is my mother's weapon of choice.

And so I was relieved that you chose passion, however restrained. I never remembered that about you. I remembered you being very stand offish, and I wanted nothing more than for you to admit that you were enamored with me. And I pouted when you didn't.

But then your reply made me rummage through your old writings and it was there. I couldn't escape it. I was blind to think you didn't care for me as much as I cared for you, and for that I am sorry. Sorry for many things. But I am glad that fate has forced my hand.

Stanley

October 25, 1956

Stanley,

As you have probably gathered, I gave in and opened your letters. I opened them all at once. Hearing that all of the men under your command died made me weep uncontrollably and I was ill all day. I was reminded of how I once prayed daily, first for Carl and then for you all. And the confirmation that my prayers were not enough was despair on top of it.

Write me if you must, but I do not want to hear any more of this war. I would ask you more about your current life. About if you have a family and children, but I don't want *to hear about that either. Not yet. I won't say ever. I've begun to pity myself less and find joy in the fact that you are alive. Even though it means that you may have never actually cared for me. If you are a father I do eventually want to know. If you are a husband I do want to know that too. But I can't say that I want to know it all. Nor do I want to tell you anything about me.*

Camille

October 27, 1956

Camille,

It was a joy to receive a response but then my heart was broken when I opened and read. I have hurt you again and I'm sorry. To think that I never cared for you would be anathema. Forgive me, as soon as you are ready.

I have a family in name only. I found a young woman to take pity on me, a widow with two children of her own. She was left destitute after her husband gambled all her money away and died mysteriously, most likely as his debt settlement. Certain injuries from the war left me unable to conceive children, which I am glad of because I don't think that I could love them, as I do not love hers as I should. But they understand I am not their father and they are forgiving.

Our first years were a blur. I was confronted constantly with my fractured state. Besides you and the few inter-ludes during the war, I had very little idea of what kind of man I could be to a woman. I remember wanting to do a good job. But the failures were so brutal, and then I woke every morning fresh from nightmares. I watched her love for me fade to nothing, as I had warned her would happen.

I vowed to take care of her and that is what I do.

I thank God every day that I had the presence of mind not to find you and drag you into this madness. And yet I searched for you at the bottom of every bottle, and in the corner of every whorehouse, even as I hoped to never ever have you see me like that.

I am sorry that I ever wrote to you and gave you such hope. It makes me embarrassed to revisit my naivete. My wife found your picture in my wallet several years ago and destroyed it. I don't dare retrieve the one you gave Carl which is safe within his letters, which I hope you will still permit me to return.

Forgive me if this is more than you wanted to know. I want to respect your wishes. But I wanted to rush and tell you how miserable I am to put you at ease.

Stan

November 3, 1956

Stanley,

It doesn't put me at ease to know that you are miserable. I am miserable too. But I do have one consolation. I do love my job.

I have many responsibilities but virtually no supervision and it is grand. No one bothers me, because my job doesn't require it. I work for everyone and no one. I merely run things smooth like the wheel in a machine. It helps to have competent people around me who also take pride in their work and yet crave the limelight. I lend it to them freely and they think it generous. I have learned, however, that some prefer to outsmart me for it and for those I oblige them also. If I appear generous it only makes them suspicious.

If I am the recipient of the limelight, it is usually at the hand of the owner, Mr. Hargrove. Whose charity and nosy disposition we owe to this reunion. He was also in the war, heard me speaking of you and took pity. I told him not to bother. But he is white, and hopelessly privileged, and considers many impossible things reachable and surmountable. But he is different. I did not consider that he could be right and so I allowed him to interfere.

I am glad you did not find me either. The promise of your love haunts me like an apparition. But I could not function in a world where I both had you and resented you. In my dreams, we never got far beyond the moment you stepped off the bus in front of my non-existent country house. Think of it, me dreaming of something patently impossible, convinced it would happen. You were never without your uniform. Your naivete was nothing compared to mine.

Honestly, love is a myth to me. Nothing is more real than accounting. Budget sheets and deadlines. Plugging in a variable and getting a result. Promotions. I am surrounded by white people all day. I'm almost certain none of them are happy. If they have love, it hasn't helped them. And yet I know that they are almost always in pursuit of it anyway. As if they aren't left with a single other challenge in life. It is good to know there is at least one playing field on which we are somewhat level.

Camille

November 9, 1956

Camille,

I opened your letter too hastily. I receive them in record time now and still lament when I've already gotten to the end. My cheeks are sore from smiling. My lovely Camille. I swear you've begun to thaw my veins and chase away the numbness, something I believed to be impossible. I should have known better.

I am glad to hear that you have become a professional woman. You must be inspiring untold numbers of colored women, because I cannot help but see them by the dozens now, all pantyhose and pencil skirts, as if the city is growing them. Perhaps one day you can come to me in Philadelphia. When you are ready, of course. If you ever change your mind of wanting to see me. Or I can come to you. I want to see how beautiful you are. My wife says that I am now as handsome as I will ever be in my life, in case that still matters to you. But she never saw me before the war. I am a shell and I know it.

If ever I run into your boss, I owe him a beer at least.
Stanley

November 16, 1956

Stanley,

In regards to seeing each other, perhaps in time. But for now, I like how we are. I still wonder if you are just some nosy neighbor taking me for a ride, by the way. Very little has changed about my living situation, down to the neighbors. My mother complained my entire life that we were cooped up here, letting out half the building even when we could've afforded not to. But now it is ours and no one can evict me. I am considering renting both sides out and finding a place in the city to be closer to work. An

106

impossibility up until recently. I finally gained permanent employment so I am in no danger. I considered finding a roommate to be prudent, but I simply cannot live with someone else. The concerns of a spinster, I know. I hope my letters weren't always this dull.

   Camille

November 23, 1956

Camille,

You could never be dull. In fact, it makes me grin thinking of you behind the desk of a big office in a big New York skyscraper. Your family must be very proud.

Speaking of prudence, if I were you and I owned your apartment in Brooklyn, I would not move a muscle. Improve on it little by little, so that by the time you are ready to leave, you will have no trouble attracting a tenant. In the meantime, save your money and watch the market. Buy when the time is right and never sell. One way or the other, you will die a millionaire.

I want to come see you and make love to you. I've decided. Would this be okay?

   Stan

December 2, 1956

Stanley,

I spoke to my father and he agreed with you. About the former thing, not the latter. I did not tell him about the latter.

That sentence is sitting at the bottom of my stomach like a spoiled sorry lump. I don't know how to answer you. So I won't.

One day I will, but not today.
Camille

11

Chapter 11

It was technically her third Christmas party as an employee at Hargrove and Chase.

The first was two weeks after she'd started and she spent the entirety of it working. She'd only made it halfway through the C's of the A-L at that time and she couldn't conceive of letting the office see her taking a break.

For the second, the dynamic was almost entirely switched. She was afraid she was perceived as snobbish and she couldn't look like the office shrew who refused to fraternize. So she pasted on a smile for a tasteful two hours and then high-tailed it out of there.

By Christmas party number three, she'd struck a bit of a balance. She was donning one of her pants suits for the second time ever— always a conversation starter— and figured that would make up for whatever sanguine act she couldn't be bothered to drum up for the occasion.

It was a Thursday and the following day was Christmas Eve. The office would be closed on the following Monday as well.

Everyone kept stopping by her office as though they'd had no intentions of working, and they did the same while she ate lunch in the break room.

"Camille, where's the record player?" Christy asked.

"Where it always is."

"I've brought my Elvis Presley records," another secretary Megan chattered excitedly.

"...Is one of them Christmas-themed?" Camille asked, chewing.

"Camille, I bet you like Elvis Presley, don't you?" Christy smirked with wide eyes.

"He's quite a character," she replied, choosing her words carefully.

"Character? He's a *dream*."

It never failed. Even Mr. Hargrove seemed to come out of hiding and find her on letter day, even though Christy could easily be found and do whatever he asked.

She just needed thirty measly minutes. Thirty minutes to get a sandwich off the cart, sit down with the latest letter from Stanley, sip coffee, and not be there. And yet, it seemed as though on every letter day there wasn't a more difficult thing to get.

Today, it seemed letter day wasn't meant to be.

2:00 had come and gone. It would be the last day she could receive a letter from him before the holiday, and with a long Christmas break ahead of her she had to assume the worst: she had wounded him with her rejection of his offer.

She thought they were on the same page. That he would understand the position he was putting her in by asking such a thing. He was a married man, and they weren't teenagers anymore.

Nothing good could come of it. Even though his offer had

reverberated through her, it'd taken her several days to even fashion a reply.

It was possible he was doing the prudent thing and simply cutting things off. But it's more likely that he couldn't bring himself to reply to her spurning. Maybe it was a combination.

Either way, it made her forlorn. Which she had to fight through if she were going to make it through the holidays.

At 4:30 the Christmas party was already in full swing. The girls were permitted escorts, which allowed the men plenty of company to fraternize. The married men who were childless or had nannies brought their wives.

Meanwhile, Camille finished up the last bit of work in her office so that she could have a worry-free holiday. She wasn't in the mood for this party, but with no other plans, she didn't mind having her door open while people popped in and asked why she was still working.

"Camille, do you know how to make a mule?"

"As a matter of fact, I do."

"We have gin, vodka, olives, lemon, and... someone brought amaretto? I'm not quite sure what we have here besides martinis."

"Any club soda?"

"Uh..."

"Check Drew's office," Camille said with a hint of mischief.

Mr. McCain and Mr. Hargrove sometimes made an unlikely appearance, but only after hours. By the time one of the bosses showed, Camille had been given full drink serving duties. And it was the one they'd least expected.

"Ken!" Ezra, one of the account men announced. Loudly. Everyone straightened up a bit.

"At ease, everyone," he said, moseying through the bunch.

"On my way to the airport, just came to wish you all a good holiday."

"And to you, Mr. Hargrove. You're just in time for the Dirty Santa game."

"Christy, did I contribute anything?"

"You did sir."

Mr. Hargrove addressed Camille's hunched back as she handed out drinks. "Miss Winters. Nice to see you in good spirits."

"I'm always in good spirits, Mr. Hargrove," she replied without looking up from her task.

"Perhaps, but it's not every day we see you with a carefully balanced tray of booze."

She conceded with a smiling huff. "A relic of my Cunard days."

Mr. Hargrove's face lit up. "You were a stewardess?"

Camille hardly noticed as she was busy removing drinks from her tray. Still, she smiled hearing his tone.

"A long time ago," she dismissed with a wave of her hand. She walked back to the makeshift bar with her empty tray.

"Were you aboard the Queen Mary?"

"I was."

"For how long?"

"Nearly four years," she said, busying herself with mixing. "A stewardess for two and a secretary for the rest."

"What happened? Travel didn't suit you?"

She shrugged, putting ice in empty tumblers. "It suited me fine," was all she said. Mr. Hargrove didn't press it further.

Christy and a few of the copywriters looked awkwardly on at the exchange.

"Well, Miss Winters I'll have a Jack and Coke if you're still serving," he said.

"All we have is vodka and vermouth."

"Then I'll leave you to surprise me."

"Will Mr. McCain be joining us?" Christy asked.

"Shortly, why?"

"We raided his cabinet," Josh outed themselves.

"Ah. Well, if you can replace it by the time he returns next year, your secret's safe with me," Mr. Hargrove replied.

No one could exactly relax with the boss at the party. But everyone liked introducing their family and friends to the man whose name was on the door.

As the two office sticks-in-the-mud, Camille kept Mr. Hargrove busy enough to let everyone mingle in peace.

"You have permission to raid my cabinet as well, Miss Winters," Mr. Hargrove offered.

"That shouldn't be necessary."

"I believe I have some absinthe hidden behind the couch. For emergencies."

"Heaven forbid," Camille exclaimed, taking a sip of her own creation. "The maintenance crew will never do a thing for us again."

Mr. Hargrove regarded her, smiling. "Did you ever receive any more letters from your soldier fella?"

Camille chuckled. "He's not my 'fella' but yes, I did."

"He isn't? Why ever not?" he asked, perplexed.

"We're estranged penpals, at best. We're simply catching up, that's all."

"Penpals, you say? Has he married?"

"He has," Camille accidentally smiled. She couldn't believe he was interested at all. Though she supposed he would want to know how his reuniting plan had worked out.

"Well then, it's simple. Don't let your correspondence go

beyond the New Year, Miss Winters."

"Shall I cut him loose, Mr. Hargrove?" she laughed.

"Naturally."

She laughed again, hearing Kenneth Hargrove's old-fashioned courting advice.

"First you want me to reach out to him, and now you want me to shun him if he won't upend his life for me?"

"As a married man and a veteran myself, I'm merely suggesting that an accumulation of letters from a lady friend could get him in trouble. And a man that would continue a clandestine affair isn't fit for a relationship."

She had to look away from his crystal blue gaze as he dug inadvertently through her most intimate places.

"So I shouldn't take him up on his offer to abandon his children and take me away from this place?" she quipped with a stoic face.

Mr. Hargrove gave her an uncharacteristic laugh. "Certainly we would miss you, but we would manage."

"Well, I don't think you would have to worry about that, but I appreciate the gesture, Mr. Hargrove. It's nice to be missed."

"Perhaps it's selfish, but I was hoping you'd stay long enough to one day get comfortable enough to call me Ken," a smile on his unusually full lips. *Hell's bells.*

"It'll be a cold day in hell, Mr. Hargrove. But you can call me Camille at any time."

"Two can play at this game, Miss Winters," he said with a wink. She grinned and noticed peripherally the room get quiet enough to demand a switch in the conversation.

Thankfully, Mr. McCain came in and stole much of the attention.

"Merry Christmas, peasants!" he bellowed. The room howled.

For the account managers and staff, being able to introduce their wives and girlfriends to Mr. Hargrove was an important courtesy. But the creative department wanted to introduce Andrew McCain.

Andrew tapped out after only a few minutes of mingling. He sat directly between Camille and Mr. Hargrove, picking up a random drink off an abandoned end table.

"Mr. McCain," Mr. Hargrove nodded.

"Ken. What are you still doing here?"

"My flight doesn't leave for another two hours," he explained.

"I could join you, if you like. I wouldn't mind tagging along. You know, keep the client happy and all that," Andrew volunteered.

"Williams-Sonoma's happy, last I checked," Mr. Hargrove insisted.

"I know, I'm just saying. As long as I'm avoiding my family I may as well work. Grace them with the face of Creative," Mr. McCain suggested with a confident inebriated smirk.

Yikes. Mr. Hargrove just gave him a look that told Camille everything she didn't need to know. Mr. McCain was getting harder to control.

"Nonsense. Enjoy The Bahamas," Mr. Hargrove diplomatically suggested.

"Can you captains of industry take this discussion somewhere else?" Mr. Shaw suggested, hearing the tail end. The copywriters gathered in formation around Mr. McCain.

"I'm just here to make sure the party will still be going when I get back," Mr. McCain eluded with a raised eyebrow.

Everyone looked at Mr. Hargrove.

"It's up to Miss Winters."

"Oh, *honestly,*" she groaned. She was free of the pressure of being liked, but it didn't always mean she was jumping at the chance to be hated.

He smiled. Obviously, it was a joke. Mr. Hargrove could simply override her if she told the whole office to take their debauched selves home.

If she hadn't already anticipated their dwindling work pace all week, she might've told him no.

"If you want us to still be here, you're going to have to do a booze run," Camille told Mr. McCain.

"Way to go, Camille!"

"Not for me, obviously. Which doesn't mean I'll be babysitting all night either, I'm going home. And you're out of gin, by the way."

"Let's go to the village and find Camille a colored fella."

"The maintenance crew's here all night," Mr. Shaw volunteered. Some of the guys snickered but the girls were conspicuously silent.

Camille couldn't decipher what that could possibly mean, so she shrugged it off.

"I'll make you sad sacks one more round of drinks and then I'm off. And no using the conference room," nagged Camille.

"Aw, you're no fun."

"The best thing I can do for the maintenance crew is to keep you from leaving your fluids all over the 14th floor. There are no trash cans down there. Or doors. Or blinds. Keep in mind they turn the heat down after 7pm."

Mr. Hargrove gave them all a lazy, irresistible smirk with smiling blue eyes. "Well, you all heard the warden."

"Ken, you coming with?" Mr. McCain inquired on his way out.

"My flight, remember?"

"C'mon, I need a wingman."

"To go get booze?" Camille wondered.

"I'll come!" Ezra shouted a little too enthusiastically. Everyone looked at him as though he were a troll. Compared to Mr. McCain, he was.

"Never mind," he scoffed. He looked over at Mr. Hargrove. "You better be gone by the time I get back."

"Merry Christmas, Andrew."

"And to you. Chet, go dig out that Santa costume, I'm concocting a plan," Mr. McCain directed him with a point of his finger.

* * *

"Pour me another, Miss Winters."

Camille finished off the last of Mr. Hargrove's gin from his office cabinet and split the last of the cocktail between the both of them.

After an hour, the married folk had gone and Mr. McCain still hadn't returned. Camille made the journey to Mr. Hargrove's office and rationed what they had left.

It was far too late for everyone to still be at work, but they clearly had hopes of getting wasted and finding some abandoned nook or cranny to do wasted things and they weren't giving up, even if Mr. Hargrove did insist on hanging around.

Camille kept him sober company. Though after a few drinks, she had half a mind to sneak into his office and sleep on that comfortable couch of his for the night.

"And what do you have planned for the holiday, Miss Winters?"

"My parents bought a house in Levittown. Our first suburban Christmas."

"You don't sound enthusiastic."

"I was just there a month ago. Besides, is anyone enthusiastic to spend the weekend with their parents?"

"You don't get along?"

"Of course. It's just the longer I go unmarried, the less sure I become of that."

"You haven't told them of your pen pal?"

Camille smiled with a devious squint. "Don't you have a flight to catch?"

He smiled. "Itching to get rid of me, Miss Winters?"

"Not at all. The rest of the office, however..."

"I see," he gave her a knowing nod. "Then perhaps I should get out of your hair."

"I should be on my way as well," she sighed, standing up and walking to her office. Mr. Hargrove trailed behind.

"Let me walk you out."

Camille's heartbeat doubled. She'd never seen him offer to do such a thing for anyone else. Not even his own secretary.

"....That won't be necessary, Mr. Hargrove. But thank you."

"Then let me call you a cab."

"I'm perfectly fine taking the subway."

"Absolutely not," he replied sternly.

"Mr. Hargrove—"

"Humor me, Miss Winters, if you're too ashamed to be seen with me. How else will I live with myself if I can't see you off safely tonight?"

Camille rolled her eyes while she smiled, charmed. "What a dramatic thing you are."

Suddenly a cluster of co-workers began filing toward the lobby entrance.

"Party's over?" Camille asked, somewhat relieved.

"Party's moving. To Gleeson's," one said.

"You're welcome to come along, Camille," said another. Though she could tell they were just being nice. They were young and dumb and all the rest. And she was a half-breed buzzkill.

"Thank you, but, I'm heading home."

"Can we walk you out, Camille?" Christy offered.

At that, Camille's pulse shot to the moon.

It sounded innocent enough but as good as Camille's radar had gotten, she could never rest on it. Surely, Christy had just assumed that no one wanted to hang around while the boss was still there.

Certainly, she hadn't meant it as a gesture to keep Camille from impropriety.

Camille knew very well what impropriety looked like, and didn't need Christy's or anyone else's help guarding against it.

Was Christy so bent on embarrassing her that she didn't even seem to mind implicating her very own boss??

"Camille and I are running away together, Christy. Don't try and stop us," Mr. Hargrove answered before she had a chance to reply.

The entire group laughed as if satisfied, as if it were even an answer. They walked out without another word.

She'd never had a rich white man take heat for her before. It was incredible. His words were like spells.

"Well, you've certainly missed your flight by now," Camille said once they were gone. She turned her focus to cleaning.

The maintenance crew could handle it, of course, but this was beyond their usual duties. And if they were anything like her brother's hourly jobs, they would not be compensated for it.

"There's another flight to L.A. leaving in two hours," he said, finishing his drink left on a random secretary's desk.

"The family's not expecting you?"

"It's bad enough that I'm here 300 days out of the year. The last thing they want is to be stuck with me for the holidays."

"That sounds terrible," Camille opined between the clang of empty bottles and the rustling of plastic.

"You don't seem to be in a rush to be at home either, Miss Winters," he pointed out.

She stopped, looking over at him. "No, I meant your... nevermind."

"My what?"

"It's nothing, sir."

"There's no one here, Camille."

Camille stopped again.

Well, that was fast. Mr. Hargrove was the first to break the first name rule.

And he would be the only. If it was his way of getting her to open up, he underestimated her.

"Whether someone's here or not is not the issue, Mr. Hargrove."

"Then what *is* the issue, Miss Winters?"

Is that why he was still here? Did he sense her contempt, subtle and buried, even to her?

"My personal beliefs about your life should never be part of any discussion."

"Not even if I request them?"

Camille looked around, satisfied with her cleanup job so far. She sighed.

"I stopped myself because I'm uncomfortable, suddenly, Mr. Hargrove."

"If I were Mr. McCain would you be so uncomfortable?"

What on Earth could he possibly mean by that?

"Of course not," she said.

"Why is that?"

"Because Mr. McCain is a buffoon. And not my boss."

Mr. Hargrove laughed. "I see. So your high opinion of me is to blame."

She smiled, with her hand on the hip of her pin-striped pants. "To blame for what, Mr. Hargrove?"

"For your inability to tell me your true opinions."

"No, sir."

"No?"

She made her way past him and back to her office, gathering her things. "It's my high opinion of *me* that is to blame."

He stood outside the threshold of her door, drink casually in hand.

"You know I would never do anything to jeopardize your future with this company, don't you? And there's nothing you could do that could make you lose my respect, Miss Hargrove."

Camille stopped, fighting a shiver as she gripped her purse. She was desperate to hope that he hadn't noticed at all.

"...Winters, you mean," she said.

"Pardon?"

"You called me... Miss Hargrove."

"Did I?" he said in a faint voice. He cleared his throat.

"And I didn't know that. But thank you, Mr. Hargrove," Camille said as she ignored his close proximity. She locked the door to her office and shut it behind her.

"And now I find myself in the uncomfortable position of envying Mr. McCain," he said watching her, unmoving.

Camille made her way back down the hallway, to the open sea of empty desks, each typewriter topped dutifully with a vinyl cover. The offices along the perimeter's blinds were all drawn like lashes to closed eyes.

"The last thing Mr. McCain wants to hear from me are my true opinions."

Mr. Hargrove lazily trailed behind. "Now that's where you're wrong."

"I'll have to take your word for it," Camille said, returning to her drink on one of the end tables where she left it.

"Where on Earth did you acquire these exquisite pants?" Mr. Hargrove leaned on the desk opposite her when he asked.

She looked down at herself. "I had them made."

"It beats all I've ever seen."

Camille giggled. He put one of his hands in his pockets and she mimicked his movements. He smiled an exquisite smile and she forgot herself for a moment in it.

"You're not exactly helping the rumors around the office about you with these kinds of outfits," he said, savoring his next-to-last sip.

Camille's smile didn't move an inch. "Beg your pardon?"

He lowered his head slowly. "I've said too much."

She tilted her head with another squint. "And now you must continue."

Ice clinked in his glass every time he moved his arm.

"Surely you've noticed how the office seems to gossip about everyone. Except whoever is present."

"I'm mostly curious how any rumors have made their way to you."

"The conference room is just one big locker room once you've left, you must know."

Camille felt a deep pit and she wanted her legs to move. Out of the office, so that the next part of the discussion could never have a chance to take place.

She could always just ignore it. She was certain if she just ignored it, Mr. Hargrove would leave it be.

"So... you all have been discussing me?"

"A bit. What's in these drinks again, Miss Winters?" he asked, though he barely sounded curious.

"Why do you ask?"

"It's just that I can't imagine I would land myself in such hot water with you normally."

"Nothing that you can't handle, I'm sure," she assured him.

"Are you telling me that I'm hammered right now?"

She chuckled a little at the implication. "Certainly not... surely not."

It was at that moment that she realized something was wrong. Had been wrong. Terribly so. For awhile.

She looked down at the nearly empty glass in his hand.

"What have you had, two? And whatever's in your glass? You handle more liquor in the morning account meetings."

"Looks can be deceiving, Miss Hargrove," he replied.

12

Chapter 12

And at the second switching of her name with his, she realized they might have a problem. A big one.

Mr. Hargrove studied the swirling contents of his glass, as if too drunk to be as panicked as he would've liked.

Camille suddenly got the darkest of feelings looking on at Mr. Hargrove as he hastily finished the rest, and then reached for hers with barely a sip left in it. She nearly dropped it when their hands made contact.

He picked it up and studied it, taking his time bringing it to his lips, and closed his eyes as he savored every last drop.

Camille got off the desk, picked up her purse, and shakily put on her coat.

"You really do make an exquisite drink, Miss Winters. Any more talents I should know about?"

She ignored him. "I'm not sure I want to know anymore. What the rumors are."

As Mr. Hargrove began taking casual steps towards her, Camille slowly, instinctively backed away toward the wall behind her, further and further from the front door.

"Mr. McCain has started a betting pool on whether or not he can out you as a lesbian. There were talks about attempting to seduce you. Jokes, of course, but I put a stop to it. Aside from the fact that the conversation filled me with an obscene amount of rage, it's been mostly agreed that chasing mulatto pussy isn't worth losing our very capable head of personnel over. Or incurring the wrath of every woman we know."

Silence stretched endlessly. Ruthlessly. Until Camille began in a stringy voice.

"I confess, I made them a little strong, sir, but... it's a party. Before the long holiday. We only had vodka. And gin."

"Would you like to know a secret Miss Winters?"

Dear God. After the rumors, she didn't know if she could bear the secrets. She gulped, bracing herself for a barrage of naked truth. "I... I don't know."

"You may as well know that I have officially fallen off the wagon."

She tried to catch her breath, tried to believe her ears.

"What?"

"Is there... any more?" he suddenly asked.

"I gave you the last. Mr. Hargrove, I... don't know what to say. Please, I'm so sorry," she began, racking her brain.

Absolutely nothing in his behavior indicated that he had a drinking problem, or that he was even abstaining.

"When I came back from the war I... acquired a bit of a bad habit, you see. Not an addiction, but... a crutch nonetheless. The equivalent of a grown man sucking his thumb."

He moved dangerously closer to her. So close that she had to strain to look at his eyes, giving her an excuse to avoid them.

He looked down at her like she was a child. Not a sound could be heard, not even her breathing.

"I'd like to tell you that I looked in the mirror one day and simply willed myself better, somehow. Because the moment you think any less of me is the moment that I might throw myself off the ledge of this very building."

Her heartbeat was wild. Her face and chest burned as if from his gaze and he wouldn't stop saying the most unbelievable things.

And yet, she couldn't shake her blunder. She'd practically spiked her boss's drinks. How could she be so careless?

"You don't look like... like you have a problem," she offered. "Forgive me, but don't you have to be completely dry to fall off the wagon?"

He chuckled. "Perhaps. I suppose there's no real term for what I am. I manage to keep it at bay most days. In my line of work, you can hardly avoid it. I merely do what I can to function, essentially. I make sure my drinks are watered down and everyone else's are twice as strong. If I make a mistake I sleep it off in the office, nowhere else. Always save clients until the end of the day, in case I decide that I don't quite want the headiness to stop while I'm alone..." he ran a slender digit down the front of her blouse. "But it's been a while since I've been genuinely impaired."

"Mr. Hargrove, I didn't know," she pleaded in a near whisper.

"You said that."

"Because I truly didn't."

"How could you?"

"I'm so sorry."

"I like hearing your apologies," he confessed in a coo that sent a rush down below. He draped one arm above as he leaned in front of her. Like a cad from those movies, like Lawrence had in the lobby of her building.

His big body in his suit jacket blocked the view of the entrance like a tent. Was he going to pull his dick out too?

She should put a stop to this right now. She should laugh it off, reprimand him. Tell him to go to his office and sleep it off. Pretend it never happened. Pretend she knew nothing.

But she was so tired of pretending. She didn't even know what she was pretending. Or why. Everything was just so horribly quiet. Including her conscience. Why had it left her?

"Why didn't you... you should've told me."

His other arm traveled low to her middle, his hand to the dainty metal clasp of her pants zipper.

"You're right. I should've. But... I wanted to drink. You made it for me. It was so good. And sweet."

They both watched as his thumb and forefinger slowly un-zipped her trousers. Neither seemed to be in the place to stop what was happening.

She licked her dry lips. Her mouth felt unnatural, as though it were about to fall off.

Everything was happening too fast. Everything was falling apart. She was going to fall apart. In front of him. She'd never be able to face him.

"Sir I... need this job. Mr. Hargrove—"

"No, you don't," he shook his head almost imperceptibly.

"I do," she insisted.

"Then you'll have to live with whatever decision I'm about to make," he stoically answered.

"I can," she bluffed. "Can you?"

She breathed like she'd been plunged in cold water as she felt his hand invading. Grazing the skin on her thigh, the fabric of her panties. An unconscious breath left her mouth.

"I'm in hell, Miss Winters. Practically all of the time. I can make it so that none of this ever happened."

And just like that, she was on the other side of it. Mr. Hargrove's hand was between her legs, and the only thing strange about it now was that it didn't seem as though their relationship had changed in the slightest. In fact, she only felt like she knew him less.

"Why go through with this at all? If you won't remember it?" she wondered aloud, looking down at his palm that seemed to be attached to her.

He found her opening.

"I've come this far already. I have to see it through."

All she could do was hold on to his right arm now pinned against her, stiff and unyielding at the wrist but light wherever it touched her.

She squirmed. She unconsciously fought his abrupt closeness, confusing her mind. It felt wrong where she wanted to feel right, and right where she wanted to feel wrong.

This was nothing like Lawrence in the hallway. This was a bombardment of the senses.

Her chest heaved. Her temperature skyrocketed, but she didn't even think to shed her coat. It was uncomfortable but she couldn't deny the pleasure on the back end, each time she tried backing herself further against the wall as if there was somewhere to hide.

She turned her head away from him as her breath quickened out of her control in terrified gusts. She clawed at him as if he were holding her under a current. Her mind was cleared of everything beyond just surviving.

He was deathly quiet as he looked down at his own hand, slick and shiny with Miss Winter's juices, more viscous by the second each time it disappeared beyond the open zipper of her trousers.

He eyed the black lace of her underwear and heard himself make a desperate noise, pulling the messy fabric down and across her mound, gorging himself on the sight of Camille's tenderly exposed center, the rest of her dutifully clothed.

She finally stilled and relaxed her grip on his bicep and complied with a desperate noise of her own, her left hand on his chest. To the passing stranger, they may have looked like they were in an uncomfortably tense exchange, or threatening one another with secrets and heavy blackmail. If they didn't look down to see Mr. Hargrove's hand furiously hovering around in Camille's trousers it would've only looked vaguely sexual.

She let out another desperate groan as she gripped his lapel. The hand gripping his bicep trailed down to his forearm as if to try to control it.

She didn't know how to simply tell him to keep going, or that it was even an option. She could only let out a satisfied grunting every time his fingers folded pleasure through her entire body.

The more noise she made the more his speed gradually got faster and faster, her grunting turning simply to quiet shock as he continued to command her body the way no other man ever had.

Finally, she seized. Blinding hot pleasure engulfed her until all she could see were the backs of her eyelids. Her stomach muscles tightened until they felt like fire. She felt as though she were in the midst of falling until she crashed into Mr. Hargrove's mouth suddenly engulfing hers, stifling her moans, coating her tongue with the taste of gin.

They suddenly heard a distant dull roar and an elevator ding.

The elevator doors yielded and the boisterous laughter of women cascaded out.

Mr. Hargrove sobered up in record time, stuffing Camille into the darkest corner of the closest available office.

There was no time to close the door so they simply hid behind it as the voices grew close.

Eventually, they heard Mr. McCain's arrogant wasted baritone, followed by the drunken and oddly foreign-sounding giggle of the two women he'd brought. What was it with war veterans and hookers?

The pair waited for them to retreat to the privacy of his corner office, but instead, they plopped themselves down in the middle of the party ruins Camille was trying to clean.

Camille couldn't see what was happening on the other side of the open door, only hear what sound like two women, laughing and giggling and cooing seductively.

Her post-orgasm high had wrecked any chance of tension growing in her loins at the sounds of Mr. McCain getting fellatio by two women in the middle of the office but she could feel Mr. Hargrove behind her wound tight enough to snap like a bowstring.

He grabbed the belt loops of her pants, pulling her close enough to feel him, hard and imposing. She felt his breath on her earlobe where he kissed.

"When I give you the signal, head to my office," he whispered.

"What?!" she mouthed in disbelief.

"We can't wait out Drew in here. We'll give it an hour. If the coast is clear we'll share a cab."

"Sir, your flight," she dared to whisper.

Mr. Hargrove pointed to the window where Camille had somehow failed to notice the blinding, steady deluge of snow.

He seemed to be of the opinion that there would be no flight. He traveled enough to know without traffic control giving him the message.

As the voices trailed further and further off, he left his place behind her and inched past the door frame quieter than anything she had ever seen.

He ventured out, looking this way and that.

Camille left her place behind the door just in time to see him with her purse in his hand, signaling her from the hallway.

"Take those heels off and follow me."

* * *

Camille was behind him like a shadow, afraid to turn around for fear that she would see Mr. McCain looking straight at her from down the hall.

After an eternity, they turned the first corner where all was clearly and truly quiet. The conference room door was open as though the staff had gone against her orders before they left for the bar, but everything looked to be in order as she passed it by and walked straight ahead, past Christy's desk to Mr. Hargrove's office.

The curtains were still open in front of the tall narrow windows that boasted the best view in the building. She couldn't stop staring there in the dark at the white cakey precipitation slowly and soundlessly covering the city skyline in the distance. They didn't dare turn on any lights.

She felt the hands of a man that could only be Mr. Hargrove envelop her from behind. But she could hardly believe it.

"You're so soft," he suddenly said, "softer than I ever imagined."

"It must be well past 7 pm by now, but I don't feel the difference. In fact, it feels hotter."

He smiled, his mouth on her neck as he peeled off her coat.

"We should get you out of those clothes, then."

Her voice was sober as she turned to face him. "Sir, what you are proposing is... insanity."

He ignored her, turning his attention toward the buttons on her untucked blouse. "Have you any idea how hard it is to see you in the office every day? Miss Winters..."

She gulped, her heart in her stomach. "No, sir."

"I suppose it would be foolish to think that you might feel the same?"

"Truly it never once crossed my mind, Mr. Hargrove," she confessed, apologetic.

"Not once?" he asked, freeing her crisp white shirt from her shoulders, revealing her tan bra.

"You're a handsome man, Mr. Hargrove. If that is what you're after."

"It is not," he replied, unbuttoning her exquisite pants.

She looked down at his dark hair, wondering if she could put her hands in it. She wasn't quite sure what she was allowed— oddly the only source of her nerves.

"It's nothing personal, sir, it's just that dalliances like these happen to... other types of women."

He peeled her trousers off and they fell to the floor, unveiling her garter belt and stockings underneath.

"'Other types?' Do you think you're incapable of catching a man's eye, Miss Winters?"

"No."

"Do you imagine these other types of women are somehow more alluring than you?"

"...No."

"Ah. You simply look down on them, do you?"

"Yes."

She could see the look in his eye from the reflection bouncing off the streetlamps outside, one she recognized but didn't understand. He grabbed her as if in a fever, turning her around so that the shadow of the blinds streaked across her exposed buttery skin.

"Shall I ravish you in front of the window? For all the world to see?" he asked in her ear.

She licked her lips. "We shouldn't do this," she reminded him. Though the way he held her, the tender way he undressed her made it harder to remember why.

"No. We shouldn't," he agreed.

"You may be a drunk, but what excuse do I have?"

"You don't need any excuses. At some point, you have to let go, Miss Winters," he counseled her.

She nearly laughed out loud.

"Is that so? Should it be as easy for me as it is for you?"

"Letting go is impossible for me. But not for you," he said.

She stiffened in his arms. "How can you say that? I'm a colored secretary. You own the building. How can I afford to let go?"

"It's because you don't own the building that you can, Miss Winters. Can't you let yourself have one night? One night of freedom from all this... this... wretched business?"

He didn't specify which wretched business he could be referring to. Her race? His position? His marriage? All of it??

"It will cost me. More than you or I could ever earn in our lives."

"Then we better not get caught," he cooed.

She left his grasp. She looked into his soft eyes, hers dark and demanding. "You mean I shouldn't..."

Camille walked to the closed door and stopped. Mr. Hargrove's heart nearly leaped out from his throat as he watched her reach for the doorknob. Then again as he heard the subtle latch of the door lock.

"You don't like me, do you, Miss Winters?" he deduced, leaning onto his office desk.

"You don't pay me to like you, Mr. Hargrove."

"Sure I do."

"Then yes," she said. She could barely see his smile in the dark. He tried to find her eyes but she wouldn't give them to him.

"Something wrong, Miss Winters?"

She shook her lowered head.

"Nothing, I just... I've never done *anything* like this," she hastily confessed with a swallow. "And I do mean anything."

"I'll be gentle."

"This is crazy," she muttered to herself.

"Yes, it is."

"I cannot have a baby," she aired her unspoken worries.

So direct. She was getting ahead of herself but the sentence mysteriously shattered his insides.

"Nor can I," was all he answered with.

"Didn't you say you had absinthe?"

Mr. Hargrove walked lazily behind his couch, found his hidden stash, and took a swig before handing it to Camille. She sputtered through her own swig before handing it back to a chuckling Mr. Hargrove, who took one more for good luck.

Hopefully, he hadn't spoiled the night already, but he felt good and warm. Nothing Camille could say now could do him harm.

"Please don't kiss me," she whispered, leaning away from him.

Well, so much for that. "Why?"

134

"Please, Mr. Hargrove."

"Anywhere?"

"I don't know. Maybe."

"You want me to ignore this mouth?" he asked, running his thumb across her bottom lip as he cupped her face. She closed her eyes as if in agony.

She opened her eyes when nothing had happened yet.

Mr. Hargrove recoiled a bit, swaying her as he pondered her face. She thought maybe he was going to pass out. His breath quickened to near hyperventilation.

She searched his eyes for signs of alarm. He was too young for a heart attack.

"Mr. Hargrove?"

His eyes shut tight like a frightened child under a bed.

"I have to tell you something," he ventured. "I have to. But I... don't know if I can."

She didn't know her boss. At all. But she knew enough to know that he never looked the way that he did right now, in front of anyone else, in his life. Sympathy enveloped her. "What is it?"

"I've imagined you... this... many times. Too many times and now... now that it's close enough for me to touch, I can... something about you... I can hear the bombs," he stammered.

Something inside her melted and she became utterly unguarded. Disarmed. She took his hands and led him to the long couch in the sitting area.

"What can I do?" she pleaded.

"No, it's okay... it's okay I want to remember," he whimpered.

"Why?"

"Because it's you," he whispered. "Were it anyone else, I'd jump out of that office window and to my death to escape it."

Camille was shocked. Her boss? Felt this way? About her?

"I'm sorry, I shouldn't speak that way in front of you," he sniffed.

She studied him quietly while he only looked off in the distance at nothing. But with intention, rather than vacant. As if passing through something.

"Was it really that bad?" she suddenly asked.

Mr. Hargrove looked up at her. He laughed suddenly at the absurd question that no one had ever before dared ask. He looked like a boy. She couldn't help smiling.

He quieted, preparing to answer the genuine question with an equally genuine response.

"The worst part was that every man had a look in their eyes, even after the fear had been shocked out of them, that they'd simply rather be doing anything else but what they were doing. Even the enemy, sometimes."

"Why didn't they?"

His eyes gathered moisture, slivers of blinding light from the snow shown through the blinds.

"Because... every man thought he would die and yet every man wanted to come home. Even if home had been tragic. And it was them or us."

"You don't think it was worth it?"

His eyes focused on the same nonsense spot as before. "Some days, I don't know. I'll never know."

Anger turned black and pooled at the bottom of her heart. It sent a shock through her veins and she thought she may have poisoned herself.

"It wasn't. I know that it wasn't."

His eyes turned back to hers, making one of his tears fall. "Don't say that."

She sighed, exasperated and bitter. She felt for him. For all of them. But not at the expense of her own feelings.

"If you're going to take me, Mr. Hargrove, do it now. Before the liquor wears off."

His brow wrinkled. "Miss Winters...you're being cold."

"Fine, I'll do it myself."

"How, do you figure??"

Camille began unbuttoning his shirt.

"The pants seem more pertinent," Mr. Hargrove pointed out. Camille pretended not to notice him as she got to the last button.

"I will not do this halfway, Mr. Hargrove."

He relinquished his dress shirt, his undershirt still on. He raised his arms in surrender as she moved her attention to his belt buckle.

"Will you at least tell me what I've done to offend you?"

"You've done nothing."

"Miss Winters—"

"It's late and I'm drunk and all of this is all wrong but I can't go back and change any of it. You were right. The only way out is through," she said, tugging at the hem of his undershirt until he'd come out of it. The sight of his bare lean shoulders made her mouth water.

"But I think we understand each other. And while I believe we are the last two people in the world that should venture to do what we're doing, I don't know that I'll find a better chance in my life."

He scoured her scantily clad body with his eyes, the haunted past having obviously retreated.

"A chance for what?"

She climbed on top of him there on the couch. "I never fought in the war, but it haunts me too, Mr. Hargrove."

He grabbed her up in his arms, pressing her neck against his lips. "Feel free to think about him, if it helps, Miss Winters."

"Think about who?" she asked, stiffening.

Mr. Hargrove was silent.

"Who did you mean?"

"Forgive me. Miss Winters. I misunderstood you."

"What did you misunderstand?" she interrogated him.

"I thought we were being honest, but I see now that it was only me."

Camille recoiled out of his grasp. "Where the hell do you get off?"

"It's okay to admit that you lost someone in the war and that it broke your heart."

"I don't want to be anywhere but the present, Mr. Hargrove," she dug at him, defensive. Poised.

"Take off your bra," he commanded sternly.

Camille silently, reluctantly reached behind her for the clasp. He should've known all he had to do was boss her around.

She was a bank safe. She wasn't letting him in, now or ever. But she was dutiful to a fault. In fact, she didn't know when to stop.

Slowly he alternated between wrapping his arms around her, using his hands like eyes and his eyes like hands, all over her skin. He got his mouth in on the action, tongue kissing her neck, her shoulder, her breasts.

She tossed her neck in sweet torture, in ease of access, until she'd become dizzy with arousal and longing for what she wasn't sure. She nudged her body into his in want.

"Oh, Camille," he whispered in constant refrain. She wanted to cry.

Who knew when she got up this morning that Mr. Hargrove was going to be the one? The one to make her forget them both.

The one to show her that there may not be anything wrong with her.

Suddenly she felt him shifting under her, somewhat frantic like he wanted her off. He stilled her movements with one hand and reached between them with the other.

She looked down. She could see something moving but it was too dark. The tip of his manhood caught the light for just a moment, only a moment before it disappeared underneath her.

His breath caught as his fingers fiddled with the fabric of her underwear until it was pulled taut to one side, revealing impossible wetness all over her delicate skin and mess of damp curls.

She felt pressure down below that couldn't be mistaken for anything else. Mr. Hargrove was penetrating her.

The pressure intensified. Morphed into sensation. The trivial gap between their two bodies was no more. Mr. Hargrove tossed his head back as if in relief. A bolt of lightning ricochet across her insides.

This time Camille didn't hesitate to put his hair through her fingers as she loomed over him. Her lips skimmed the rough naked skin of his jawline until finally, his lips met hers.

"I thought it was supposed to hurt?" she whispered.

"Are you saying I have a small prick, Miss Winters?" he raised a drowsy eyebrow.

"I don't know."

He laughed, a little too loud, because she was shushing him, stifling laughs of her own.

The grip on her buttocks and hips became insistent and her insides went into frenzied tingles and shocks that she couldn't believe.

"I'm going to hell for this," she said.

"That's impossible, you're an angel, my darling."

"I've let a married man ruin me."

"What's wrong with that?" he groaned, taunting her conscientiousness with his tawdry ways.

"What about your wife?"

"Screw my wife," he panted.

"Screw your wife?" she repeated. He thrashed his body with hers again and again.

"Just keep talking, Miss Winters."

"Why?"

"Because it hardens my dick."

"You can feel when it gets harder?"

He let out another quiet laugh, holding her close.

"Does it feel good?" he nudged her earnestly, quietly.

Camille thought for a moment as he kissed her. The buckles on her garter belt were digging into her right thigh. Her right leg as a whole felt crushed, on the verge of numbness. Mr. Hargrove was moving like some majestic creature underneath her, at his own mysterious pulse. His thumb dug a place in her side like it was trying to sink in.

"Yes," she whispered.

"Yeah?" he sprightly asked, as if energized by her answer.

She nodded, meeting his eyes.

"Oh, Camille," he exclaimed in a whisper, as if ecstatic. He hauled her up in his arms, his one big hand around her thigh as he held it up, thrusting her deeper and faster. As if he wanted to give her more good feelings than she could handle.

Suddenly all the sensations from his cock played together in unison. Now this, she could get used to.

She reached behind her for something to lean on until she found an armrest, her other arm hooked around his neck. She went quiet, enjoying the movement of his hips as they picked up speed.

"I'm going to come inside you, Miss Winters."

"No," she gasped.

"Please," he whispered, "it's all I want."

It was impossibly hot in his office and their bodies were entwined, slamming together in a syncopated frenzy.

"Beg me," she gritted her teeth. He eagerly complied.

"Please... let me have you now."

She didn't think she heard him right. "What?"

But he was gone.

"Please... please," his voice wavered. She wondered if he could still hear the bombs as she studied his haunted face. Her heart in knots. She thought she might cry if he kept on, but it came to an abrupt end.

All was quiet as his muscles surged into one solitary movement and then relaxed, hovered. He pulled her back on top of him dutifully before collapsing in a heap on the couch under her.

The pins holding her hair in place had become useless. She looked down at her boss, the light and shadow from the open blinds leaving streaks across his face.

Her body throbbed with heat like burning embers, refusing to cool until finally, she'd come down enough to detach herself from his grasp and lean against him, there on the couch.

13

Chapter 13

Camille shivered hard enough to wake herself from sleep. She roused to the strange whirring of machines, the taste of bad liquor breath, the feel of tweed cushions against her cheek. An ache in her back.

She brushed the disheveled hair from her face and slowly came to the sober realization that she was far from her bed. She was still in Mr. Hargrove's office and it was morning.

Mr. Hargrove was nowhere to be found. Naturally. Thankfully. But there could be no doubt that last night happened. She felt it in her body. Saw traces of it all over the room. Tasted it. Smelled it.

It was the next day. Friday. The snowfall had stopped.

She heard the distant whirring sound of a vacuum as she hastily found her pants and put them on. She buttoned her shirt and thought of what to do.

She had no hope of not being found out so crawling around on her hands and knees was out. She began to smooth her wrinkled appearance the best she could without the aid of a mirror.

She'd come in early before. Or stayed late. Copywriters stayed overnight all the time. Surely Mr. McCain was long gone.

When the dread became just as unbearable as seeing who was on the other side of the door she reached for the doorknob and slowly turned it.

The sound of the vacuum got louder and then waned. Further and further she creaked the door until she was face to face with the vacant office floor. Light from the fallen snow reflected well through the windows despite having no help from the fluorescent lights above.

Luckily the emergency stairs were within sight of Mr. Hargrove's office. She could simply go down one floor, go through the mailroom and the art department and take the elevator from there.

But it was locked. She took off her heels and prepared for a 19-floor hike down to the lobby. She took a chance around the 8th and found an unlocked door.

The city was eerily quiet. Taxis stilled as stragglers like herself roamed the city sidewalks looking like solitary blades of grass poking out of the snow. She felt trapped in a giant snow globe.

"Do you have the time?" she asked a random old couple.

"Half-past nine," the man answered.

The family was likely already on the way to her parent's house and she would be late. It would take her an hour at least to get showered and changed.

She nursed a headache on the train ride back to her apartment. She hadn't felt hungover but she must've been.

It certainly explained the goings-on after the party. Her skin warmed and the front of her shirt grew tight as she recalled the activity of last night.

She skimmed the flesh of her neck thinking about his lips, his own fingers where he had found her wetness and violated their boundary. Violently and in so many ways.

Strange, how easy it had been. Though it had been impulsive and daring, it hadn't been salacious or perverted. It was a moment of weakness.

She just hadn't known she was something he'd had to be strong over. Camille undid one of the buttons on her blouse as the tunnel temporarily plunged her into darkness.

* * *

All five of her siblings and their families crammed into the three-bedroom two-bath empty nest of her parents' newly warmed house.

"Well, your father's going to work with the government on the new highway project."

"Daddy, you must be excited," Camille's sister beamed.

"Don't 'Daddy' him. He's supposed to be taking me to see my family," their mother frowned.

"You can go alone, Pigeon."

"Daddy, if you say that to Mom she might not come back," her other sister joked.

"You're supposed to be retired, Roy," their mother insisted.

Father was indignant. "Why are we talking about this on Christmas?"

"Camille, you awfully quiet in there."

"I'm just waiting for the chicken patties," Camille bellowed from the kitchen.

"You know the Campbell's finally had their baby?" Donna informed her, the youngest sister responsible for her serendipitous blind date.

Camille feigned a polite interest. "How is Lawrence?"

"Wonderful. Thinking about transferring to Chicago," Donna broke the news.

"Chicago? It's so brutish over there."

"Maybe, but they're offering him more. And the cost of living is even lower. He could buy a mansion."

Camille made the exhausting effort of a response. "Well, send him my love. And his wife, of course."

"It's really a shame," Donna's husband lamented. Overtly. "I thought for sure you would fall head over heels for him."

"He was impressive, I won't deny," offered Camille.

Her grandmother couldn't hold back anymore and finally chimed in.

"Royston, talk sense into your baby."

"She got plenty sense," her father chewed.

"Thank you, Daddy."

"She could be married to a doctor by now if it wasn't for that stubborn head of hers," her grandmother insisted.

"I could also be moving to Chicago," Camille argued.

"Not so," her grandmother argued in her accented English, "You could talk sense into the man, get him to stay."

"If I thought it worked that way I would've married him."

"Tell her, sweetheart," her father defended her playfully.

"How's that job of yours coming along?" another brother-in-law asked.

"Good."

"It's a dead end."

"Grandmother, please."

"It is! Meanwhile, your childbearing years are wasting away!"

"I'm not going to have a child with some man I don't love just because it's time."

"You're not going to want to work forever. You'll be old and tired and lonely. And worthless. With no one to take care of you."

Camille wasn't prepared for the perfect storm she'd walked into with her grandmother. A strong, neurotic woman who carried her entire family on her back, even her abusive husband who died mysteriously on the way to America. There wasn't a woman in the world she respected more.

"Excuse me," Camille simply said, getting up from the table.

There weren't many places in the house to go besides outside onto the cold front porch or the backyard. She settled for a bathroom. She craved a cigarette, but she'd left them in her purse in the dining room.

"*Ayaga,* Mom!" her mother chastised in a sharp hushed tone.

"If none of you will remind her then let me be the one," her grandmother continued at full voice. "What sane colored woman *chooses* to work? When she is that beautiful? Your daughter is crazy. You will be an old woman taking care of her."

There's got to be a secret stash in here somewhere, she thought, eyeing an ashtray. She raided the cabinets.

"Her beau got shipped off to die, and so did the other that had written," her father said in an attempt at sympathy.

She stood in front of the sink, cringing as she looked back at her own reflection. Her father thought she was simply heartbroken. Which meant he didn't really respect her independence. He was giving her excuses for being defective.

"That was a long time ago, Royston. No, she is stubborn."

"They don't grow back, Mom, all the men her age got shipped off to die!"

"Not all of them. She threw away a perfectly good doctor boy and you let her. Thirty years old and she would've had the life of a young woman!"

146

"The man never asked, Pearl."

"You know why *that* is, eh?"

"That'll do, Pearl. Now I know you frettin' over your grand-baby, but I can't tolerate much more disrespect in my house. This is supposed to be a family gathering."

Pearl turned to her daughter, Camille's mother.

"You are spoiled, and you raised a spoiled child. You found a man the moment we got off the boat! And you are not beautiful as she is!"

"Everyone at this table is willing to take care of Camille, Miss Pearl. But we all know we won't have to," Donna's husband spoke up in a rare display.

Camille had to turn the sink in to hide her appreciation, coming out in pitiful sobs. Her brother-in-law's humble appeal made Pearl relent, but she could only shake her head and mutter under her breath.

Camille kept the water running in the sink until she could compose herself. Then she washed her face, collected her things, and left without another word.

* * *

"The usual, Mr. Hargrove?"

"Actually, can you make a mule?"

"Of course. Gin?"

"Vodka, if you have it. Make it minty."

"Coming right up, sir."

Mr. Hargrove had three days to pull himself together. The office would be back from Christmas break on Tuesday. It was plenty of time to put distance between himself and the Christmas party, and he trusted Camille knew what to do.

So he had no excuses. Especially with an extra day or two to pull rank and get away with skipping practically everything until the first quarter account meeting.

So why did it seem like his sleepless nights were about more than just nightmares?

He'd lost control with Camille. It was embarrassing to recall.

He barely made his meeting in L.A. and when he got there he was more useless than usual. He was paranoid that when he arrived in the office her letter of resignation would be staring him in the face.

He couldn't wait to get sloshed on the way back to New York. He'd been sober for a day and a half since the Christmas party and it was unbearable.

His mind and body burned with the memory of Camille's soft nakedness, her orchid smell, her brown nipples, her disheveled hair. Her soft whispy moans, her clenching thighs...

This was worse than when he drank so much that he woke up on the other side of the world. Or in the middle of a fight. Or whimpering under a table at the sight of a Jap walking his dog.

This was worse than any drunken relapse he could've indulged. Because none of those was an open door. How was he supposed to make it like it never happened without using booze?

By the time he landed, Mr. Hargrove was sobering up with a cup of coffee. He still had three more modes of transportation left before he had to worry about resting.

The children would hopefully be asleep by the time he got to his home in Westchester. The commute was positively grueling. For a normal person. But Mr. Hargrove wasn't normal.

Mr. Hargrove felt the chill of the city as he hailed a cab outside of the bustling airport. He couldn't believe there were this many men in the same boat as he was, and he despised them for it.

By now he could tell which ones had been to war and who hadn't. He knew why he dreaded going home on Christmas Eve. But these other men had no excuse to be filling up the airports, arriving as he was leaving.

They were dirtbags. Entitled. They despised the order that peace brought about. They were tame in the ways they should be wild and wild where they should be tame.

The train was much less crowded on the way to Westchester. He enjoyed a half-empty car and put his feet up with the paper until he'd made it to the terminal and took his Cadillac the rest of the way home.

The lights were on in the house and it filled him with dread. What on Earth was everyone doing awake past 8pm?

Sure, it was Christmas Eve but there were presents to wrap. He walked in to the sound of tinkering on the piano.

"Dad!"

He turned around to see a young man nearly as tall as him.

"Daniel?"

"Mother didn't expect you in until tomorrow."

"I came straight home after my meeting. Where's your sister?"

"With Mom in the kitchen."

Ken abandoned his coat and briefcase in the hallway to make a brief appearance. Katie, unfortunately, looked almost as large her brother. It seemed as though it was yesterday that they were five and seven, staring back curiously at him from the floor, cross-legged and under the breakfast nook.

He was even more terrified now, looking at them. Soon they would be unleashed upon the world. What kind of people had he made? He didn't know and wasn't confident. He didn't even realize how old they were.

Katie instantly saw him appear in the doorway, dried her hands, and wrapped him in a hug. His wife Trish didn't look up from her place at the sink.

"You made it," she said with a surprised tone.

"I expected everyone to be asleep."

"Honestly, Dad, my bedtime hasn't been this early since I was 12."

"Wasn't that long ago, Katie dear."

"I spoke to Christy," his wife interjected. "She said the snow delayed your flight and you wouldn't be in until tomorrow."

By now, Christy knew how to stretch his timeline far enough out that when he finally did come home, he seemed like a hero by comparison.

"One of the passengers needed a later flight and we offered to trade."

"Certainly lucky he was there."

"Indeed. I take it your mother had no trouble picking you up?" he asked his daughter.

"She didn't need to. Daniel drove."

"Didn't you see the car out front?" wondered Trish.

"I confess I didn't. Who's is it?"

"A classmate of ours. He said he wasn't using it."

"Well, get some rest. Breakfast starts bright and early in the morning and then we're going to my parents," Trish reminded him.

"What about presents?"

"Dad," Katie chuckled.

"Don't tell me we're not opening presents this year just because your brother can drive."

"There'll be plenty of presents, Kenneth, just go upstairs."

"Meet me in 20 minutes?" he softly suggested.

His wife looked at him like an alien. "Why?"

"I've missed you."

She turned back to her task at the sink, briefly widening her eyes. "Who's got you in such a good mood?"

"I'm not in a good mood."

"Ah. So this is a therapy session."

Her icy tone wasn't enough to discourage him. She was right to be skeptical.

He touched her elbow and gave it a squeeze— a private joke.

"It's Christmas. You can have whatever you want."

"I'm frightened to believe you," she said without turning around.

Mr. Hargrove wasn't sure if that meant she would or wouldn't take him up on the offer. He trudged upstairs, undressed, and left the bathroom light on before retreating under the covers.

He imagined there in the dark that Camille was on the other side of the door, fiddling around in the kitchen and keeping him waiting. Unfortunately, wearing a pencil skirt and not a flowing negligee. He couldn't picture much beyond the office, but now that he'd taken a taste of her, maybe it would make this part of his life easier.

But it was worse than before. Because when he heard his wife enter the bedroom he detected her blonde hair at once. She smelled sharply of perfume and his insides went limp.

She didn't want him, and she hadn't for a long time. But there was no danger of being interrupted by sick children or haunting dreams, and she clearly had hoped that he would be kind and make good on his word. He closed his eyes.

He was beyond repair. If the memory of Camille couldn't get him through a night with his wife then this had nothing to do with his libido. Maybe he only wanted things if they were wrong.

Trisha moved closer and closer, finally stopping when it was clear that he had no intentions of acknowledging her. Wordlessly she turned down the covers and for a moment, he thought he was in the clear.

"When we got married, I understood what this was," his wife softly began. "You'd been so matter-of-fact. The war made you even more closed off, but I accepted that. And even though you weren't my first choice I was taken in by your honesty. Your sense of loyalty. I'm embarrassed to say it now but there was a glimmer of hope that one day you would stop your restlessness. One day I would be enough for you."

He was rendered still by her resentful gaze that he felt burning through him, even though his eyes were still closed and he was turned away from her on his side.

"I was wrong about that. But I said I would be the wife and mother that I agreed to be and I am. I promised to attend all the parties and client outings I was obligated to attend as a rich man's wife and I have. And I may not be happy, but I am grateful," she said, still sitting up in bed, facing the bedroom window.

"I knew there would be others. I'm not naive," she sighed, her face grimacing with pain and anger.

"But the way you have paraded this colored girl around in front of my eyes..." she sobbed.

She knew him well enough to know he was faking unconsciousness. Guilt left his insides charred the longer she laid still next to him.

"What, no snide remarks about being paranoid? Overreacting? I'll take that as a confession," she sniffed. "Has your guilty conscience finally caught up with you?"

She was right. She knew him after all.

Ken laid still, outed fully by her speech. He could've said "I'm sorry," but he wasn't. So he couldn't say anything.

Her disdain was off-putting and unnecessary. He'd delivered everything that he'd promised her, including the hard times.

She couldn't have prepared for them, he admitted readily, but he was prepared to take care of her for the rest of his life.

She was perfectly welcome to find happiness wherever she could if she could do so discreetly, but she was incapable of that, and anyway, it didn't matter. She was miserable, but nothing about her reeked of desperation. She turned off every mark she came across.

"I can take a lot of things, Kenneth. But not this. You never said you would make a fool of me. I wouldn't have agreed to any of it if you had. Maybe I never deserved love, Kenneth, but you certainly don't."

They lay in a silent standoff until she finally faced the opposite way in bed. He didn't move a muscle, fearing at any moment she would simply rise up and scream at the top of her lungs. The paranoia of it kept him on edge until his body finally relented, and the next time he opened his eyes it was morning.

14

Present Day, Winter 1958

January 21, 1957

Stan,

*I have to confess something. To someone. Something
that I cannot ever tell anyone. But I can tell you. I've
waited for sometime to even speak of it. What seemed like
a lifetime.*

*I was supposed to make it like it never happened. I told
him that I could. I thought that I could. I don't know why
I even want to tell you this, but I cannot keep it from you.
Especially after your last proposal.*

*If it changes your opinion of me I have to know imme-
diately. But I know that keeping it from you would be for
my sake more than yours. But you know me. You may be
the only person. And you love me. And you know what
life truly is. That there is nothing to be afraid of because
there's nothing worth preserving. Nothing we can hold
on to. But if we're lucky we can gather experiences. And
sometimes people.*

My boss made a pass at me at work. But that isn't the truth, is it? He seduced me. And I, in turn, seduced him back. I couldn't feel guilty if I tried. And that is what I feel guilty about. He is married. He is white. He was drunk. I was not.

It was scary, of course. Don't misunderstand. In the moment it felt as though God himself was watching me. Watching a man put his hands on me truly, for the first time. But after a long while none of that mattered. All that mattered was what he was doing to me.

I thought about you. I hesitated so long thinking about you. It's a wonder that I'm not still standing there. If someone told me that even after a decade of thinking you were dead— knowing you were— that I was still hoping against hope that you'd be the first to do those things to me, I would laugh and call them a liar. I'd threaten them with violence if they didn't promise to take it back.

But it would've been true.

I felt such shame and grief and despair, such a swirl of emotions as he laid me bare in his office. It was nothing like any of my dreams. It was sterile and matter of fact and wrong. Cynical. And then I had the strangest desire to be wrecked. I just wanted him to wreck me. And then it was as though I couldn't be wrecked fast enough.

I'm not explaining this correctly. At all. I wish I could tell you in person. Even a phone call would suffice. I think I would like to hear your voice. At least. I know things may be complicated where you are, I no longer want to be a burden if seeing me would cause that.

Camille

January 24, 1957

Camille,

Seeing you would not be a burden. I do have access to a phone but I can think of nothing more conspicuous than me speaking with you for countless hours in the middle of the hallway about nothing of real consequence should someone overhear. And considering what you have just told me it would be impossible.

I went outside on my roof and thought about what you confessed to me. Are you saying that he was your first? You were very guarded about your experience in general so I deduced the breadth of your inexperience from that. Experienced women have a certain air that you do not, even in letters. So it was jarring for a long moment. In a good way. Still, you never told me that you wanted me to be your first. Or that I would have been your first. Or that you dreamed of it. Perhaps for the same reason that I didn't ask. Making plans was so excruciating then. Poor little old us.

It made me wonder if my whole life had been a mistake. Should I have thrown caution to the wind and found you then, and wrecked you before anyone else had the chance? Before you would've even discovered the desire? Should I have ever even enlisted? Should I have been born?

But eventually I settled back into reality. This is the way it ought to have been.

You should be crazy to suppose that I would think less of you after I have told you over and over to find bliss as soon as possible. My only hope is that he indeed wrecked you in the way you strangely desired. It is more common than you think. Oddly, I wish I could've been there. A morbid thing to say. Years of letter writing has taught me to not only want you but want to live vicariously through you and be in your skin. Feeling every sensation as though it were the first again. Weren't you afraid of being caught by someone? Did he wreck you to your liking?

Are you in love with him?

Stanley

January 31, 1957

Stanley,

In love with him? As if that could possibly be relevant. Can all the stars in the universe fit onto the head of a pin? I could never be with him, in this world or any other. And now we avoid each other enough to rouse suspicion. Well, at least I do. He has an obscenely cool and unshakable demeanor at all times. Truthfully I think he could chop me up into pieces and no one would know or suspect, so unflappable his status makes him.

I think I'll have to move on professionally, which pains me. It's caused me to hate him, which I loathe. I do not want to hate this man. I don't know why. And yet, I should be grateful. If my good luck in this industry could run out with anyone, I'm glad it was with him. He respects me and doesn't want to see me ruined. Professionally, at least.

I do confess, however, I fear his retaliation. Though it seems vain to do so. I don't see myself as one in a million, nor do I see myself as one in a pattern. I don't know how long I can go with my hours heavy with dread by the end of the day. I will have to take a pay cut. I may have to go crawling back to the agency that once hired me.

I wish I had more to say to you that wasn't so narcissistic but it is the only thing on my mind and I have no other outlet besides you. I won't address your reaction to my confession because I am too shy. I am glad that you're here again. I'm certain I would go crazy if you weren't.

And yes. He did.

Camille

February 5, 1957

Camille,

I wouldn't worry about retaliation as he has as much to lose as you do. You should, however, probably have a reasonable conversation with him before you do anything rash. Men in powerful positions don't like being made to feel powerless, it's true. But from what you've told me he sounds like he can be leveled with. I'm sure much of your dread is imagined. That he looms so large in your imagination is evidence that communication is needed. A young woman who has never been in a position like this is bound to need guidance.

Let me know if you would like anything for Valentine's Day.

Stan

P.S. You never answered the last question.

February 12, 1957

Stan,

You are lovely but please do not send me anything for Valentine's Day, unless it is another letter.

I don't think that I could be in love with him. The things that make him lovable to me make him lovable to everyone. He is handsome and dapper. Intelligent, mature, gracious. Rich to a degree that seems mythical. Meticulous. Sure. Unavailable in every possible sense of the word.

But something peculiar happened. During. He said something about me was making him hear the bombs. And I don't think I've ever felt such tenderness for a human.

Honestly, what is wrong with me? Why do I despise a fully present man? A young man was in love with me once. A surgeon. Perhaps he still is. In love with me, that is. Who knows if he's still a surgeon, though I imagine even if he ever wanted to pursue his dreams as a beat poet that would be out of the question.

He invited me to his wedding, and even now I can't shake how pointed his performance of bliss seemed to be. I went to show that I was a good sport. He seemed inordinately relieved to know that my brother was my date.

We were incompatible, but it's hardly an excuse. I could've approached our marriage with the same ambition I approach my job and likely have been as happy. I would've certainly had more to show for it. A spinster like me landing a colored surgeon! The bragging rights I would've had.

But the truth was, he was simply too whole. And I couldn't stand the sight of him for much more than an hour.

You are my only friend. I love you.

February 23, 1957

159

Camille,
Then another letter you shall have.
I love you too.

Stan

Chapter 15

C amille showed up to the office in a stunning hunter-green dress that sang the praises of her shape and her butterscotch skin.

She didn't start dressing sexier per se. Just dressing to be noticed. She let her hair cascade down her shoulders and end in a foam of curls.

When Camille returned to work after the Christmas break, hoping against all hope that Mr. Hargrove would never come into the office again, it almost seemed as though he never would. He wasn't seen again by anyone in the office until the 31st of January.

She couldn't look Mr. McCain in the eye as long as she lived. Couldn't look at Christy as she typed away on her desk that may have had spunk on it when the cleaning crews came in. Couldn't look at booze, couldn't look at certain walls.

She certainly wouldn't be able to look at the inside of Mr. Hargrove's office. Tomorrow would be the first account meeting of the year. She had to get her mind right by then.

She had to get over what happened. And never want for it

again. She didn't know why she was taking his adherence to his own word so personally.

But somewhere deep inside of her, she was resolved. If she was to suffer the overcompensation of Mr. Hargove's uber professional demeanor the rest of her life, she would do it while titillating his subconscious. Until he dreamed of laying on a bed made of honey covered in mint and dollar bills.

Unfortunately, people that weren't Mr. Hargrove began noticing.

"It's about time you started dressing for the men around here, Camille," Josh oozed. The room filled with a mixed potency of tension that Camille dutifully brushed off.

"Do you have your list yet, Mr. Manning?"

"Not yet."

"The department heads need it by the end of the day," she reminded him.

"Duly noted."

"Which means I'm coming back after lunch."

"What is this about Camille?" Max inquired.

"I don't know, I just do what I'm told," Camille assured them.

"Save it. Mr. Hargrove is in love with you," scoffed Josh.

Camille ruthlessly ignored him. "Be that as it may, I know as much as you do."

"We don't need Camille, any moron could figure out what they're doing. They're selling the company."

"Ridiculous."

"Do you see any rousing speeches to boost morale? Do you not know what quietly counting the money means?"

"Maybe they're expanding. Ken's had his sights on LA for years."

"All I know is today is the deadline to have everyone in your department accounted for," Camille repeated as she reached for the door of Josh's office.

"Are we to believe they don't already have this?"

"I would tell you the same thing in another way but American Negroes only speak English."

"Not in my neighborhood."

"Camille, you barely qualify," Josh sharply taunted her.

"I qualify just fine, let your father tell it," Camille ragged on her way out. She had three brothers and a master of fine arts in playing the dozens.

She closed the door behind her and let the bomb she dropped detonate in her wake, not waiting for Josh to scramble together some clever retort. As she walked off she could hear the room consoling him with muffled guffaws of ridicule.

She wore a faint smirk when she eyed Christy standing near her office with crossed arms.

"My my, aren't you the prized pearl?" she crooned with mocking in her voice.

"Beg your pardon?"

"Mr. Hargrove needs you in his office."

Camille followed behind as Christy wordlessly returned to her desk, not sure if whatever was going on with Christy would need to be addressed or not. Mr. Hargrove's door was open and he summoned her without looking up.

"Shut the door," was the last thing Christy heard as it clicked behind Camille.

Now that she was in the office again for the first time since the Christmas party, she regretted the dress.

She willed her eyes away from the couch in the corner. Mr. Hargrove busied himself at the liquor cart behind his desk.

"You wanted to see me?" she began.

"I did. I have news."

"Is this about the merger?"

Mr. Hargrove stopped mid-pour, eyeing her above his reading glasses. "So you've heard."

"The office has been sniffing around since the... 'restructuring.' Apparently, they got Delores to talk. Also, Josh has his theories."

"Delores?"

"One of the ladies on the switchboard," Camille filled in.

Mr. Hargrove's mouth went down at the corners. "Clever."

She watched as he filled one tumbler and began to fill another. "Are we the ones eating or being eaten?"

"A little of both. Hargrove, Bower, Chase, and.... McCain."

"You're kidding."

"It was the only way, without a contract. He's earned it," explained Mr. Hargrove as he handed her the strong drink.

She would say he was carrying on as if nothing happened but it wasn't even that. The door was closed. He was giving her booze.

"When?"

"Publicly? Summer. But effective immediately. Bower will be handing over the roster, I'll need you to go through and find any conflicts."

"Am I to be next?" Camille ventured.

"Next for what?"

"Next to be... redundant."

"No. Actually, it's quite the opposite," he smirked, raising his glass as if to toast. He seemed very pleased with himself as he eyed her.

Camille looked down at her brandy. "The opposite? How so?"

"The next growing markets on the horizon will be working women such as yourself, and believe it or not, the middle-class negro. A 10 billion dollar market. Bower wasn't in love with the pitch but they'll come around," Mr. Hargrove smiled.

"I'm sorry, I don't follow."

"How would you like to be an account man?"

Camille put her unsampled drink back on his desk. "With all due respect, Mr. Hargrove, I... wouldn't. Like that."

"You wouldn't report to me, directly, you would report to Mr. Daniels."

"That sounds even less appealing, sir."

She was forced to consider the couch as he made his way over to it and sat down.

He sat on the edge with an arm next to him, as if inviting her to sit. She was waiting for him to give the couch seat a few light taps.

"I suppose I could insist you report to me, but it would be favoritism of the highest order. I could certainly get away with it, but I'd... rather not."

"I certainly wouldn't want to be the recipient of whatever gossip that would earn me," Camille scoffed with her folded arms.

Mr. Hargrove's smile waned. "You want to be a secretary the rest of your life? Is that it?"

Camille suddenly felt panicked walking into a conflict she was blindsided by.

"I'm not a secretary, I'm head of personnel."

"Okay, a glorified secretary."

"Mr. Hargrove... with all due respect, why would I want to go from having my hand in every account to the heavy lifting of just a handful?"

Mr. Hargrove sat forward, looking deeply offended. "I'm trying to promote you, Miss Winters. You'll be the first account woman ever. A colored woman. This is the opportunity of a lifetime."

She knew it. How did she always know it? He'd done her a favor. That she didn't want done. He couldn't even see how it was completely disastrous.

"You're feeding me to wolves is what you're doing. Is this because of the Christmas party?"

Mr. Hargrove's anger blazed behind his stoic gaze. "*What* Christmas party, Miss Winters? This is about your future. About having a career. I thought that's what you wanted?"

"If being the glue that holds this place together can't be considered a 'career' then no, I suppose that's not what I want. I'm perfectly happy—"

"Someday, Miss Winters, you're going to need more than $100 a week to survive. I cannot continue to overpay you to do the job any two college graduates off the street could do. You will eventually have to venture out beyond your comfort zone."

Why was he was demeaning her?

"I don't see why. There are plenty of people who stay in the same position until they retire."

"You *will* run out of challenges, Miss Winters."

And now he was insulting her.

"And you assume I'll be a spinster my entire life. I'm certainly not young but—"

"Don't tell me you still one day intend to marry? Let me guess... your woebegone pen pal? Perhaps you'll catch the eye of some handsome old widower? With seven children? Teach them songs and sew them clothes out of curtains?"

Was he drunk??

"This *is* about the Christmas party."

"No, Miss Winters. This is about you changing course midstream. You had me fooled. I thought you'd chosen your path as a career woman. But it seems you don't want that either. You are simply damaged goods, resting on your natural talents, secretly still hoping that some impossible love story will fall into your lap. You pity them, but you're no different from the rest."

He was definitely drunk.

"Are you sure this conversation is still about me, Mr. Hargrove?"

"Get out, Miss Winters."

"Of course, Mr. Hargrove." Camille turned and reached for the doorknob with a quaking hand.

"Open or closed?"

"Closed," Mr. Hargrove replied.

* * *

Camille avoided eye contact all the way back to her office, praying that no one would try and spark up conversation. She was liable to chew someone's head off and she was noticing that some in the office were starting to bare their teeth after two years.

This might've been her first big city job, but her habit of getting promoted didn't sit well with many people here. The elevator operator, the mail clerk, the sandwich cart guy, these were the kinds of negroes they were used to working alongside.

They were starting to get confused, starting to not see the point of it. And now Mr. Hargrove wanted to give his "overpaid secretary" a man's job.

She felt the eyes of everyone all the time already. Everyone except Mr. Hargrove's, of course, who seemed unable to perceive his own limitations.

Going on to Jacob Bower about a colored account woman, of all things. She was embarrassed for him just thinking about it. What was going on in his head?

It felt like a good time to use a chunk of one of those sick days she'd saved up. She grabbed her coat, purse, and headed for the door.

"Going to lunch, Camille?" McCain's secretary asked.

"Actually I'm done for the day."

"Is everything okay?"

"Not sure. Feeling a little under the weather, I should be back tomorrow."

"I hope so. Quarterly meeting's tomorrow," she reminded her.

"I know. I'll be here."

Before enjoying a congestion-free trip back to Brooklyn she spent a few hours in the city. She shopped at Macy's and got deli soup and a sandwich for lunch.

8:00 am came and went the following morning. Camille was wide awake when her alarm clock blared, having tossed and turned for what seemed like hours before it'd finally gone off. When sunrise came, the bedroom lightened very little. The clouds were ominous and heavy but no rain came.

She decided to call in sick. Some unconscious part of her wondered if she was retaliating for yesterday's insult by missing the account meeting.

What a mess. She was in limbo. She didn't know if she was fired and she didn't even want to know. Christy would love nothing more than to tell her it just wasn't working out.

She assured herself that she was essential but Mr. Hargrove's drunken tirade corroded her confidence. How was it an insult that two people could do her job?

She sat in the kitchen in her robe and pink curlers, with the paper laid out in front of her and a bowl of ice cream for breakfast. An announcer garbled the afternoon report on the radio in the background.

Suddenly she heard the buzz indicating someone was at the apartment door.

She thought perhaps it was the upstairs tenant locked out again. He was lucky she was home in the middle of a random afternoon.

When she got to the door she could hardly believe her eyes.

"Mr. Hargrove!" her voice echoed through the empty foyer. Hastily she unlocked the door, cracking it open.

He looked... slightly disheveled. Gorgeous.

How had she managed to ignore it? For years??

"Miss Winters."

"Come inside," she rushed him in quick with a hand on his back. Someone had probably already seen him. She led him into her apartment looking this way and that before closing the door.

"What on Earth are you doing here?"

"Why weren't you at work?" he questioned her.

"Why do you think?" she asked, tying her robe. She motioned for him to follow her out of the foyer and into her apartment.

"I feel terrible for how I handled our conversation yesterday. It was absolutely monstrous," he began as he stood in the living room while she fixed him a drink in the adjacent kitchen.

"Were you drunk, Mr. Hargrove?" she accused him.

Mr. Hargrove hesitated. "...Yes, but... only a little. I'm not an angry drunk."

"No, just Jekyll and Hyde."

"You will never see me like that again. I promise."

"Sounds like the promise of a drunk, to be honest," she replied, picking at ice from the icebox and collecting it in a glass.

"I met with Bower that afternoon and he's a fish. Selling you as an account woman took an unusual level of... finesse."

"You didn't have to do it at all," she sighed.

"I did."

"I don't want it," she insisted.

"I know, and I'm sorry," he said, watching her drown his gin and simple syrup in tonic water. "I wanted it to be a surprise but I couldn't wait. I thought you would be pleased."

He walked toward the bar separating the two spaces. Camille set his drink down and he took it. She leaned with both arms stiffly on the kitchen counter as she watched him take a sip.

"I... I thought I could make it as though it never happened, but I can't," she admitted.

"So do you mean to quit?" he fretted.

"I don't know what I mean to do."

"I need you to be there."

The notion wasn't comforting, as he had meant it. It sounded needy and weighty. More than she thought she could give him.

"Mr. Hargrove..."

"I'm not going back on what I said. It indeed never happened," he said, pushing up against her on the counter. "Be that as it may, I still need you there."

Camille didn't move, despite his closeness. "Christy could do my job."

"Not yours and hers. That's not what I meant and you know it."

She felt his gaze but refused to give in and meet it. "We've made a mess of things haven't we, Mr. Hargrove?"

He breathed deep, grinning. He was growing to like these little transcendent talks of theirs. Shedding their skins and candidly ignoring the expectations of others.

"It was worth it."

"I disagree."

"You regret it?" he asked.

"A little."

He trailed his hand down the smooth satin of her robe. "Only a little?"

"Why do you need me there?"

He took note of her beautiful face, accentuated by the helmet of pink curlers. Her lips were a colorless heart.

"You're different at home."

"Everyone's different at home," she insisted.

"I know. Care to show me around?"

A sober Mr. Hargrove was even more irresistible than his drunken counterpart. And strangely more irresponsible. "Are you like this with your other mistresses?"

"I don't keep a mistress, Miss Winters."

"Certainly I'm not your first."

"You are indeed."

"I believe there was a Caroline that came around more than twice."

"If you say so," Mr. Hargrove shrugged a bit.

"Are you saying you don't remember these women?"

"Are you saying that you *do* remember them?"

"It was my job to remember them."

"No, it wasn't," he said with a lazy smirk.

"Mr. Hargrove, I resent the implication," she sourly replied, still avoiding his eyes somehow. She wriggled away from his imposing body to put the booze back in the cabinet. He whirled around to watch her, drink in hand.

"You were going to show me around."

"I never agreed to that."

"Don't be shy, Miss Winters."

"When are you expected back?"

"Any minute," he said with a stern look of caution that soon melted. Camille huffed a laugh. Mr. Hargrove was really in her Brooklyn apartment. It was scandalous and electric.

Camille sighed and did a little twirl to indicate there wasn't much else. Reluctantly she faced his entranced expression before guiding him deeper into the apartment.

"My father owns the building. We have tenants upstairs."

Camille took him to a large room with a Murphy bed doing the job of guest room, library, and office. They went down the hall to the bedroom.

"It's small, but it's my favorite room in the house. Even with everyone out, I refuse to take the master for myself."

"It's full of light. Like its owner."

"Mr. Hargrove..." she blushed.

He smiled, cautiously walking towards her. "You still won't call me by my first name? Even now?"

"Especially now."

He caressed her arms at her sides, cupped her chin in one hand, and gazed at her longingly until she finally met his eyes and stared.

"Let me take care of you now, my dear."

"How do you mean?"

He donned a sheepish grin, hands going to her robe. "A romp in my office is hardly my best work."

"A damp old Brooklyn apartment isn't much of a step up," she replied, frozen as her robe fell to the floor. She wore a nightgown underneath.

"A fine bed is all we need."

"For what?"

She barely got the words out before he had engulfed her mouth with a kiss. Lightning struck and it took her aback. She realized that she hadn't let him kiss her in his office.

Had their first kiss not been cut short by Mr. McCain's drunken entrance, she would've known that it wasn't the booze turning her upside down. She might've let him make love to her right there. Her thighs clenched as they broke apart, panting.

"You couldn't forget either," she outed him.

"No," he breathed, "but then again... I didn't want to."

He nipped her lip, grabbed both her hands, and led her in front of him as he sat on the edge of the bed, the open blinds revealing the brick wall of another building yards away. His hands trailed up her thighs where they found no traces of underwear.

"You're not wearing anything."

Camille lifted the nightgown over her head exposing her naked body to him. She stood there like the Venus de Milo and he prayed to her there on the bed.

He was in love with her, he realized. He'd made an obscene amount of money from the merger and it meant nothing. Nothing like this moment, charging his cells like an electric wire.

He caressed her arm and brought the skin to his lips, moving them up and down before he finally kissed. She rewarded him with the soft touch of her fingertips to his face.

He took off his shoes and scooted back to the head of the bed, encouraging her to follow suit. She looked like some ginger-skinned medusa with her black hair enmeshed in pink rollers as she crawled in bed next to him.

He'd never made love to a woman in rollers. He could feel her bare chest against him as she lay in his arms and he felt content enough to sleep. But he didn't.

"What are you doing," she giggled as slowly he left her side and loomed over her naked form, kissing down her body to her center.

"Mr. Hargrove... be careful," Camille blurted as his kisses sunk lower and lower.

Mr. Hargrove raised his head. "...What?"

"I don't know."

He grinned. "Seeing you flustered is flustering me."

"Just hurry up and do it," Camille snapped with her eyes lowered.

"It won't hurt."

"I know that."

"It doesn't make you dirty," he assured her.

"Of course it does, if you have to say it."

Mr. Hargrove licked his lips. "I take full responsibility for everything."

"How can you say something so patently false?"

"Do I strike you as a man with public and private beliefs?"

"Yes, as a matter of fact. As if it matters. Once is a mistake. Twice makes me a harlot."

Mr. Hargrove completed the journey, hiking up one of her legs and surveying her moist center like a jewel. "What will three times make you?"

"Un-salvageable."

His clear sky eyes cut sharply to her black ones, already watching him carefully.

"So that no other man will want you?"

Camille sighed, laying back. "I saw my life going a very different way once."

Mr. Hargrove commenced inducting her into the council of unforeseen life paths, finding her sex and latching onto it with

174

his mouth like a vampire savoring its bite. And like a vampire's victim, she thrashed in conflicted pleasure, powerless to stop her descent.

* * *

Mr. Hargrove soundlessly puffed on one of Camille's cigarettes as she rested on his chest.

The radio was still on blaring faintly from the kitchen. A soap opera, which meant it must be around 2 o'clock.

"Do you really think I could do it?" Camille suddenly asked in the quiet.

"Do what?" Mr. Hargrove asked, caressing her naked back under the covers.

"Be an account woman?"

Mr. Hargrove took another drag. "I know that you could," he said through a plume of smoke.

"What made you think I would want to do what you do? You're miserable."

Mr. Hargrove rested his cigarette in the ashtray on the nightstand. He checked his watch, the only thing he was wearing.

"I'm miserable because I have no talent at it."

"Stop that. You're the best at what you do."

"I'm simply the best at Hargrove and Chase. There are better account men."

"I can't do what you do. What Mr. Daniels does. Mr. Shaw," she aired her insecurities as she fiddle with his chest hairs. "Be all things to all people and... schmooze and... lie... frankly, I was insulted when you told me."

He stroked her fine hair as well as he could with her curlers still there, now significantly loosened.

"No. You're no-nonsense and unexpectedly funny. And frank and competent-looking. I'd trust you to do heart surgery on me right now."

She smiled a glowing smile. "You're buttering me up."

"Maybe I'm not."

She rested her chin on his chest to look at him. "Like I said. I can never be like you."

"Which is why I want you to be like yourself. I didn't pitch you as one of the boys. The world is changing, Camille. It's too late for me to change with it, but not you."

"We're practically the same age, Mr. Hargrove."

"Yes, but my breed, it's a dying one. We are dinosaurs. Fighting over scraps. You have something we don't."

"A vagina?"

"Among other things," he said with a dazed look, taking in her dramatic beauty. He still couldn't believe his fortune.

"You're the entire future, wrapped all in one. All the other agencies are frightened of the negro market. We're going to make millions."

Camille focused on his chest, where she was connecting freckles with imaginary lines using her finger.

"You still care about such things?" she asked.

"I care about being more successful than my father was."

Her brow furrowed a little. "I didn't know that."

"Now you know."

Her dark eyes flew up to his and he felt a shiver. He had to get used to her looking at him like this.

"If I say 'no' you'll be cruel to me," she said.

"I won't. I promise."

"How do you know it won't backfire?"

Mr. Hargrove shrugged, indicating he didn't know. "We will either become a laughing stock or force the entire industry to change."

Camille shook her head and used an elbow to prop herself up on one side next to him. She wasn't sure if she wanted to be responsible for changing the whole damn industry.

"Probably both. In that order."

"We'll pretend to be sullen. Dress up like paupers."

"Can I have my old job back if it doesn't work out?"

"No."

Camille sighed a heavy sigh before conceding, begrudgingly. "Fine."

Mr. Hargrove sat up on his elbows, not believing his ears. "Really?"

Camille looked down as if preoccupied with her sheets. "I'll get a bonus from whatever account I land?"

"You'll get a bonus from a *meeting*, Camille."

"A per diem?"

"Now you're getting it," he said, with an air of almost mischief. He shifted to mirror her position. "Bring in accounts no one would dare try to take away from you. You can make yourself invaluable. Irreplaceable."

"Will I get to travel?"

"If necessary."

"With you?"

It was his turn to look down at the sheets. He skimmed them with a finger before shyly locking eyes. "You've discovered my secret plan, Miss Winters."

She shook her head again, chuckling. Was he really saying what she thought he was?

"People would catch on, Mr. Hargrove."

177

"Perhaps. Eventually. But they wouldn't dare say a word."

He was talking crazy. Which was making her think crazy.

That wasn't like her. She was always the one with the level head when folks started talking crazy. Camille donned a far-off, calculating look.

"We'd have a perfectly valid reason to cavort in public. Business dinners. Hotels. With propriety of course."

"Of course."

"All on the company dime."

"We could go to a movie," he grinned in a low voice. Camille scoffed.

"So that's why you tore my head off. Had it all planned, did you?"

He inched closer to her, until his head was resting in her bosom.

"Every part except your refusal, I'm afraid," he confessed. "I've had this idea for a while. Before Christmas happened. But I admit, it did... accelerate things. I got caught up in the plan being so perfect, I left you behind. I'm sorry. Forgive me."

Camille studied the fan at a standstill on the ceiling, stroking his hair in silence.

"You were right," she admitted with a watery eye, his chin near her heart. "I need to stop kidding myself. The marriage ship has sailed."

"Camille—"

"I can't count on you, I know that. I want to. I hate that I want to. But maybe if I'm successful. If I'm truly successful. It'll be enough."

He felt her body simmering again as he stroked her smooth skin under the sheets.

"Take it from a man. It won't be. But you'll never have to

178

worry. And that's almost as good. Especially, I should think, for a colored woman."

Camille lay still as he kissed across her chest.

"Why would you do this for me?" she breathed.

Mr. Hargrove loomed over her again, lifting her chin with his fingers, forcing her gaze to meet his. A long piece of hair dangled playfully out of place in front of his eyes.

"You've got what it takes, Camille. I'll make sure you never have to cower before a man. I'll die making sure of it."

Chapter 16

C amille took a whiff of the adoring bouquet sitting on her desk when she came into work.

Her mustard blouse and long plaid skirt perfectly matched the sensory-bombarding assortment of colorful tulips sitting in a glass vase like they were part of her outfit. It shielded the entire view of anyone walking past when she sat down.

"So you're the one we're all supposed to be jealous of," Mr. McCain's secretary Cheryl chimed in with a soft smile that matched her white mohair sweater. She leaned against Camille's doorway.

"What's the occasion?"

There was a simple hand-written note attached. "*Just be-cause.*"

"None, apparently," Camille tried and failed to hide a grin.

"It's about time you found a beau, Camille."

Camille smiled a smile of secrecy. "He's not really a beau, per se."

"Don't tell me these are from your anonymous soldier," Lillian, one of the new girls gasped as she loitered.

Camille's would-be love story had reached mythical status among the secretaries, and much of it behind Camille's back. All the girls knew what it meant when Camille headed to a corner of the break room alone and earlier than everyone else. They shooed the others away on her behalf.

They longed to read whatever kept Camille beaming like a school girl the entire 30 minutes and sometimes well into the day. Sometimes even blushing. After nearly a year, they were still going strong.

"Okay, I won't. And he's not anonymous."

"Could've fooled me. Where's the signature?"

"He doesn't need one," Camille bragged.

"You sent these to yourself, admit it."

"You still haven't met him?" another secretary wondered. Now they were piling in and taking turns breathing them in. Soon everyone would notice that no one was getting their phones answered.

"We... making plans."

"So romantic," Lillian sighed rapturously.

"Isn't he married?"

"It's not that kind of meeting," Camille lied.

"If it was me, it certainly would be," muttered Cheryl.

"You're terrible."

"A year of letters describing all the things he would do in person," Lillian said in a low whisper. Camille let out a rare cackle that amused them all.

Suddenly Christy appeared in the doorway looking accusingly at the others. A few of the new girls made themselves scarce without a word while the veterans stayed put.

Of all the secretaries who'd survived getting married, fired, or quitting, Christy was still one of the newest and the other girls never let her forget. They knew being the secretary of the boss still wasn't a management position, and they liked to remind Camille of the same whenever Christy wasn't around.

"Camille?"

"Yes, Christy?"

"Mr. Hargrove would like to see you."

Camille only nodded politely, addressing her remaining visitors. "Duty calls."

"Want me to put these in water for you, Camille?" Cheryl said, making a show of carrying the flowers directly into Christy's face.

"Put them in the breakroom, please Cheryl. They need sunlight."

Camille had an odd spring in her step on the way to Mr. Hargrove's office. It should definitely feel much worse than it did to be a hussy. What was she doing wrong?

Mr. McCain looked stern coming out of Mr. Hargrove's office but softened when he saw Camille headed his way.

"Someone's in a good mood," Mr. McCain discerned with a smile on his way down the hall.

"You didn't happen to send me any flowers, did you?" she flattered him, goading him to take the credit. He met her in the middle.

"I'm sure I don't know what you're talking about," he said with a wink.

"Miss Winters," Mr. Hargrove bellowed impatiently.

Camille gave Mr. McCain an uncharacteristic eye roll of solidarity before shutting the door behind her.

Camille stood, confident she wouldn't be offered a seat. "You beckoned?" she sighed.

"You'll be accompanying Mr. Daniels to his meeting with

Kraft foods."

Camille was stunned into silence for a moment, feeling like the passenger on a runaway train.

"That's a big fish, Mr. Hargrove. Aren't they already with Bradford Hudson?"

"They're premiering a new brand drink. A sweetener, really. Goes right into a glass of water. A dietary supplement with vitamins and minerals."

"A weight loss drink?"

"Aimed at women," he looked up at her from his desk and back down.

"My word," she replied. She took a deep breath.

This was it. She was really grabbing a bat and stepping up to the plate. He was really making her a player.

"They're giving all the agencies a crack at it."

"And if we land it, we'll get the rest?"

"It's certainly a foot in the door. Which is why Mr. Daniels won't object to sharing a bit of the credit on this one, whichever way it falls."

"This is really happening."

"It is."

"When?"

"Friday. There won't be much to say. He'll introduce you, show you how it's done. Take what you think works, leave the rest. You'll shadow him when he goes to Creative. If it lands, you'll share the account. We'll go from there."

"Very well," Camille accepted in an unsure tone.

"Calm down, you'll do fine."

"Easy for you to say," she breathed.

"Phil likes you, you know that."

"Anything else?"

"No.

Without being dismissed Camille turned to walk out, in a bit of a daze.

"Did you like the flowers?" she suddenly heard behind her.

Camille froze as she drew a blank, ignoring a strange wave of paranoia attempting to wash over her.

"Pardon?"

"The flowers I had delivered," he silently confirmed, breaking character for a brief moment.

Camille's heart pounded her whole body stiff.

She turned a little, feeling woozy.

"You had them... delivered?"

"Cryptic, I know. Reckless," he said with a wink, his voice lowered even further. "I promise it won't happen again until there's a true occasion."

As Mr. Hargrove returned to his role as her dutiful employer, Camille was left between worlds.

She turned out the door with a dead expression and slowly went straight back to her office.

"Open," he said after her when she didn't ask. He did nothing when she didn't answer.

"Mr. Hargrove?" Christy broke in through his intercom.

"What is it?"

"The Dvorak Group would like to know if they can reschedule? They have a conflict."

"Joel?" Mr. Hargrove verified.

"Yes, sir," Christy confirmed.

"Where is he?"

"He just flew in. The Roosevelt, I believe."

"Ring him in five minutes. Let him know I'm on the way."

"Very well, Mr. Hargrove."

* * *

"Of course, I'd jump at the chance, Ken. I can hardly understand why you'd want to work with a fledgling investment firm like mine," Joel Dvorak grinned over a pastrami sandwich in the hotel restaurant.

"*Boutique*, Joel. Boutique. It's the personal attention. The average man is bored. Works 9–5, comes home to one woman. He deserves to be rewarded."

"The average man doesn't trade the stock market, Mr. Hargrove."

"We can change that. No one remembers the crash anymore."

"Isn't your wunderkind supposed to be the one selling me?"

"Nonsense, you're my friend. Plus, he's become a bit of a diva now that he's made partner."

A young woman from the lobby made the long trek into the dining room to the table where they sat.

"Sorry to interrupt, Mr. Hargrove, but there's an urgent phone call from your office?" the woman interjected.

Mr. Hargrove furrowed his brow. "From a Miss Winters?"

"I believe from a Miss Caldwell."

He didn't want to heed the interruption at all, but Christy knew better. Whatever it was, it had to be a doozie.

"Excuse me," Mr. Hargrove addressed his friend and potential client. He braced himself as he took the receiver at the front desk.

"Miss Caldwell."

"Mr. Hargrove? You might want to come down here."

He furrowed his brow. "What's going on, Christy?"

"It's Miss Winters, I think she's gone crazy."

Mr. Hargrove turned away from the receptionist, switching to the other ear. "Care to be more specific?"

"She came to your office, looking for you, I suppose. I told her you weren't in, but she barged right past me and started looking through your desk."

Mr. Hargrove practically went into combat mode right there in the lobby. His guilty heart panicked.

Camille was looking through his desk as we speak. Everything was locked but it didn't matter. Clearly, he'd buggered himself. The jig was up.

But how?

"Where is she now?"

"I told her to stop. I even threatened to call the police but it's like she's completely lost her mind. She's tearing the place up."

Mr. Hargrove's mind was spinning.

"Tell her to meet me here. Twenty minutes."

Christy was sick.

"Mr. Hargrove, you can't be serious."

"...Do you have something to say, Christy?"

Christy's tone turned stoic. "I'm simply thinking about the client, Mr. Hargrove."

"That's commendable, Christy, but let me handle that."

"You don't know what she's like. What if she refuses to leave? What if she assaults someone?"

"Just do as I ask, Christy."

"...Did you sleep with her?" she accused in a repulsed tone.

"I won't ask again."

"I suppose I have my answer."

Mr. Hargrove chuckled in rare astonishment. "My word. You really don't care about this job at all, do you? Have you been hanging on all this time? Waiting for me to come to my senses or something?"

"*You* sent her those flowers, didn't you?"

Mr. Hargrove was stunned.

She was bluffing. She had to be.

She knew nothing. How was this getting away from him *this* goddamned fast?

"Tell her I've left a note with the front desk with instructions," he stayed composed, on task. "Be sure to clean out your desk once it's done."

"That's all we are to you, isn't it?" marveled Christy.

"You'll be paid to the end of the month."

"Well, that is generous, Ken," she spat.

"You were an excellent sport, Chris. For a while."

"I should've had the courage to leave long ago. I should at least thank you for that."

Mr. Hargrove took a long time catching his breath. "You're smart, Miss Caldwell. So do what I've asked. Or you'll have to find another industry."

"I wouldn't dream of doing anything else. Mr. Hargrove."

"Thank you, Christy."

"Go to hell," she said with a click of the line.

"Do you have a pad and paper?" he asked after he'd hung up the receiver. He grabbed the notepad and a pen from his pocket.

Hastily he began to scribble. As he did, he nearly doubled over with nausea, thinking of his own stupidity.

The fucking note.

He hadn't signed it with any name. But... he didn't need to, did he?

All he had to do was keep his fucking head down and be her boss. It was the one thing he had to do. But no.

So. *This* is how terrible this was going to end. Huh.

It was always destined to, but at least it would've been on his terms. Now it was fucked. Totally fucked. Sad. He'd been so close. Mere days away.

The story of his life.

"Is the penthouse vacant?"

"No sir. I have an executive suite on the third floor."

"Perfect. I have another client meeting. If you could put this in an envelope and leave this for a Miss Camille Winters when she gets here. She'll be expecting it."

"Of course, Mr. Hargrove, anything else?"

"Nothing for now," he said in a rushed manner.

He finished the meeting with Joel Dvorak in a fog. Then made a show of leaving the hotel, greeting the front desk on the way out. He made his way around the corner, then down the back alley through the service entrance.

* * *

Camille had never been inside a hotel room as luxurious as this one. Burgundy embroidered drapes adorned the dramatically long windows. A tray of room service mysteriously appeared after 20 minutes had come and gone.

But Camille hardly noticed. Time had folded in on itself since she last spoke to Mr. Hargrove, and all she could do was replay the moment. She was at once desperate to know the truth while dreading it just as much.

The last letter she'd written was clutched in her hand. Well, at least the envelope that'd contained the letter. The contents were nowhere to be found. She'd had to dump out the wastepaper basket in his office to find the little that she did.

She couldn't do much besides sit on the edge of the bed and stare at the wallpaper, waiting for Mr. Hargrove to come. If he ever would come. She just needed to get out of that office.

A knock on the door forced Camille out of her stupor.

"Miss Winters? It's me."

She walked slowly to the disembodied voice on the other side. It had to be Mr. Hargrove but there was a sudden wall of mistrust between them that even his voice sounded strange.

"Camille, sweetheart, open the door."

"Mr. Hargrove?"

"Yes, Miss Winters, it's me."

"Why do you have his letters?"

Mr. Hargrove didn't quite know how to answer. He didn't know which letters she was referring to. There were oh so many.

"My bag, the one with the medals. Did you look there?"

"Why do you have his letters?"

Mr. Hargrove licked his dry lips. "Did you bring it?"

"Answer me!" Camille shrieked.

"Lower your voice," he pleaded in his own low tone.

"These are *his* letters. Why do you have them?"

She must be talking about Stanley's letters, but he couldn't think if he'd left his desk unlocked. He never left his desk unlocked.

"I can explain everything, Camille. Let me in."

"You think I'm letting you anywhere near me? You have a dead, *colored man's* letters, his *private* letters, in your office."

Oh no. The mailcart.

Had Winston slipped a fresh one under his door?

"Camille, please..."

"Please tell me you're not the one sending me these. Please, Mr. Hargrove. Please, don't tell me that," she wept.

Mr. Hargrove's tongue was like glue.

"Please tell me that you're not some *sick*... I have to get out of here."

189

Mr. Hargrove didn't know what she meant by that but he heard a familiar tone of desperation. He tried the door feverishly. When that didn't work, he frantically willed his mind to some type of order.

"Okay, Miss Winters, alright. You don't have to open the door. But if you'll indulge me, I must tell you a story. Please."

Finally, a frail, weeping voice answered back. "I can't stay."

"I know that. Please. Just listen. And try to forgive me. I should've done this long ago."

He took a breath, suddenly glad she wasn't able to see him.

"When you asked me if I knew of any colored regiments stationed in Asia, I lied. I did know of one."

Silence. He'd hoped his opening line was enough to keep her attention on the other side of the door.

"My father never wanted me to join the Marines. At the time I thought it was because I was his only son. But now I think he hated the thought of sharing any glory with me. He was a marine in the first war, you see. No one wanted me to go. They didn't understand it. Why a boy from a wealthy family would want to be a number in a sea of faceless, poor men, huddled together facing death in the dirt. But to me it was obvious. It was glorious. It was hard. The hardest thing I will ever do. So many of those men I carry with me. I carry them with me and it makes me go still. To think that so many of them would trade places with me now. Though I suspect a few would be ashamed of me."

He had to stop as emotion threatened to grip him. It was deathly quiet on the other end of the door. The hallway outside the executive suite remained bare.

"Camille?"

"Go on."

"I couldn't completely abandon my status. I came in as an

officer. I had a good education. Good breeding, they said. When I became a Lieutenant, I got a... peculiar assignment. It was in the Pacific. The negro regiment had been sent where the action had been the least. The Marines hadn't yet been integrated and they needed white officers to report to. The lieutenant who was there had been sent to Europe. I had a feeling it was my father's doing, pulling me out of Patton's unit where he thought I would be out of harm's way. He was wrong, of course. Harm was everywhere in 1943. But for once, I'm eternally grateful to him for interfering because it changed my life.

"To this day I don't know how he found out where I was at all. I was using an alias, you see. I couldn't very well waltz in there with the name Hargrove and expect to be treated fairly. That's the way it had always been for me. I didn't know any better. Turns out I had nothing to worry about. No one looks rich taking cover from bombs and shitting their pants. None of that matters there. But I didn't know that. I picked a name that I thought sounded pedestrian enough. And the surname of my favorite poet."

Suddenly the door flew open. Mr. Hargrove was confronted with Camille's dumbfounded, tear-stained expression.

"Mr. Hargrove—"

"Please, call me Ken."

"I... no."

Just then he looked at her. He probed her eyes, willing her to look at him. But she could only lean further away in fear as breath heaved up and out of her. The only sound was her breathing.

He moved slow, as if for a weapon. Slowly making his way inside the room until he could shut the door behind him, never taking his eyes off of hers.

He went down on his knees in front of her, at her feet with both her hands in his.

He wanted her to be put at ease but he could see there was no hope. He was who he was to her. He was just going to have to say it.

"Camille," he swallowed in a half-whisper. "Sweetheart, it's me. It's your Stanley."

"My what? Is this a joke?"

"It's no joke."

"Then you're a liar. You're a lying, drunk... miserable wretch."

"I am all those things, but I am telling you the truth."

"You'd say anything, wouldn't you? To make me... I don't know. To control me. You're obsessed with me."

"I am."

"I don't... how... why do you have his letters?"

"Because they're mine."

"So what you... found them and bought them? Are you even a war vet?"

Mr. Hargrove smiled. "My little Brooklyn nobody with the strange mind."

Camille froze in terror, in bewilderment.

"I have his letters because they are my letters, Camille. The ones you let me keep."

"That's impossible. Stanley's colored. He's... from Alabama. The drawing..."

"Was of my Private First-Class Briggs. He volunteered to do it."

"You said you drew it."

"I never said that I drew it."

"You said it was your likeness."

"I know. I'm sorry."

"Because you never intended to tell me the truth."

"I never intended to make it at all. I just knew I didn't want it to end. That's all."

"You lied. About the magnolias, about your family. You're from Rochester. That day... at Cadillac..."

"Wayne said your name in passing. I had to see for myself that it was you."

"So you could toy with me in real life? The way you couldn't in letters anymore?"

"No."

"No? You're a married man. Writing me letters, seducing me while your wife raises your children..."

"No, Camille."

"I have to go. I have to..." Camille couldn't breathe. Her world was being turned upside down. Work. She had to get back to work. But her boss was...

She recoiled from his grasp. She headed for the doorway that separated the bedroom from the rest of the suite but the more she walked, the further away the doorway drifted.

She held an arm out to steady herself against the wall, but there seemed to be no wall there. She tried to collect her balance before she collapsed into the rolling cart carrying a tray of silver.

She heard a crash, felt an arm underneath hers. The room spun relentlessly once she stilled and she gave up trying to walk. She could only breathe and shut her eyes tight to try and make it stop, make it all stop.

Mr. Hargrove. The first white man she was willing to say that she trusted. Turned out to be the one responsible for breaking her heart. And now she had to find out he was worse than a liar.

She cried there on the floor, exhausted. Feeling pity. Everything was turning white and she was sure she was going blind on top of it.

She tried to stand up when she felt Mr. Hargrove's hands on her skin again. She scrambled poorly to her feet and felt herself falling again, dramatically swooping back and unable to catch herself.

Suddenly she was stilled as if suspended. Lifted. Slowly she was hovering and she realized Mr. Hargrove was carrying her. She held onto his shoulder for one glorious moment, her eyes still closed. And she felt the bed beneath her.

She felt panicked and she wished that she wouldn't. She wished she could've enjoyed Mr. Hargrove carry her in his deceptively strong grasp like she were a precious work of art.

She continued her confused crying on the grand white bed-clothes. Tossing her body away from him as she sobbed louder and louder. She could only distantly ponder herself coming undone.

There was no point in looking composed, the jig was up. Had been up, since the day he hired her. Since the day he had laid eyes on her and there she was, ten years later still not over either of them. Still unable to move beyond their decade-old fevers.

She was lonely and sad. She wasn't even sure of any compliment he'd ever paid her. She was a doll in his menagerie. A sad one. Worthy of pity and ridicule. Had nothing ever been her own to claim?

"I wish I knew why you were crying, my dear," she heard behind her patiently. "I wish you would tell me what you're thinking."

"I'm embarrassed, Mr. Hargrove," she quivered, "and sad."

"You're not angry with me?"

"No, sir."

Her professionalism was like knives in him. His sleeves were rolled up to his forearms. He reached out, desperate to touch her still. After all these years. After everything between them.

She was so close. But not his. Not as his true self. He retracted his hand. "Please look at me. Camille."

She didn't. She kept her body turned but she quieted down, proving she was listening.

"I assume you're sad because... I'm not the man you wanted me to be."

"The man I wanted? No, I'm sad because the man I wanted doesn't even exist."

"He does."

"It was ridiculous, to begin with," she lamented, her dripping red nose saturating the pillow. "Sending fanciful letters to a stranger. Letting him... fill my mind with all kinds of nonsense. But then, it wasn't even that, was it? It was dress-up. Vaudeville."

"Not for me. I always knew who were, Camille."

"You're some kind of rich sicko? Playing sick games with colored women—"

"You really think I ever gave a damn that you're colored? After all these years you've known me?"

"Well, aren't you a saint!" she barked, looking over her shoulder at him. "Forgive me, Mr. Hargrove. I hate to break it to you but I do care that you're... *white*."

"I know."

"And I care that you're married. And... a liar."

"But you love me. The real me. And I love you."

"You don't know me."

"Camille—"

"You don't! What's a book's worth of letters? Look how much I knew Stanley! He's not even real."

"Please don't say that."

"Just stop, Mr..."

"I never lied, Camille."

"Of course you did."

"Not about this. Not about us."

"This is too much to take in. I'm not sure I believe you," Camille hopped up soberly, wiping her face with her hands. "I don't know how you have Carl's letters. Or how you know what was in Stanley's, but I have to leave now."

Camille clumsily grabbed her things, sniffing her emotions away until they were neatly contained again. She reached for the door handle, barely able to face the direction of the bed where Mr. Hargrove was sitting on the edge.

"I don't know when I'll be returning to work. I'm sorry, I can't tell you much more than that."

"Of course," he replied, as he watched Camille disappear on the other side of the quietly closed door.

* * *

Mr. Hargrove sat there on the bed in a daze, enveloped by silence.

"She's gone," he finally said out loud.

He did it. He finally did it. The last of his secrets had been exorcised.

So why was regret closing in on him?

You should've just denied it, he faintly thought. He could've doubled down. Called her crazy. He could've maintained control.

Who was he kidding? It would've happened just like this.

His mind surged with pathological clarity. He could fall apart. Right here, right now.

They could bring enough booze to kill an elephant. He

wouldn't even have to leave the suite.

But he'd just made a million dollars for shaking hands with a man. And he now had a much larger company to run and virtually no one to help. Salaries to pay. Including hers, perhaps. If she doesn't leave.

So he couldn't fall apart. Not yet.

He was frightened to go back to the office, but he knew that he should. He doubted Camille was there, but Christy likely still was.

The day was surreal enough, but seemed to be hungry for more. No one could get a hold of him. The hotel was under the impression he'd left long ago. He decided to wait it out as close to the end of the day as he could.

When he showed back up to the office it was eerily quiet, even for 5:00. Nearly everyone had gone. Everyone except for Chet, who was making coffee in the break room.

Chet was startled as Mr. Hargrove walked by, and again when he saw who it was.

"Ken," he nearly gasped.

"Where is everyone?"

"Where've you been?" Chet uncharacteristically chided him. It gave him an ominous feeling.

"I had meetings," he replied with a furrowed brow. "What happened."

"Christy quit."

Mr. Hargrove jostled his head. "She didn't quit, I fired her."

"She accused Camille of doing things. Horrible things."

Mr. Hargrove sickened. "What kinds of things?"

"She said she was sleeping with everyone and that's how she got her job. That your wife had been warning her since she was hired."

Mr. Hargrove tilted his head, his brow still in a knit. "Hold on... when was this?"

"This afternoon. After you left."

It certainly wasn't like Christy to fly off the handle. Though he had to admit he had no real reason to have that impression.

"Follow me, Chet."

They passed Camille's office, dutifully locked. They made their way past the conference room to his office.

"Did anyone fill you in on what happened?" Chet asked as he fast-walked to keep up.

"No. It's a good thing you're here, isn't it, Chet?"

Mr. Hargrove saw the mess at Christy's desk. He got to his office door that had been left open, surveying the damage.

"Christy did most of that."

"I see."

Papers were strewn everywhere. A plant had been toppled over.

"Did security finally escort her out?"

"Camille convinced them to let her leave on her own."

Mr. Hargrove turned to him. "Miss Winters?"

"She was the only one in the office who'd kept a level head."

Surely all that didn't happen in twenty minutes...

"Didn't she... Miss Caldwell told me that Camille had ransacked my office."

"I was sitting with the secretaries so I didn't hear any of that. In fact, all I saw was Christy screaming and carrying on about Miss Winters. And then when Camille came back from lunch, Christy started screaming at her."

What the devil?

Mr. Hargrove pretended to be more in the dark than he was. Though it wasn't too hard.

"Camille left? And then came back?"

"Not for long. She stayed long enough to make sure Christy left the building, closed the door to her office, and then came out looking for Winston. Then she left."

Winston??

The mailcart.

"Winston still here?" Mr. Hargrove asked.

"I don't know, sir."

"As you were, Chet."

"Yes, sir."

Mr. Hargrove left everything as it was. Tomorrow, he could deal with all this easily.

What he couldn't do, is go another second without knowing if Camille had written him another letter.

He got to the stairwell and raced down to the mailroom floor below where the elderly black man was sorting.

Winston saw Mr. Hargrove standing wordlessly in the doorway and halted his work.

"Gunny," Mr. Hargrove began.

"Captain."

Mr. Hargrove couldn't help his desperate look. "Please tell me you have something for me, sir."

Winston knew what he meant. He reached up into a cubby hole where he'd placed the letter especially. "Right here, Captain."

Mr. Hargrove couldn't help snatching it from his grasp, hardly believing his eyes. He flipped it upside down with his thumbs and forefingers, inspecting the sealed, pristine thing.

"Everything alright?"

Mr. Hargrove eyed the letter with both hope and suspicion. Like a cyanide pill.

He shook his head, squinting. "I fucked up, Sergeant. Beyond all repair."

"Worse than Iwo Jima?"

"I wasn't in Iwo Jima."

"Worse than Peleliu?"

Mr. Hargrove sighed. "No sir, not worse than Peleliu."

"Then I'll see you tomorrow morning, Captain."

Mr. Hargrove put the letter in his coat pocket, his hope renewed for at least another afternoon.

"Yes, sir."

17

Present Day, Spring 1957

March 2, 1957

Stanley,

Things have gotten progressively worse. But not for the reasons you might imagine. The boss whom I slept with tried to promote me. When I refused it, he became angry. He accused me of being lazy and inconsiderate of my future. He says I'm more talented than I give myself credit for and that I need to think about securing my future. The implication being that since I'll never be married, I need to be preparing to earn my keep among unscrupulous men until I die. And apparently, Mr. Hargrove doesn't think he'll be around much longer to do that for me.

I admit, it caught me off guard to think about my entire future in an instant, but I suppose it is overdue. I'm well past my prime. And the men that I want who also want me have chosen others to devote themselves to, and cannot go back on that.

I honestly don't know what I was thinking. I do not see

myself married, nor do I see myself being alone forever. I suppose I imagined companionship. Eventually. I think deep down I am waiting for your wife to keel over and die. Waiting seems to be my strong suit, anyway.

I made the mistake of mentioning you during this argument. I don't know why. I was feeling defensive. He was making it seem as though I had nothing. I just wanted to prove to him that he was wrong. And then mentioning you made him so livid. It was simply awful.

I don't have anything else on my mind.

Camille

March 9, 1957

Camille,

It pains me to see you distressed. And I'm glad that you felt comfortable enough to confide in me. It does sound like a precarious situation, one that I wish you didn't suffer at all. I wish your only suffering were wondering what to cook for dinner and how to keep up with your many children. But I won't go on about my wishes for your life.

Stan

March 16, 1957

Stanley,

Since we last spoke, my boss has confessed more of his feelings. He came over and we made love.

I could never be a mother. Or a wife. If there's one thing my life has taught me, it's that. So don't waste your pity, Stanley. By all accounts it sounds like we would've been miserable had you caught up with me. Maybe not right away, but eventually. If anything, I'm grateful that you've come back in my life and allowed me to see that. At best, I would have done whatever you wanted out of love. At worst, out of obligation. Our love would've turned bitter. Our treasured memories to ash until nothing was left.

I don't know if I am in love with him but I am certainly addicted to him. He has pried me open. But I know that it is not real. I didn't think I could ever abide it but luckily you and Carl have given me years of practice in hoping for doomed things. I am being cruel now, so I will end this letter.

Camille

March 25, 1957

Camille,

No, you aren't. You are being honest. Forgive me if I offended you. I confess that in the afterglow of your confession it has slowly and surely made me a little jealous but I keep it at bay for your sake. To be honest, I want to find him and choke him and bruise his airway and watch the life slowly go out of him. Were he not a fellow Marine, I might still. And yet I know that I could not have wrecked you in the way that you wanted. There are many things I've meditated on, so hard and so long that it almost became real, but wrecking you has never been in them.

Stanley

March 30, 1957

Stan,

So you do think less of me, Stanley Whitman. Admit it. When will you come to me? I'm tired of letters.

203

Camille

April 7, 1957

Camille,

I will come to you whenever you want. D–Day is coming up. That is a joke, of course.

I could meet you in the city. Or you could come to me. My house is just outside Philadelphia, about an hour from you.

April 14, 1957

Stan,

Perhaps I will come to you. I've scarcely been out of the city since my Cunard days. Do send me the address. And make it a week before. Say, the 28th? As romantic as D–Day sounds, it seems destined to fail. If I am in danger of making a fool of myself by showing up mysteriously at a stranger's doorstep, please tell me now. I am old and in no mood for surprises.

April 20, 1957

Camille,

No surprises here. I only ask that if we endeavor to make this plan that you give me your word that you will be here on the intended date come hell or high water. I don't think my heart could withstand this being postponed. I should warn you however that if you come to see me, I have every intention of wrecking you now as well as I can. Should I manage to successfully talk you into it.

The 28th seems too far away. I should've known better

than to set a date with you for the future. It instantly filled me with anxiety. How about two weeks? The 7th? There is a bus that comes right by my house, if you can believe it. Every two hours.

Stan

April 27, 1957

You,

Very well. But it will have to be the 10th now, since your letter. Monday is prickly for you, I'm sure, as it is for most people but find an excuse. Don't worry about me, I will be there. I have every intention of letting myself be wrecked.

Me

May 5, 1957

Dear Stanley,

The strangest thing happened today. Strange. The owner of my company, the one who seduced me, said that the flowers you sent me had been sent by him. A strange thing to lie about, since the card was in your handwriting. It didn't make sense that he would know I received flowers, or that I'd gotten them from you. It didn't make sense that he would know anything about you. It drove me mad. Then I started to think that it was him. He was the insidious neighbor, taking me for a ride. I had to know.

I broke into his office. Scoured his desk. Much of it was locked away except for an envelope in the wastebasket. It was your letter.

Then I became utterly inconsolable. I looked through everything that wasn't nailed down. I looked through his war memorabilia and nearly screamed in terror. He had Carl's letters. In his office.

The moment I saw them I thought I was going to float out of my body. I couldn't think. The nightmare got more and more diabolical. First, I thought he was somehow sneaking through my private things. Then, when I saw that they were my letters to you, not yours to me, I realized that it was worse than I originally thought. Worse than I could imagine. In fact, I didn't want to imagine any more.

I confronted him, all the while outside of myself. He had nothing to say, of course. Eventually, he came up with something. He admitted that he was the one writing me and saying he was you. He said that he was you all along.

Which is impossible. I don't know why he would say something like that, of all things.

I don't know. I don't know what's real. I don't know if you're real and I never have known. I don't know how long I will write dead men. But now I'm lost and desperate.

Please tell me the truth, Stanley. And I won't be angry. Whatever it is. But I need to hear it from you.

May 8, 1957

Camille,

The flowers. Of course. I'm an idiot. I'm sorry if that moment caused you distress, and I'm sorry to hear you describe it. And you will hear it from me. In person. I promise.

I won't waste your time pleading. I don't deserve anything. I can't speak for your boss. I can only speak for *myself. My plans haven't changed. I don't know if I can stand to disappoint you any more than I already have, but I'll answer you the best way I can, if you decide you still want to meet. It's the least I can do. Monday afternoon. Please be there.*

   Yours,

   Stan

18

Chapter 18

The sun beat down just enough to make an unusually warm spring day.

Ken sat in the kitchen of his country house, smoking a cigarette and enjoying the fresh air from the open doors.

He'd smoked a pile of them since he'd heard the first bus of the day stop by his house around 9 am. His heart nearly lunged when he saw someone get off from his upstairs bedroom window.

But it wasn't her. It was a balding black man holding a suitcase. From the window, Ken watched him head down the one endless stretch of country road visible by his property, unconcerned with how long it would take him to get wherever he was going.

Since then he'd showered, got dressed in a wife-beater and slacks, made breakfast, and couldn't tear himself away from his kitchen table in the quiet, where he had a perfect view of the road from the wall of kitchen windows.

For four hours he listened for the bus's engine coming to a stop, but in the two times it passed, there were none.

After the sixth hour, he was finally rewarded with a screech of the brakes.

Slowly he closed his eyes, feeling his exploding heart. Bravely he approached the kitchen window to look out at the road.

After an eternity the bus began to move again, revealing a young woman holding only her purse, wearing a coral dress with white polka dots and a matching scarf tied around her hair.

Camille.

He hurried through the living room to the front door. His legs were rubber as he walked out onto his porch. He shielded his eyes to get a better look as she strode towards him.

He expected her to still be stunned to see him somewhat. After all, she had come to see Stanley. But it was him there instead.

She didn't seem surprised, but she didn't seem happy either. The guarded look she hid behind in the office was gone and that was enough to turn him into a coward.

"Come inside," he offered when she got close enough to the porch. He left the screen door open with his arm as she entered fully into his world for the first time.

"You came," he said.

"Of course," she replied, looking around. "You weren't expecting me?"

"It's just the way that we left things, I didn't know. You never answered back."

"How'd it feel?"

He grinned as he grabbed her hand, pulling it towards his chest. "Like the bleakest hell. I'm sorry."

Camille ignored him. "I didn't know if I was going to come until today."

"You hungry?"

"I ate."

"Coffee?"

"Sure."

Ken pulled her further into the house, past the dining room, and into the kitchen where there was a massive fireplace in the corner. An old-fashioned coffee pot was there on the stove and she helped herself.

On the mantle was the familiar canvas tote he kept in his office with the medals attached.

"Please sit," he said as he grabbed it, using a chair for a footstool as he sat atop the table in front of her. "I have something to give you."

Camille reluctantly took the seat in front of him, dreading whatever speech he was about to give her. She still wasn't sure that she liked him this way. Groveling and repentant. Mr. Hargrove had been a facade. And so had Stanley Whitman.

"This was my war bag. I took it with me everywhere. Everywhere. I never wanted to be found without it. Especially towards the end. The enemy could strike at any time and we'd have to move. I'd die going back for it. I'd die thinking about it more than my own men. My instincts were right because it saved my life."

Mr. Hargrove produced the contents of the bullet-torn bag. Letters. Yellowed by time, a brown halo around the cursive ink hand she recognized anywhere. He took out one set that was bundled together with string.

"You don't have to do this now," Camille said.

"Of course I do. They're yours."

"I don't want them."

"I said I would. I'm only here at all because I said I would."

Camille relented and took the bundle.

"You're here," he repeated, as if in shock. There were no more secrets between them and he felt a bit naked.

"Yes," she smiled.

"Why did you write again? After the hotel?"

Camille shrugged helplessly reliving it. "What else could I do? At that moment? I was completely turned around."

"The note I wrote. With the flowers," he recalled with a faint sickness. "You realized it was me?"

She finished her sip of coffee that was black, same as his.

"I don't know that I realized so much as I came to grips that I already knew. Or should've known. Why would the letters just suddenly start up again? Why on Earth would a man like you poach a colored secretary from a car salesman in Jersey?"

"Don't say it like that. Like you're not good at what you do. I didn't expect you to be so good, in fact."

"I never told Stanley that Mr. Hargrove was a Marine."

"...Could've been a lucky guess," Ken shrugged.

"You'd been so careful up to now."

"Hardly."

"Don't sell yourself short, Mr. Hargrove."

"Call me Stan."

"What on Earth for?" Camille furrowed her brow in exasperation and awe.

"Because you won't call me by my first name. Because... that's who I am to you. Who I was. To all of them."

Camille sighed, bewildered. "Why didn't you just tell me? Back then? That you were white?"

Stan took the seat next to her, hunched over and sitting sideways to face her.

"I'd just wanted you to know how much good your letter had done, that's all. And then when you replied I was petrified, really. It certainly never occurred to me to tell you the truth."

"So... you never planned on meeting me? After the war?"

"No. Well...yes I did," he lowered his head sheepishly, his

brow furrowed. "While I was writing you, over there, I planned it every day. Like a mad man. I didn't see the point in vexing you further in the likely event I didn't even survive.

"But then I barely made it out alive. I lost my men. I got home and...there was no need to fake my death. Because I was dead. I wasn't anything like Stanley Whitman let alone myself. I was a soldier without a war.

"Eventually my mother dressed me, stood me upright, and wheeled me about town. She forced me to take over the company since it was losing money. I did business. Kept clients. I made money. I somehow gained a wife, a family. I had plenty to do, plenty to keep me from offing myself. But I gave up being happy."

Camille pieced together the parts in Mr. Hargrove's story with Stanley's. Not everything was a lie, then.

"Ten years? Why? You never looked for me? Weren't you curious?"

"It wasn't easy trying to find a reason to be in Bedford-Stuyvesant, trying not to stick out like a sore thumb. Sometimes I drove, sometimes walked. Sometimes took the Subway. But never managed to catch a glimpse. Must've been during your stewardess days, I think."

"I don't believe it," Camille exhaled.

"I couldn't see how or why we could ever be together. It was simply a habit. A tortuous one. Then life went on. Family and such. I let the agency consume me and abandoned the search, practically. And I couldn't entrust it to anyone else, I was too paranoid. I was convinced it wouldn't make sense to anyone else and they would figure me out. But I felt you. In the strangest places. Sometimes I'd feel you and it made me so frightened that I didn't want to turn around. Even though it would be impossible for you to ever know me, it didn't feel that way.

"And then one day a colleague told me about this new agency girl he had working for him. Named Camille."

He looked up at her with those pale blue eyes. A smile bloomed over his face, crinkling his eyes in the corners.

"I went to Jersey. I decided to buy a Cadillac. And there you were. Come to life like a princess from a storybook, walking around. And then I heard that voice. Answering phones. After all those thousands of days, you came to me. Right on time. You don't understand, I could hardly contain it."

He was lost in remembering, looking off to something behind her, reliving their reunion. He was still handsome this way, vulnerable and scruffy from not shaving.

But he was shrinking. He looked shorter, even sitting down. His head was close enough for her to pet his hair like he was a farm animal.

"I was still dead but... I just wanted to keep you close. What was the harm in it?"

"You lied. For years. How could you do something like this to someone you say you love?" she argued.

"I never wanted you to find out it was me. Not at first," he insisted, unapologetic. "The way you looked at me when you first saw me. When I first hired you. I never wanted you looking at me any different.

"But after a while... it wasn't enough anymore," he divulged, grabbing her hand. It sent a tingle between her legs. "I wanted to hear you talk to him the way you would never talk to me. My God, Camille, I wanted it so much. Even though I saw how much I'd done, and I couldn't... I didn't want to hurt you any more than I had."

"How much you'd done?"

He met her bewildered look, choosing his words carefully.

"You brought him up. Out of the blue. After a year and nine months, one week and two days. You said his name."

She pulled her hand away. "I didn't say his name."

"You did—"

"Listen to me," Camille confronted him standing up from her chair, eyes darting back and forth as they probed his. "I would *never* utter his name. At *work*. To you or anyone else."

Stan looked up at her from his chair. "Perhaps. But I heard it all the same. And I could not keep what happened next from happening."

"What would he say to you now, hm?" she asked softly, glaring. "Watching you toy with me?"

His stare hardened. He didn't blink. "Don't do that."

Camille was undeterred. "Did you swear to take care of me, is that it? While he died in your arms?"

Stanley was on his feet in front of her abruptly, his towering height returning, but Camille didn't flinch.

"Stop... talking."

"How did he die?" she interrogated him.

"It doesn't matter."

"You saw what happened? Does it haunt you? Do you want to know what it looks like in my mind? Nothing, Stanley. It looks like nothing. It's just a blank page. But I guess I'm never allowed to be as broken as you? We only had what, two dances? Not like I lost anything I wasn't already missing. Everyone knew Carl better than I did. You certainly know Stanley better than I do."

"You *do* know me. I may have known Carl more than you did, but you know me. Better than any of them ever did. Better than anyone. As well as I hid, you still found me."

"You messed up, that's all. You could've written letters to me until I shriveled, couldn't you? Look at our lives, Stanley, it was a waste."

"Don't say stupid things, Camille. Out of anger. That you can't take back."

It wasn't anger, it was guilt. Perhaps in a way it was anger, in that guilt seemed to be the only appropriate emotion between them now. The last shred of denial she harbored about their dalliances was now impossible to hold on to.

"You don't get it, do you? I'm *tired* of soldiers," Camille sobbed and it broke his heart. There was nothing so deflating as seeing the impact of the war on everyone else.

"I don't care about your stupid war and your stupid honor, don't you get that? He died for nothing!! And so did you! And so did I! I hate you! And I hate him!"

There was nothing she could say that could make him feel any less for her. "You're not dead, Camille."

"Yes. I am."

He palmed her face with one of his big hands. "You're not. We both know you're not."

Camille's breath quickened. "...This doesn't prove anything."

"Sure it does," he said, capturing her lips with his own. The sound of afternoon birds colored the silence there in the country kitchen through the open back door. Camille winced as his mouth trailed her neck, injecting bursts of arousal through her blood.

"When I opened your letter," he whispered, "the one after the Christmas party, I put my body through such a punishment. Did you know that?"

"Stanley," she gasped, before he was gathering her in his arms and carrying her down the hall to the four-post bed in the downstairs guest room.

"I can't believe it's you," she whispered, again and again, her eyelashes clogged with moisture. Stanley didn't answer as he laid her down and crushed her in his arms with his weight, tasting her salty tears.

Kissing, they clung to each other's embrace, still fully clothed, squeezing the life out of one another as Camille quietly wept.

For the first time in over a decade, it felt safe enough for celebration. But even the secluded country house wasn't safe from her heart's perpetual gloom.

"Do you think... he can see us?"

"Maybe."

Their foreheads touched. "Would he be... angry?"

"At you? Never," he said.

"He was the most beautiful boy I ever saw."

"They all were."

Her head began to toss, as if in unseen agony. She lost her breath.

"Make love to me. Right now."

It didn't feel right. At all. Maybe she knew that. Maybe that's the reason why she wanted to. Shaky hands began navigating his belt buckle.

Stanley was powerless to deny her. With her polka dot dress, she was as close to the girl in the torn-up picture as she would ever get.

And now the picture was begging him, the same way it did all those years ago when he was covered in mud, only now he wasn't sick with impotence.

As he felt Camille clawing at her own garter belts underneath him he knew he'd been right. Her guilt and sorrow were raw and palpable and for a moment he thought, maybe this would do it. Maybe they could exorcise this together.

He reached down into the depths of him, that sinister lightless dark. Feeling around for that noble young man's hope, praying that nothing else came dislodged.

She gasped as the first thrust jarred the posts of the headboard. The second did the same.

She wrapped her legs around his torso as if to anchor him. He grabbed them underneath each knee and adjusted her crudely, gripping the supple warm flesh of her inner thigh with one hand, and her delicate calf in the other, still covered in nylon.

"Oh God, my heart," she wailed pitifully in her low, feminine timbre.

Stanley didn't hold back anymore, smearing the sight of her grief all over his soul, letting the gruesome flashbacks intervene, determined now to let them play, let them land on something good. When they landed on Carl's vacant countenance he had to squeeze his eyes tight.

"I shouldn't be here. I'm so sorry."

"How could you do it?" she whispered. He didn't know what she meant and was afraid to ask. But he knew that he wanted to take the blame.

"I don't know. I'm sorry."

He let go of her limbs and caught his breath, collapsing on top of her before rolling next to her on his back. His forehead beaded sweat.

"Get on top," he said.

She didn't want to. She wanted him to unleash all his mad fury on her but for some reason, he pulled back at the last second.

Reluctantly she mounted him, feeling the scruff of his un-shaved face on hers. His kiss was boyish, no longer tantalizing or hungry. She felt his hands on the zipper at her back.

When he'd gotten it all the way down she sat up, peeling down the front of her dress and unhooking her bra. She didn't get it all the way off when he reached up and cupped her face in his hand.

"You're the most beautiful woman."

The tears fell and she shut her eyes. She knew it wasn't true. She was old. Cynical.

He was simply haunted by his memories. The decade-old delusion was falling apart one moment at a time.

"How can I make you happy now, Camille?"

"You can't," she sobbed. "Just fuck me."

Her words made his blood simmer, his hands tighten their grip.

"Just fuck you?"

"Yes."

"Do you like getting fucked, Miss Winters?"

"Yes, I do."

"By me?"

"Yes."

His dirty interrogation continued as they slowly whipped each other into a deliciously tense frenzy. He couldn't maintain his erection as Stanley anymore, and luckily it wasn't who Camille wanted anyway. Not in the bedroom, at least.

Her makeup was smudged, her hair disheveled. He commanded her body, giving her tasks and enduring her torturous moans until orgasm broke the fever between them and they collapsed in a heap, still semi-clothed and fused together.

* * *

Camille emerged from the shower and retrieved her discarded dress from the empty bed. From the window, she could see

Stanley outside in the yard. She studied the time on the bedroom clock that suddenly seemed to be blaring. Almost two. Another bus would be coming soon.

She dressed, found her shoes downstairs in the kitchen, and headed out to where he was.

"You wasted your energy putting that dress back on," he smirked. He wrapped an arm around her waist. "There's a Cadillac back seat with your name on it," he cooed.

Camille shivered. "I didn't come here to make love."

"Why did you come?"

"To tell you goodbye," she confessed.

His stomach lurched but he was good at hiding these things. "Where are you going?"

"I don't know. Away."

"What will you do?" he asked.

"What I've been doing. What I've always done. Find the chaos and offer my services."

"You know I'll help you. Whatever you need."

"You're not going to try and stop me?" Camille wondered aloud.

"Is that what you want?"

She shook her head. "It's not fair. You seem... different. Lighter."

Stanley gave her a serene smile as he studied her face with a tilted head like a patron at the Met.

He reached out and touched the forbidden canvas of her cheeks, under her chin, like oil paints still undried after years on display. He caught a strand of her hair and curled it around his finger.

"Come with me down to the water," invited Stan.

Camille trailed behind him, rounding the back of the house to a screened-in porch overlooking the greenest grass she'd ever seen.

"The next bus is in half an hour," she reminded him.

"I know. Would you like a sarsparilla?"

"No thanks."

He popped the top of an old-fashioned bottle from an old-fashioned icebox off the porch. She followed him down the grassy hill where there was a long pier that seemed to hover over a quaint, smooth lake, bordered all around by wild weeds and tall flowers.

"This house looks like it's been passed down at least 15 times," she commented.

"It's been updated."

"I only meant that the size and location indicate it has been in the hands of Hargrove men for many years."

"Actually in the hands of Handley men for many years, and then one Handley woman. And *then* many Hargrove men."

"You must have at least 100 acres."

"143 to be exact."

"Strangely I feel claustrophobic somehow."

"The city will do that to you."

Stanley went to the edge of the deck, stripped down to his birthday suit, and fell backward into the lake. Camille laughed.

"Join me."

"You're crazy if you think I'm getting my hair wet."

"At least dip a toe in. The water's wonderful."

Camille took off her shoes and sat cross-legged at the edge of the pier.

He tread water as he looked at her perfect legs, still as dainty as they were in the picture she'd sent him. Her knee was propping up her arm, chin in hand. Her creamy smile melted him like sherbet in the sun.

She was here. Smiling at him. At the real him. Just like the picture he used to stare at in his bunker. Or kept under his helmet so that he would never be caught dead with it off.

He was so happy he could cry. But like everything else he kept it inside.

"This is the house isn't it?" Camille deduced.

"Hm?"

"The country house. That you saw yourself coming to? When you got home?"

"...I suppose."

"We've come full circle, Stanley Whitman."

"It seems we have."

"Who would've thought?"

He squinted through the sun's glare, his arms busy swimming. "Get in."

"No."

He splashed her with a huge gust of water. She gasped, soaked. Mouth agape.

"You can say goodbye tomorrow."

Camille wasn't amused. "I can still get on a bus soaking wet, Stanley."

"Let me put them in the wash. Hang them out in the sun."

"Where's your family?" she reminded him.

"Westchester."

"Does your wife know where you are?"

"She does."

"Does she know why?"

"I need a lot of space, she knows that."

"Not exactly what I meant."

"She thinks we've been having an affair since you started

working there."

Camille remembered his wife's rude first impression.

"And you didn't correct her?"

"No."

"Why?"

He shrugged, treading water. "Because I liked the thought. And it served her right for destroying your picture."

Camille closed her eyes, recalling his wife's icy demeanor. Christy's initial rapport slowly and sporadically deteriorating. She shook her head.

"Why don't you love her?"

"That's not what our marriage is."

"How can you torture her like that?"

"She doesn't care about me, Camille. I don't want to talk anymore about it. I don't want to talk about her out here."

"I don't like being lied to. Hidden."

"I know. And I'm sorry. I've never done anything else, I suppose. It feels rather normal to me."

She felt an odd comfort hearing him say that. He wasn't the person outside that anyone saw.

Being himself was a private thing. A freeing thing.

"Do you pretend we're married? When we're together?" she asked.

He smiled as he waded up to her dangling feet over the dock, caressing one of her calves. "Do you?"

"No. I don't pretend anything."

"Please stay."

Camille gnawed at her lip. "Perhaps I could stay for a night."

"I have so many things to tell you. So many things I want to know."

"Really?"

"Of course. Catch me up on everything. Do you still have your stewardess outfit?"

She laughed. "You're bad."

"Surely you have questions for me."

"You'll answer them?"

"Of course."

"All of them?" she raised her skeptical brow.

He shrugged. "I don't see why not, not anymore. I'll certainly do my best."

Chapter 19

Camille pinned her hair back as well as she could in a modest bun that'd begun to frizz. Her wet clothes dried on a clothesline outside.

Stanley retrieved a chest underneath the bed filled with vintage robes and dresses made of silk. She chose a peacock patterned smock and emerged from the guest room, hearing water boiling. Stanley smiled when he saw her.

"Whose dress am I wearing?"

"Trish's," he said, cutting a tomato. Camille took a seat at the kitchen table, watching.

"Is it true about her being a widow? That her husband died penniless?"

"That is true. He was a friend of friends."

"And that you can't have children?"

"Yes."

The kitchen smelled of fresh air from the screen door. Camille crossed her bare feet and lit a cigarette.

"Your daughter Katie. And the boy I met when you came into the dealership."

"They are my stepchildren."

Stanley cooked a simple dinner of pasta, oil, and fresh tomatoes with basil. They split a porterhouse from the butcher and he told stories in vivid detail about Carl.

He told her about valiantly hand-delivering ammo during the battle when the guns jammed. How they were starving and Carl stole army supplies on the 'Canal. Carl stealing some Commander's shoes that his wife had sent him. Leaving the picture because the wife had been too ugly.

She laughed until her stomach was sore as he described it all as if it'd just happened. Seeing Camille laugh like that made the last ten years seem merely like a bad dream.

Afterward, they cleared the table, standing over the sink while Camille washed and Stanley dried.

"Am I your first colored woman?" she asked, handing him a dish.

"An odd question."

"I don't think so."

"I've piqued your curiosity haven't I?" he smirked with a tone of regret.

"More like my paranoia. Your letters take on a whole new meaning now."

"How so?"

"Are you refusing to answer the question?"

"No," he chuckled, wiping the inside of a cup with his dish-towel. Finally, he confessed.

"You were. At the time."

"I see," Camille raised her eyebrows with a smile, masking her mysterious pain and jealousy for the time being. "So colored women are your true preference."

He took a wet plate from her grasp. "You're my preference."

225

Camille didn't press further. She rummaged around for silverware at the bottom of the basin.

"Your regimen knew you were writing a black woman?"

"Of course," he grinned. "You were famous."

"What did they think of that?"

"Of me writing you? They found it amusing that I got you to write me back," he smiled, drying his plate and reminiscing. "They all thought I was some yokel from Alabama with no family. They didn't even know I'd written you until you replied, see."

"Why Alabama?"

"The home of my maternal grandmother. Mobile was a place I thought I knew well enough to fake it."

"So what happened when a new letter arrived? Addressed to you?"

He looked up at the kitchen window, the sun still holding out in the dark blue sky.

"A few objected to it. I proclaimed my innocence to them. I simply didn't want you to think your letter went nowhere when it had impacted us so. I didn't have to explain myself at all and they knew that."

"Us?"

Stan took his time answering. His demeanor seemed to turn sullen as he recalled it. "Everyone read their letters aloud. Some of us were lonely and received nothing. And those of us who had loved ones wanted us all to feel loved."

"I see. So this wasn't just an impulse of Carl's."

"Not at all."

She smiled, having the gaps filled in of that admittedly fond time in her life.

"Some of them objected. On behalf of Carl's memory, but I suspect there was some... moral objection to it. Perhaps jealousy."

"They never confronted you about it?"

Stan shook his head, still taking time with his answers. As if wanting to make sure they were as close to the truth as he could get them before he uttered them.

"I was still their lieutenant. But they made their annoyance known. I reminded them that you probably assumed I was black and they seemed comforted by that."

She thought he was done answering. She didn't have another question. But he continued.

"We'd taken back the beach not long after that and no one gave a flying shit about morals. We would've stabbed each other for a can of tuna. We had to find new reasons to live. The one who objected most was the one who eventually drew me the picture. Everyone else made a bet to see how long I could keep you writing back."

"Stanley Whitman," she huffed with faux outrage, her hands on her hips.

He dried his hands and then put them over her own. "I don't think you understand how long it'd been since any of us had seen a woman. And besides, it wasn't purely chauvinist. You meant something to us all at that point. Yours were our favorite letters. After we came back from shore leave in Australia, everyone was much less ornery. Women took their rightful place in the world again. For a while, at least."

"And just what place is that?" she raised her eyebrow again.

He smirked. "I'm afraid you wouldn't like my answer." He guided her to the middle of the floor between the sink and the kitchen table. He grabbed her around her waist and held her right hand in his. She laughed.

"We can't dance without music."

"What do you suggest?"

"You don't have a record player?"

"No," he grinned as he began to sway her.

"Criminal," she smiled, wondering how long he'd been waiting to do that. "You knew you'd never be able to take me out dancing when you wrote that."

"And yet here we are," he grinned, his eyes threatening to glisten. "The world can't stop a man from having dreams. Or making a woman feel good."

There was only the sound of their feet shuffling across the floor as a song unconsciously played in Camille's head. She lay her head on his shoulder as Stan kept talking.

"It was the regimen's idea to send you back Carl's belongings."

"And so the trap was set," she shook her head a little, remembering. After their first correspondence, it was clear that there was nothing more to say to each other otherwise. "I was courting all of you, it seems."

"As I said, after shore leave, they more or less lost interest. Or were receiving letters of their own. I was sent to New Britain to a completely new company. Once you expressly told me that you were uncomfortable knowing others were seeing the letters they did indeed remain private."

There was silence as Camille broke away from him and resumed her task at the sink. Stanley watched her.

"I shouldn't have told you."

"Stop that. I'm glad you did."

He stood behind her and grabbed her around the middle.

"You think less of me. Or you think... you didn't mean as much to me as you thought."

"I understand. You were all young and lonely and expecting

to die."

"The way that you say it, I know that you don't understand. I can't explain it any better than I have."

"I was a young girl, I had no concept of what you were going through. Every one of my days was flippant compared to yours. You somehow survived hell and made sure the letters survived as well. The last thing I can accuse you of is capriciousness."

He grazed her neck with his lips. She had no idea that the frock she was wearing was laced with the aroma of his life's memories. He let them mingle and trick his mind into thinking she was part of them.

"Do you still have mine? The ones I sent?" he asked

"Of course."

He wanted to clear the table they'd just set, hike up his wife's dress and make love to her right there.

"Did you show them to anyone?"

Camille spun around, facing him. "What do you think?"

He smiled, still pressed against her. "No one knew about me?"

"No, they knew. My mother encouraged me to keep writing to you. We all thought you were colored, of course."

"Of course."

"Mother was being practical. She loved the idea of having a soldier in the family and I could tell she hated losing Carl, perhaps more than me," Camille scoffed. She reached for Stan's belt buckle. He licked his lips.

"I suppose it was... wrong. To hope that we... I mean if everything would've happened the way I hoped— you coming home from the war completely whole and somehow colored— how would we have explained it to everyone without being simply awful people?"

He hooked an arm around her, nuzzling her collarbone, his

other hand trailing up her dress to feel her fleshy thighs.

"We would've told them the truth. That we struck up a friendship through letters. Though loss. That you saved my life."

Camille tossed her head to accommodate his kiss, spreading across her neck, her jawline. His hand inched up to her under-garments and gripped the flesh there.

"Did you fantasize about me?"

"As well as I could," she admitted.

"What was I doing to you?" he whispered.

"Something close to this," she breathed.

He situated her in front of the sink behind them, unbuckled his trousers, and slinked both hands up her skirts until they found her knees, parting them.

"You can be as loud as you want here," he said, not bothering to draw the curtains as he pulled her frock down in front of the kitchen window.

* * *

The next morning he came downstairs to see Camille in the living room, in his wife's untied robe. Her hair was puffy and pulled back, the texture of wavy cotton thread.

The old, frail letters from his war bag untied from its ribbon and stacked in front of her. One was in her hands and she was smiling.

She looked up to see his shy grin in the doorway. He was wearing a plaid long sleeve shirt and suspenders. Like a regular lumberjack.

She scanned him up and down, with an amused look that he ignored.

"Hungry?" he asked.

"Sure."

"I may have to make a trip to the market."

"Let's go together. I'll make you dinner."

He smiled. He didn't know what he'd done to make Camille Winters completely carefree about their association, but he enjoyed the moment a little longer before he had to break the news.

"Might be better to give me a list. The Hargroves are pretty prominent around here."

"Of course," she said sheepishly.

"I'd love to parade you around, Camille, I think you know that."

"Maybe I could go? The list is pretty specific. In fact, I'm not confident I would find all that I needed out here."

Stan gave her a quizzical look. "Can you... drive?"

"I'm an old pro," she lied. "I may need a little refresher."

"There will be plenty of time for driving lessons when I get back."

"Fine. I'll make you a list. But if the right things aren't there I'll need suitable replacements."

After nearly an hour of Stan being gone, the sky became overcast and the clouds doused the afternoon in every bit of its moisture. She went out to the screened-in porch at the back of the guest room, completely naked and waiting for Stanley's return.

She saw the car a ways off, smoothly disappearing and reappearing across the hilly two-way street. She doubted he could spot her from the side of the house.

Instead of stopping in the gravelly driveway, he drove across the field until he was directly in front of the porch. He got out with a sack and a bottle of milk, letting the rain pelt him as he approached the door. Camille got up to open it and he pushed her back inside.

"What on Earth are you doing?"

Camille looked panicked. "You could see me from the road?"

"Of course."

She was mortified.

"No one else drove by, I swear it," she promised, regretful.

Stanley burst out laughing. He grabbed her hand and led her outside in the rain while she squealed for him to stop. He got in the back seat and shut the door behind him.

She could've easily retreated back to the porch. But for some reason, she kept trying the door that he'd hastily locked.

Finally, he relented with a chuckle. She scrambled her naked self inside the car and walloped him a few good times before he finally got hold of her wrists.

He was incredibly strong, she mused, her own breathless giggles making her stomach tighten. She couldn't believe how effortlessly she'd changed just being with him for a day. As if he were an entirely different man.

Easily he hoisted her atop his lap. She spread her legs until her knees were touching the plush leather of the back seat. They tasted the cold raindrops on each other's skin.

The rain picked up in unison with their passion as he breathlessly unbuckled his trousers. His heart beat so fast he thought he might be dying.

"I've never behaved like this in my life."

"Neither have I."

"I want you so much."

"So, take me."

He gripped her backside, inching himself deeper in, as deep as

232

he could get. She arched her back suddenly, as if it still wasn't enough.

One hand left her bottom to steady her. He held on to her frame, just under her breasts, watching them tumble with every thrust. His jaw went slack as the humidity of their breath heated the backseat.

He wished he could go back in time and add this to his fantasies. He wished he still had the stamina and the enthusiasm of that young lieutenant that'd memorized her after just one look. Maybe he wouldn't have lasted more than a second but he would've touched heaven in that second.

There was a symphony of bodies grazing across leather and metal as they wrestled with abandon in his Cadillac. He grabbed her like a baby in his arms, inching up to the edge of the spacious backseat. Camille leaned back gripping the shoulder of both front seats as his clamped on her narrow waist. At that, she began filling the steamy backseat with her cries of pleasure.

He never thought it could be like this. Stan didn't deserve the passion he'd unleashed in Camille but he was going to lap up every spilled drop. He only wished he had a third hand to rub her to ecstasy. He had to settle for his filthy mouth.

"Come on my cock, my dear. You can do it," he encouraged her. He wasn't going to be able to finish without it. Camille quieted, as if concentrating.

"Right there?" he asked. She faintly nodded. He summoned the filthiest desires he could muster, looking into each other's eyes, coaching her to orgasm.

Finally, he felt the spasm. The crease in her brow deepened.

"Yes, that's it Camille, baby," he moaned, spilling over the edge without warning. Climax gripped him powerfully as Camille seized in his hands and her eyes floated up into her head.

He could barely hang on to her slick flesh as his thrusts continue to die down. He gathered Camille's rubbery body back into his arms, fading in and out of slumber until the sun returned to its perch and all was quiet, besides the sound of chirping robins.

* * *

Stan came back with everything but the coconut milk and curry powder, as she feared. Not the best for making potato curry but she would make it work. She also made roti, cook-up rice, and a modest attempt at her mother's chicken patties.

"I thought you said you didn't cook?" he chewed as he smiled, wiping his fingers on a napkin.

"I don't. Aside from the chicken patties, no one in my family would consider this cooking."

He looked at all the plates sprawled out in front of him until his eyes landed down at his bowl. "So this is cook-up rice."

"As well as I could get it without coconut milk," Camille sighed with a hand under her chin. "I wish this wasn't your first introduction to it."

"You can make it for me again," he said, eyeing her across the table, contentment in his face. She mirrored him but there was a ribbon of sadness in it.

"I wish you could come to my house," lamented Camille. "I wish you could meet my mother. She could make it for you."

"I wish that too."

"Do you?"

"Of course," he said, taking another heaping bite on his fork.

"We could've made it work, Stanley. We could've told the whole world to go to hell. You were a war hero. A lieutenant to a colored regiment."

He finished his bite and took a sip of water before replying, "A captain."

"A captain!"

"Who stole another dead colored soldier's fiancee," he elaborated with a burp.

Camille sat back in her chair. "...Well, we wouldn't tell them that part."

"Someone would. Carl's family. Yours, perhaps."

"I'm not saying it wouldn't have been hard."

He reached for a fresh chicken patty, biting it in the center. "The first years were dark. Incredibly dark."

"I would've loved you through it."

He shook his head, finishing his bite.

"The only way you would've gotten through it is if you didn't love me at all. Otherwise, you would've ended up hating me more than you loved me."

"You can't presume to know that."

"I would cheat on you. Even though I loved you. I would be too ashamed to make love to you, let alone wreck you."

Camille felt the sting of his hypothetical actions as he spoke.

"You would be childless. You would have no one to comfort you. You wouldn't work, because you wouldn't need to. I wouldn't allow it besides. Your job would be to lunch. Every day, until you died."

She had to snicker after a pitiful silence. He'd obviously thought it out more than she had.

She smiled. He smiled back.

He was purposely leaving out the good times they were sure to have had, she knew. He didn't need any reasons to not go on living his life.

It was surreal to think about, first as her boss and second as her long-time love. Surreal to even be sitting at this table.

Tomorrow she would have to leave. They both would.

"I like it here," she said. "I like you here."

"Say you'll come back."

"When?"

"Whenever you want. Write to me."

Write to him. She suddenly realized she had nowhere to go back to.

She couldn't go back to work. She didn't want to. She just wanted to be with Stanley, being Stanley.

Though she feared leaving Mr. Hargrove stranded. Herself by extension.

"People will talk. Without Christy or me, it'll be a disaster."

"I'll pay you to train someone. A consultant's fee. You can come and go as you please."

Camille thought for a moment. "As long as you're gone when I'm there. It's too bizarre otherwise."

He raised the cup to his lips.

"We should stage a falling out," he said before his sip. Camille chuckled.

"Now I know why it took you so long to finally acknowledge me when I started working there."

"I didn't expect it to take so long to work up the nerve to talk to you."

"Awww," she chuckled sympathetically. She reached over and grabbed his chin, kissing him on the cheek as he continued to eat.

* * *

That night, sleep was hard to come by. Their time together was nearing its end and each of them knew it. The real world was calling and it made her sick. They laid down after dinner and didn't move, though neither of them were tired.

"Carl," she whispered in the blue of near darkness, the sun almost setting and threatening to shroud the house in complete blackness.

"You saw him die?"

"I did not," he confessed in a strained voice after a moment.

It was generous of him, she understood, to be talking of it at all. It was better for him to bury it. But he was resurrecting it for her.

"But I know the manner of how he died."

"What happened?"

There was no answer. His energy assured her that there wouldn't be.

"Was it... swift?" she ventured.

It was so quiet she thought he was asleep.

"No," his reply finally came.

Camille stiffened. She didn't know if she wanted to push any further. She closed her eyes, starting to drift.

"It's my fault that he died," he muttered, rousing her.

"How could it possibly be?"

"One day I will tell you. But not now."

"Okay," she said. The old house creaked and she didn't flinch.

She didn't worry that someone was in the big house anymore while they were upstairs. No one could see in a pitch dark like this. She'd hear them in the grass first anyway.

The quiet wasn't scary at all, she realized. It was peaceful.

A shame. She was just getting used to the country, she lamented. And now she had to leave.

"Stanley?"

"Yes," he answered sleepily.

"Thank you. For writing me back."

He huffed, feeling a lump in his throat as gratitude mixed with guilt.

"No. Thank you, Camille."

20

Present Day, Fall 1957

October 19, 1957

Stan,

I got the most awful feeling that you may be trying to reach me and that you have been unable to. Since turning in my resignation I decided to take some time off and go with my mother to Guyana to visit family before going straight back to work. I figured since I have a lifetime of long labor in my future, now was the time to see more of the world, more of my heritage. The last time I was here I was too young to remember it. It's quite lush and beautiful. Paradise really, and I wish you were here. Perhaps one day we could go and I could show you around. Provided your professional and personal obligations could stand your absence.

I will be here for at least a month, but it may be longer. Please write to the enclosed address. The mail is not as prompt as it is in the states but we are no strangers to that. Just know that I am not intentionally avoiding you. I think about our weekend at the country house often. And the subsequent rendezvous in the city, though it was terrifying, I admit. I suppose I'm not the type to be thrilled by danger. And though you assured me that there could be no chance of a scandal, I hate to be put in the position to mistrust you.

I assume that you still love me and await your response. Don't do anything fun until I return.

Camille

October 27, 1957

Camille,

Thank you for writing! And you were right, I did reach out to you only once. But my internal dread that you had abandoned me was constant. I am glad to hear that you have not and that you have taken a holiday to your family home. Unfortunately, my dear, I cannot do jungles or anything of the sort. And I tolerate beaches but only if there is no greenery or seclusion. Otherwise, I would certainly come and visit you. It's embarrassing to say out loud but nonetheless true. It sometimes fills me with pain that my children have missed out on these kinds of outings because their father is sick and refuses to make the same memories that he got to make. Forgive me if it is too rude to bring them up, please tell me because I don't know.

I do like the thought of us meeting someplace remote and without context, in some other part of the world where we would not be bothered. I would love to see Australia again, as it holds no bitterness for me. But it is very long to travel. I may have some business in Italy, but based on your previous sentiments I don't think it would be wise to take advantage. Though if you were to stay within an hour's reach of me, I think it could be feasible. I would love to contribute to your seeing more of the world, not to mention seeing it through your eyes. I am now restless to do it and my mind is made up. Let's make plans whenever you return.

Stanley

March 23, 1958

Stan,

I am pleased to inform you that I am officially enrolled as a student at the Barnard College School of Business.

The thought of going back into the workforce seemed so redundant. I quickly realized there was no way to move on from Hargrove and Chase as my position had pretty well reached its zenith. No one was willing to give me the same level of responsibility or workload, and honestly, the places that responded were dismal in practically every way. I felt very self-conscious turning down offers, but I simply did not feel peaceful taking any jobs.

But I am thrilled at the thought of my schooling, so thank you for suggesting it. I can already feel the change in my confidence. I will never have to be caught unprepared in a room full of white men again. In the meantime, I have returned to temporary office work. I'm concocting a plan to come groveling back to my old boss at Hargrove and Chase once I graduate, and persuade him to let me come back under the steam of the previous promotion he offered me before the dustup.

But it is only a faint inclination at this point. Tell me

what you think I should do.
  Camille

March 30, 1958

Camille,
I assume you're referring to the old boss who took advantage of you in his office that one snowy Christmas. Personally, I think he sounds like a creep of the highest order, and you should stay far away from him. But I also know how keenly you spoke of working there, and how irreplaceable you made yourself. And I know how much you take pity on him. I say you meet him privately, make him his favorite drink, and aggressively demand more money. Make him beg. Wear those pants.

Did you ever think we would be writing again after all these years? Did you ever conceive of our meeting in real life? It's all utterly surreal.

Nothing feels as good as getting a letter from you. Let's do this as long as we are able.
  Stan

October 18, 1958

Stan,
You'll be happy to know that much of what I am learning as a first-year student I have already learned from years at working for my previous employer. Or maybe you're not happy. Or interested, I have no idea. Have you given any thought to the holidays? I can't say that I'm looking forward to mine as much. My grandmother is ill and I am frightened to death. She is old and death is expected. I simply don't want to face it. Let's plan another weekend at the country house before

*your schedule becomes inflexible. I haven't yet decided
if we should go before or after. Or during. Do I need
strength going in or relief going out? Or something to get
me through? I will let your availability decide.*

  Camille

                                    October 21, 1958

  Camille,

*If you will allow me to persuade you that New York
isn't so small we can do all three. Otherwise, I can meet
you the weekend after Halloween. If not, the weekend
before Thanksgiving. After that, I will be unavailable
until the New Year. Not that you would be happy— or
interested— but things at my current place of business
are hectic, to put things lightly. So I cannot stray too far
away. We lost an important client and the office is in a
scramble. I would tell you about the headaches that have
been brought all the way to me, but I know you would be
horrified. There is a girl that we inherited from the merger
who is quite competent and bright but inexperienced. Not
terribly aware of her surroundings. It makes me value all
the more the one employee who moved on...*

                                      May 6, 1959

  Lovely Camille,

*I am pitying myself greatly tonight because you are not
here, and I am not there, wherever you are. The last time
we were together I must've watched you for at least an
hour because you are so unnaturally beautiful. I have
deconstructed my life in every conceivable way for over
fifteen years concerning you and I am weary of defeat.*

It's as though our lives are destined to run parallel, just out of reach, never to intersect. In my intellectual haze, I hold on to a thread of gratitude for what we have, though it threatens to wear off. Which should not take away from our time together, which is immense and vital. But if we could possibly be together, without suffering intense scrutiny from everyone else on the outside, I would do away with it in a heartbeat...

May 10, 1959

Stanley,

I must admit that I have a low opinion of married life, due in large part to your very own actions. If this miracle were to take place, which would likely cost us everything, how long before you resent me enough to lie directly to my face? How long before I would be staring down my own replacement, which I honestly deserve? We would quarrel, we would hurt each other because time would be endless and we would run headlong into it, rather than stave off all unpleasantness not related to the moment, as we are free to do now...

May 14, 1959

Camille,

Honestly, my darling, I would rather fight with you than do what we are doing. I tell myself that I am doing whatever I want. That I can get in the car and solve my problem in an instant but it is all sad consolation for the reality that I am a slave, both to my passions and my obligations. I pity myself enough to die. Leaving your side is unbearable and yet seeing you is no longer a thrill.

It is natural and not enough to take the edge off of our separation...

May 16, 1959

Stanley,

You've just left me and now I find this letter waiting for me, which is as startling in its rawness as it is fitting. It is important to me that you must never lose that feeling and I will not negotiate it. If we were together, you would. You were the one to convince me of this, or don't you remember? You were right. My intense, beautiful lover! I know how it feels to wish to burn it all down if you can't have what you want, but you can't. Even if you were unburdened, our marriage would still be a tall order and you know that. We are not young anymore, I don't know where this dissatisfied angst has come from so let me remind you: you are a realist. And so am I.

I was considering prolonging my junior year and your whining has convinced me. I think it would make you feel better if I made myself available to the industry again.

Camille

January 7, 1960

My love,

You asked me once about Carl's death. Let me tell you of it now.

We were on patrol on the 'Canal. Deep in enemy territory. At that time, we were mostly unacquainted with the fighting style of the Japanese. We were warned, but we were ignorant. On that particular night, we were surrounded and took turns keeping watch. Four hours each. I let the men coordinate their watch, but I shouldn't have because Carl had chosen the dead of night for his. Everyone knew he was prone to terrible nightmares. Towards the end, he didn't like to sleep because of it. Naturally, he put it off until the last second. He let out such a howl, apparently. Someone came and woke me. He wouldn't stop. And so, I gave the order. In that moment, he was a giant flare. He was our brother, but at that moment, we all feared for our lives more. I said, 'do whatever you have to do to shut him up.' I was angry. At him, at everyone, for letting him put off his watch so late into the night.

The chap that carried it out was never the same. He was killed a few days later.

The whole thing made us despair in a way that never happened again. And it got ten times worse. But your letter came. And we bawled our eyes out. And I knew I had to live long enough to say thank you. If it weren't for you we would've died. We wouldn't have taken the beach. We would've given it to them.

Stan

January 9, 1960

Stanley,

I don't know what compelled you to tell me that but I'm glad that you did. If no one else said it, then let me be the one to. You did the right thing. I know you don't believe there was such a thing as that over there, but you did.

It's hard to imagine him like that. So tortured that he put off sleep. But I have to, don't I? So young. I'm glad that you were there. And I'm happy to have been your good luck charm.

I have more theories about you and me now, but I will spare you them. I can think of nothing else to say except to request that you stop punishing yourself. Do it for me...

21

1963

The only downside to airplane travel was the airplane travel itself. It was actually worse than the subway. And scarier.

The noise, the luggage, the turbulence. Camille would rather take a beautiful and relaxing journey that took a little more time than a five-minute trip through hell.

Just because it was faster, in her opinion, didn't mean it was better. As soon as white people invented anything they were shoving it down everyone's throat. The train was clearly well enough... *so leave it alone.*

So it was a good thing Mr. Hargrove was working on the PanAm account instead of Camille, who was still years away from handling billing like that. On this particular day, she would gladly trade places with Mr. Hargrove and work on PanAm than meet with Hanes and tell them what she had to tell them.

"Sometimes I truly do hate you for making me do this, Mr. Hargrove," Camille dramatically pouted as she pulled down her airplane window shade.

"Every account man has been here at least once."

"Do you have any medals of honor I could borrow?"

"You have something better than a medal of honor. Two of them actually."

"If I thought showing the client my tits would help I would gladly do it."

After leaving Hargrove, Bower, Chase, and McCain as head of personnel, Camille went back to school for business and marketing. She was hired back during her junior year and by 1963 had been working accounts longer than she had been a secretary. She was the first black female junior account man.

"How am I going to explain to the client that they're being outsold by a product that's cheaper to make and more expensive to advertise?"

"I think you just did."

"Tell the truth?? Mr. Hargrove, you can't be serious."

"The truth with a solution."

"Which is?"

"You'll think of something."

Even after three years of a modest roster of niche clients, even after the 60's vehemently promised to be nothing like the 50's, and yes, even though California was practically Amish country compared to New York when it came to this industry, Camille still dreaded the potential loss of a client. It was the only time she wished away her femaleness and her blackness. Perhaps then she could conceptualize faulting someone else for her failures.

"I can't convince them to appeal to blacks. You know we already tried that."

"Desperate times, Camille."

"Desperate *times*," Camille scoffed at the hapless joke. "I hope Playtex grounds them into a forgotten dust."

"I'm going to pretend you didn't say that," said Mr. Daniels, technically her boss seated across from her.

"I need a female copywriter. I can't keep trotting out this mindless uninspired drivel."

"Careful, Camille. That 'mindless drivel' gets eaten up every time," Mr. McCain defended, sitting across from Mr. Hargrove.

"Because you convince them to. Chet's the only one who has any hope of getting into the female mind."

"Ironic."

Mr. Hargrove used to sit across from Camille to avoid scandal, but that only proved worse. Especially on planes. He practically lost all ability to speak. There was no safe place to look. Not her eyes or her lips, certainly not her curve-hugging dresses. Or her legs.

It was much more natural to breathe in her perfume and feel her shifting body movements next to him. Of course, he simply had to bite the bullet when his presence was required in a client meeting.

Most of the time he made sure to pick the most remote, random chair from her vicinity. Camille adhered to this covert manner without a single conversation about it between them.

Once, she did sit across from him and he nearly had a heart attack. She never looked up at him, but she didn't have to. She may as well have crawled across the table and grabbed him by the tie.

"Max and Josh are worthless. We need an edge."

"You know where I stand, Miss Winters," Mr. Hargrove interjected. The moment you find this female George Lois, impress McCain and keep him from sleeping with her, you have my permission to hire her."

"Why me?"

"Why can't I sleep with her?" whined Mr. McCain.

"We should look in-house," Mr. Daniels suggested.

"How progressive of you, Phil," complimented Mr. Hargrove.

"We found this one, didn't we?" Mr. Daniels nodded towards Camille. "Bet you one of those hens knows how to find the benefit."

"How much?"

"Mr. McCain..." Camille chastised him.

"How long until you finally cave and call me Drew, Ms. Winters?"

"I suppose once I've been made partner, Mr. McCain."

"Not even once we've finally slept together, Camille?"

"Not even then, Mr. McCain," she retorted.

"You'll never get me to believe you're this dour in bed, Camille. You're not fooling anyone. I know you could leave me speech-less."

"Only because you can't talk with your mouth full, Mr. Mc-Cain," she deadpanned. All the men snickered.

It'd taken a few years but Mr. Daniels was finally used to Camille's unexpectedly garish humor. It, unfortunately, confirmed his assumption that all negroes were vulgar in some form.

It broke his heart at first to see that Camille was no different, though she was more discreet about it. Likely her white side. But he saw that it never failed to tickle the boss and his wonderboy lapdog.

After spending some time with her, Mr. Daniels theorized that she merely adopted the humor to fit in. She never acted that way around him, because he was respectable. Only Andy was so keen to bring it out of her.

And what could she do with such a powerful male figure corrupting her work environment? Cry harassment? A woman had no such option, let alone a colored woman.

She had no choice but to dish it out herself, or else suffer the piranhas, who smelled the blood of virtue for miles. A struggle he knew all too well.

In that sense, being colored seemed to do her a service. It certainly kept McCain in check, but barely.

Mr. Hargrove, of course, was always above board. Though he'd prefer it if she stayed at a different hotel on these trips, to absolve them all from scandal entirely. Re-hiring Camille had brought out the sordid imagination in the unlikeliest of people and it was finally starting to die down.

Phil dreaded the thought of a scandal ever arising from Camille's close relationship with the boss, which seemed to be purely that of mentor/mentee. One rumor from a disgruntled client could undo it.

But Camille was a rising star. The clients were likely afraid to disparage her for fear of the growing malcontent of the negro population. How Ken could always predict the future he'd never know.

"Two martinis?" the stewardess interjected, cart in tow. Mr. McCain and Mr. Daniels took their drinks without a word.

"Two ginger ales?"

"Thank you," Camille smiled.

Camille adored California.

Even on the flights on the *way* to California, no one batted an eye at her light-colored skin. The Mexicans never left her alone. She even started to learn a little Spanish. After so many trips she deduced it was the sunshine. Personal space was practically non-existent in California and absolutely no one was curious about her beyond why she was never in a swimsuit.

When they arrived at the hotel, the boys stayed put and Camille got out, preferring to get her first meeting over with as soon as possible. She freshened up in her room and came back downstairs to meet her clients by the pool.

She had luck pairing her professional demeanor with a relaxing or surprising location. So much of this job relied on sleight of hand.

The boys spent the day schmoozing with Pan Am until they'd successfully earned themselves a 90 day trial period. They got back to the hotel and celebrated in the poolside bar, baking to death in their suits and jackets.

Mr. Hargrove nursed a club soda. Mr. McCain slapped Mr. Daniels on the back, drink in hand.

"Why the long face, Phil?"

"I don't know why any of us are celebrating."

"It's a foot in the door, Daniels. That's all I need."

"If Bower and Mrs. Chase had come they would've given us the account," Phil insisted. "They were insulted."

"If they were insulted we wouldn't have gotten the trial," McCain replied.

"If we'd flown over all the senior partners we would've looked like amateurs," Mr. Hargrove backed him up.

"Amateur virgins. Who are desperate," McCain drilled him. He blew out a plume of smoke. "You pack a swimsuit, Phil?"

"Of course not."

"What about you, Hargrove?"

Ken just smirked in response. Just then a blonde in a bikini walked between the three of them.

"Hello there," Phil tipped his hat. She responded with a smile. Mr. McCain grabbed her hand.

"Don't talk to him, he's married," he smirked. The girl giggled.

"Mr. Ken Hargrove?" the bartender cut in, looking at the three of them. Ken nodded in acknowledgment.

The bartender set down a rotary phone in the corner of the bar, handing him the receiver. Mr. Hargrove watched the flirtatious exchange between the young woman and Mr. McCain from a corner barstool.

"This is Ken."

"Come up here."

Ken grinned as he took a drag of his cigarette.

"Miss Winters."

"Come up here. Right now."

Ken kept it cool with his professional, in-charge demeanor. "The meeting went well, I take it. I had all the faith in the world. I knew you could do it."

"Room 221. I only have an hour."

He used the cigarette puff to cover his stifled smile. "Then what's the use?"

"The use is I want you."

He ground the remains into an ashtray, blowing out the smoke.

"I have a 3:00. Minute Maid."

"Keep them waiting. They love it."

He looked at his watch. "What shall I tell them?"

"The truth. You had to congratulate your junior account man."

"I do love your reckless side, Miss Winters. But I can't."

"They'll never let you handle Coca-Cola. No matter how well we do, you know that right?"

"Now you're just being cruel."

"I didn't say we had to use the whole hour."

Mr. Hargrove smiled. "You've gotten very good at persuasion, Miss Winters."

"Just one drink. A toast. To me."

He looked up to see that Phil was already watching him.

"No drinks and come to me. It's easier," he said, refusing to break eye contact. Phil looked away.

"Suit yourself, Mr. Hargrove."

Mr. Hargrove hung up the phone and excused himself.

"Gentleman."

"Ken," Mr. Daniels eyed him.

"I'll leave you to it."

"Do I have permission to knock on your door at 2 am?" McCain asked as he walked past.

"Knock to your heart's content, Mr. McCain," Ken sent behind his back.

* * *

"I have to confess something," Camille announced with a puff of her cigarette.

She sat up in bed with her hair in a disheveled bouffant, holding the sheet across her bosom.

Mr. Hargrove laid flat on his back, his eyes closed and both hands behind his head.

"What is it?"

"I've lured you here under false pretenses," she said, dabbing the ash into her ashtray behind her.

"Oh?"

She took a breath before diving in feet first.

"Drew wanted me to talk to you."

He opened one eye.

"About?"

He was already upset, she knew. She may as well go all the way.

"Toyota."

Mr. Hargrove was instantly up and out of bed, retrieving his dress shirt from the floor.

"He knows I have your ear, that's all," she assured him.

"Horse shit. He's gone too far. Both of you."

It wasn't the time for tough love, but she pressed forward. Acting contrite would only make her seem guilty of something.

"I know I only just graduated Mr. Hargrove, but turning down a $7 million dollar account seems unwise."

He turned to look at her.

"Camille, don't make me hate you."

"Why would you hate me?"

"Because you're mixing this, with business," he gestured, standing to replace his boxers. "You're mixing it all. Miss Winters. And it's vile and distasteful."

"It's *vile?*"

"I wouldn't expect you to understand."

"Because I didn't lose anyone?"

"Because you didn't strangle a Jap with your bare hands."

Camille recoiled. She watched him make quick work of his pants and belt buckle.

"Drew did," she said. "He did worse than you."

"Oh yeah?" he huffed, buttoning his shirt with annoyance. "What else did he tell you?"

"Nothing. He doesn't need to, I can tell. We all can tell. And he's fine with it."

"Of course he is, the man doesn't have a conscience."

"That's not fair," she admonished him. He disappeared into the bathroom, raising his voice over the running sink.

"If he didn't tell you, then let me illuminate things for you. He cut gold teeth out of a decaying human skull, Miss Winters."

"Did he tell you that in confidence?"

"He did. And I'm telling you now because it's pertinent."

Camille waited until the faucet was turned off to respond. "Well. I've done nothing of the sort and I agree with him."

"Good, so go sleep with him then."

"Stan..."

Just then, Mr. Hargrove walked out of the bathroom with an awestruck look. Camille didn't flinch as he came toward the bed.

"Are you crazy? Is this arrangement making you crazy? Miss Winters?"

"No, sir," she lazily blinked.

"We are on business."

Camille shrugged. "They see what they want. Mr. Hargrove."

Mr. Hargrove continued to be dumbfounded. "I can't believe what I'm hearing. We are done having this conversation. Now and forever."

"Then I suggest, Mr. Hargrove, that you consider what the future will look like without you. Because there are young men going into advertising right now who only know what peace looks like. And they don't give a shit how many mass graves are in Japan as long as they make a superior product."

Mr. Hargrove retreated back into the bathroom, stunned into relative silence.

"If this is what school had done to you, then I'm sorry I sent you."

"Well, I'm not. Because if I couldn't foresee what your loyalty will do to your company, to my job, I would never forgive you for making me watch what will happen next."

"Because that's all you care about."

"The whole point of me being here was so that I would never have to rely on a man. Or did you forget?"

"Honestly, I did. When I promised that I didn't imagine you would ever entertain the thought of sleeping with the enemy for money."

Camille ignored his emotional tirade. "If you want to honor the memory of fallen colored Marines cut down in the prime of their lives there are better ways."

"Perhaps. But I can't think of a better way to spit in their faces."

"You gonna stop doing business with German companies too? Ford?" she tried to reason with him. "Japan is coming. They're exciting, they're cutting edge, they love design, and they want the best agencies on Madison Avenue to spare no expense bringing their products to America."

"They can ride the divine wind straight to hell for all I care."

Camille heard the sound of an electric shaver as she sat in silence. It abruptly stopped with a click and she watched from her bed as he searched for his tie.

"The rest of us didn't inherit this company, Mr. Hargrove."

"None of you raised it to the profile that it enjoys today," he snapped in calm yet short tone. She was running out of good will.

"Those people have a code, Camille. And it is unyielding. Do you really think twenty years is long enough for an ancient culture to forget about Hiroshima? Hm? We have a code too, and believe it or not, the dollar is not involved in it. I didn't get this far by selling out. There are plenty of products that need selling."

"So there are multi-million dollar companies flashing their tits at us every day now?"

"Japan is low-hanging fruit," he insisted. He snatched the tie from the floor and lassoed it around his neck, adjusting the slack.

"B&L will get this business if we don't. They'll surpass us. It won't be hard. Tobacco's not long for this world. That's 60% of our billings."

"Your concern is noted but we're done talking about this. If I am to keep doing this pointless occupation let me at least be able to do something with integrity."

"Fine. But it isn't pointless," Camille said, watching him. His steely eyes, his distinguished mannerisms. His hair turning salt and pepper.

With a few magic loops, the satiny rope became a necktie. "Don't bother reporting back to Drew, I'll handle it."

"He'll be angrier with me that way."

"I hope so," he said, straightening his knot without a mirror. "Put an end to these clandestine meetings between you and McCain at once."

"It was hardly a meeting," she said, reaching for a cigarette.

She was angry with him. The 60's had done wonders for Camille's sex appeal, he thought.

Soon he wouldn't be able to hold on to her much longer, he knew. Personally or professionally. His lungs filled with dread and he gasped for the air of the present moment.

"I suppose you're happy with how late you've made me," he cooed, ambling around to her side of the bed.

Camille blushed. "I didn't expect to take so long."

"It was your guilty conscience," he reprimanded her, kissing her atop her forehead.

"Why don't you like California?" she asked.

"When did I say I didn't like California?"

"You don't have to. Look how grumpy you are. Is it the sunshine?"

He grabbed an apple from the bowl on the small table and draped his suit jacket over his arm.

"Be gone when I get back," he said, not bothering with the automatic closing door.

Camille sighed. "Of course, Mr. Hargrove."

22

Present Day, Summer 1982

July 15, 1982

Ms. Winters,

I must have started this letter a thousand times. It has taken seven years for me to drum up the courage to finally send it. I don't know why. I suppose I've just been afraid. Ever since I started researching you and your amazing career, my anxiety to reach out to you personally has increased more and more. You seem very busy, on purpose. And I guess I fear your rejection. But lately, I've been made aware of the shortness of time. So here I go.

My name is Celeste Davies. You may not know this, but I am your daughter. My mother and father recently gave me the information regarding the agency where I was adopted through. And that's how I was able to find your name. On my file, it said that you were open to meeting once I turned 18, which I suppose is what made my parents wait until then to tell me so that I wouldn't be bogged down with the choice. I'm not mad at them, and I

261

understand why they made that decision. They are great parents and they have always made me feel included with me and my other siblings.

At any rate, I would love to have an opportunity to meet with you. If you ever find yourself in New York, please look me up. Until then, we could talk on the phone. Or you could write me back, of course, if letters will suffice. And please take all the time you need to reply. I look forward to hearing back from you.

Respectfully,

Celeste Davies

July 20, 1982

My dear Celeste:

This year must be the year of surprises. I've only just finished coming to grips with the funniest thing, just before I received your letter. It turns out my father, your grandfather, incidentally, was white.

I wish you could see my face and hear my laughter as I write that. How do you not know that your own father is actually white?

I don't know what young people are accustomed to these days. After the 60's, I'm sure that we all look like pre-historic dinosaur fossils who are ignorant. But when I was born, the world was different. The world moved slower. Nothing happened. It may as well have been the days of the acropolis. Abolishing slavery had been the most exciting that had ever happened and would ever happen in America. Many people longed for progress, but they did it through optimism and a god-like devotion to civility and diplomacy, and reputation forging. A few *of them abandoned society altogether in the pursuit of being utterly genuine and therefore despised. They did not simply whine to the government for it. But I digress.*

It didn't matter what you looked like. If a man said he was black then that's what he was. My mother, your grandmother, had relatives of all shades, and her mother, my grandmother, your great-grandmother, was very dark. My siblings were quite the light-skinned lottery. My youngest sister is the lightest of us all. So we had no real reason to suspect that my father was anything but a variation on that theme.

He said he was a product of rape. Disowned. Abused by two people who were not his parents. He didn't like to speak of his childhood which he said was rough and filled with poverty and hard times. And so we never pressed it. He missed country life, that's true. Spoke of it often but never took us to visit his home.

We suspected that his real family was dead or so disconnected that he couldn't possibly know them. He left for the north as soon as he could and landed in New York. He saw my mother as soon as he arrived.

We perceived him a gentle man of quiet strength. Humble. Not given to bragging or going on about himself. I was the only one in the family who seemed to inherit this disposition.

But guess what, Celeste? It turned out that it was only because he was in constant danger of incriminating himself. Because he had also married a second woman, a white one who lived in Rochester. Can you imagine? She also had four children with him. He has ten total, that we know of.

I can't tell you the scandal it has been for all of us. But as far as we know he loved both women and was certainly loved by them. My mother wanted for nothing. He was stable in all ways and consistently there when we arose and home for dinner.

He left a debacle upon his passing, one that my brother found unforgivable. I seem to be the only one who understands and forgives him. No surprise there.

I nearly left out the most entertaining part! At least for me. You may be wondering how my father managed to competently head two households. Well, it turns out that he was lying about his childhood. It may have indeed been miserable, but poor he was not.

He grew up wealthy on a prosperous tobacco plantation. He did some work in New York to support himself, but none that required his own labor. He made us believe that he worked from dusk 'til dawn.

For his other family, they believed its opposite. What he provided for us more than corroborated the story. My mother never worked a day in her life and we clashed on that subject constantly. I always said I got my work ethic from my father but I suppose I will have to correct that. Or maybe not!

He was quite the clever confidence man. He even went through the charade of being equally destitute during the depression when he was anything but. What a brilliant, prudent thing he was.

As far as we knew it, he never went back home but, in fact, he did. His white family visited quite often. Naturally, he couldn't bring his colored family down to visit. His alternate family at that. Though all parties admit that ours was the first conceived.

Once the dust settled, there was hardly anything to bicker about. They wanted the plantation— we didn't! In fact, most of the things they wanted we didn't even know existed and could not miss them.

At the end of it, I could find little fault with him. When I think of his stamina it honestly makes me laugh. I cannot believe I knew a man like that. Intimately. And I did know him intimately, despite the appearance of this.

From what I could make of it, he simply had more love to give than was necessary for most men. The way that he left us nothing in the way of an explanation proves it, though the last will and testament was thorough. There were no apologies in it. An eternal shrug of the highest order.

I will say that I am torn about this oral history of oppression that I have inherited about my life that is now only 50% factual, and even the purity of that is likely dubious.

I would say that the story is similar to yours of your father's, but that's the thing about it. I realize that your father was simply a coward. I gave him many benefits of the doubt but he was deserving of none. But then again, neither am I, since I too am a coward. In fact, your father knows nothing of you. How can I judge him?

Well, I don't. But I thought not judging him meant not processing the consequences of all his actions. And I simply can't do that anymore because now they are laid bare. Time has judged him. Other men have.

My father became a black man to marry my mother. And for another, he remained white. He had the self-

respect to subvert this wretched inferior world of ours and simply disregard it as a dishrag. Your father was intelligent, but not clever. Not as clever as mine.

I shouldn't speak of your father in the past tense, as he is still alive as far as I know. But we haven't talked in some time.

I have run out my typewriter ribbon speaking to you of complete strangers. Imagine how much more I have to say about myself. And how you came about. Do come and see me. I am eager, now that you have reached the proper age to really talk. You may not know but I did keep abreast on your upbringing. I asked your parents not to disclose this and I hope that they did honor me at least in that.

I don't know if they told you that I am black, however. Which I suppose means you are too. But hell's bells what does it all mean at this point?

Let's begin our correspondence officially in person. Whenever I come to New York I am very busy and it is all so gloomy. I'd much rather you come here, to L.A. Send me your available days and I will clear my schedule and fly you out.

Please come to me when you are free. So that we can talk all day.

Camille

Chapter 23

Celeste reached for the iron doorknocker on the large front door of the Encino house. She stepped back onto the bottom step, lacking the confidence to even stand on the top step with intention.

Her heart raced amid the silence that followed until finally, she heard the faint footsteps coming closer and closer, the inner workings of the lock disengaging.

She told herself to keep composed, chanting the command to her soul as the moment drew closer and finally met with reality. The door opened and removed the last of the distance between them.

She was met with the bright face of a solitary and successful woman, her high cheekbones bared as prominently as her smiling teeth.

She wore a silky-looking poncho in a colorful pattern. Her arms seemed to be outstretched but Celeste didn't want to presume.

Camille let go of the door and her arms remained wide. Instead of meeting Celeste on the porch outside, Camille waited for her to come inside.

Celeste tried to remain composed, but when she saw it was no longer necessary she rushed to her mother's joyous arms, weeping in front of the hillside house's open front door.

They sat down in a plush sunken living room area. A panel of windows replaced the walls on one side, with the woods surrounding them as if they were inside a potted plant.

Planked cedar covered the walls and enormously high ceilings, making the house seem like a mid-century modern extension of nature. There were finger sandwiches and tea on the coffee table but Celeste was too nervous to partake.

Celeste sat cross-legged on the floor, looking across at Camille from her comfortable couch. She small-talked her birth mother as long as she could stand.

It was all thrilling to know, on some level. Every small detail filled in a poorly constructed picture she'd relied on her parents to fill in. Finally, she got down to brass tax.

"So I did some digging on your family tree. Your maternal grandmother was named Sinclair?"

"That's right."

Celeste knew that Camille's family was Guyanese but that she herself had been born in America. By some miracle, Camille had managed to find the only lily-white family on an island full of multi-colored Guyanese. Her adoptive parents were Arnold and Elizabeth Davies, German ex-pats who couldn't conceive after years of trying.

"Before I came to the States I contacted them. They don't live that far from my parents."

"No kidding. I can't imagine any of my aunts and uncles are still alive."

"No, but the nieces are still alive. They found me some

pictures," Celeste offered. She flipped open her knapsack and retrieved the photos.

"Oh my goodness!" Camille exclaimed when Celeste laid out the bundle of pictures across the table.

Celeste's great-grandmother, the oldest sister, left the rest of her family behind after the first world war.

"They told me she killed her husband."

"That's what they say."

"So you didn't get the whole story either?"

"Well, my mother just said they went to disembark at Ellis Island and he never got off with them. And Ganny just told her not to worry about him."

"What did your mother say about it."

"Nothing. She says she was relieved. Which tells me all I need to know about the man."

Camille's father had apparently been white, according to her letter. Celeste assumed that was where she got her light skin.

To her German family, she seemed to stick out, but to the rest of the world, she was white. Finding out her mother was Afro-American raised more questions than it answered.

There had to be more than just a white grandfather. Celeste's father must be white also.

"Your accent is absolutely thrilling."

"Thank you," Celeste laughed with a shy flip of her auburn hair behind her ear, not sure how to respond.

"Reminds me of Ganny."

"There's a bit of German in it too."

"Is that what that is?" Camille smiled.

"Yes, everyone makes fun of us on the island."

Camille shook her head in wonder. "I wish Ganny could've seen you."

269

"Is *my* grandmother still living?"

"She is. In New York, we'll have to visit."

"Does she know about me?" asked Celeste.

"She helped deliver you."

Celeste wanted to cry about that but instead she braced herself, feeling her window approaching.

"I was hoping you had some information about my father."

"What would you like to know?"

"Do you have any pictures of him?"

Camille scoffed in amusement, her brow furrowed. Searching her memory. She sat back in wonder.

"You know, I don't think I have a single picture of that man."

"Certainly none of you together, I imagine."

"I'm sure there's a few floating around. Not that anyone would know we were someone's parents in them, of course."

"Of course," Celeste smiled, instinctively piecing together the small crumbs into a narrative. "I gather he was white."

"He was. Is."

"Is it possible for me to meet him?"

"Well he doesn't know about you, but... yes, I believe that can be arranged."

"Is he... close?"

"He's back in New York."

Her heart skipped a beat. He was in the same city as her.

"I suppose I could meet him without telling him."

"Don't be silly."

"Will he be... angry?"

Camille thought for a moment, her brow knit in uncertainty.

"I don't know," she whimsically answered, stroking the back of her hair. "If he is, it won't be at you. He'll certainly be surprised."

The prospect seemed to make her a bit nervous but there was a trust and familiarity in Camille's tone about her father, and that was enough to make Celeste's heart skip again.

Celeste deduced that perhaps they were estranged but there were mostly fond memories. And it seemed as though she hadn't been the product of a one-night stand. Or maybe she had, but they were still very close. Perhaps they'd worked together.

She wanted to know everything about him. And Camille's face was worth about a thousand words.

"How did the two of you meet?"

Camille let out an abrupt cackle, shaking her head.

"Would you care to hear a very long story?"

Celeste nodded emphatically with a smile.

* * *

Mr. Hargrove sat in his office, taking another drag of his cigarette as he scrolled down his list of leads. He held it between his fingers and rubbed his forehead back and forth with a thumb. Days like this made him want to take a vacation.

After so many years he marveled at his ability to still get nervous about this part of the job. Jumping feet first into that cold pool. Still hearing his father's voice in his head. *You want a vacation? I can make that happen.*

"Mr. Hargrove?" the receptionist buzzed over the office intercom.

"Yes, Linda."

"There's a Celeste Davies here to see you."

Celeste Davies. He was certain Nabisco wasn't sending over a woman.

"Did she say what it was regarding?"

"She said she can only discuss it with you."

Wha??

"Uh...okay. I'll be right out." Mr. Hargrove cleared his throat, putting his Winston out in the ashtray.

He made his way out into the lobby. A beautiful dark-haired woman with piercing blue eyes sat waiting. Perhaps the most beautiful young woman he'd ever seen. She looked up at him with uncertainty.

"Mr. Hargrove?"

"Yes. Miss... Davies, is it?"

"I'm sorry, I... This is Hargrove and Associates, correct?"

"Name's on the door."

"Did you know a Camille Winters that used to work here?"

Mr. Hargrove searched his memory of the few employees that'd made themselves memorable in the time he'd been there. He'd certainly remember a name like that.

"I'm afraid it doesn't ring a bell."

"This was a long time ago and frankly... you look a bit too young to remember."

"Ms. Winters, of course," he nodded with recollection. "You're looking for my father, then."

"Oh goodness, I hadn't even considered. I'm so sorry for the confusion."

"Don't mention it. I'm Daniel, by the way. The old man doesn't get in for another hour."

"I can come back," Celeste offered with a smiling anxiety.

"Nonsense. Linda, can you get Miss Davies some coffee?"

Linda made a gesture with her outstretched hands on the desk, as if there were cuffs on them. "You want me to leave the switchboard, Mr. Hargrove?"

Linda was the kind of old lady that was so old everyone 60

and under was still a child. And he had a suspicion that she was probably the same way in her youth.

"Never mind. Miss Davies, come with me."

"It's Celeste, please."

They went past the front lobby doors and into the belly of the offices. All the while, Mr. Hargrove gave her the tour until they reached the conference room. Daniel was so determined to impress the young woman that he realized he forgot to inquire what the ultimate purpose of her visit was.

"So are you... a student?"

"I am. At Pace."

"Good school. Looking to get into advertising?"

"Um, actually no, I'm a journalism major."

"I see. Is this for a project?"

"You could say that."

Celeste followed Mr. Hargrove into a large room with a conference table and a phone placed in front of each chair. He gestured for her to have a seat, then took the seat next to hers. He had work to do, but didn't feel right leaving her alone.

"We've had some inquiry in the past about Ms. Winters. Magazines, a documentary or two. Most before I started but we still get a few here and there," he boasted.

"Is that right?"

"Oh, yeah. The last person that remembered her, besides my father, retired a few years ago. She made quite an impact, it seems."

"I didn't realize she was so... infamous."

"Well, she was the first black woman to make partner at a major advertising firm. That movie, Glenda Garrison, was based on her career, right?"

"Explains why she hates it."

Daniel's eyebrows raised in intrigue. "You've met Ms. Winters?"

"I have. We're close relatives."

"How nice."

Just then, the boss was making his way through the office.

"Danny boy."

"In here, Pop."

A tall elderly figure appeared in the hallway dressed in a fine suit. His eyes went to his son but immediately averted to Celeste's with a happy but confused anticipation.

"Dad, this is Miss Davies."

"Celeste."

"She's a journalism student from Pace. Here to do a profile on Camille Winters."

The senior Mr. Hargrove wiped the dust from his heart, hearing the name outside of his own mind for the first time in ages. He felt a strange pride, seeing the name live on in the mouth of a young person.

"Well, I'll be," he grinned.

"It's more of a personal research project," Celeste clarified. "She's my mother."

Before he could understand why, his dusted-off heart was falling. For an impossibly long time. Down a chasm, until it shattered.

"Oh. Well, of course," he nodded, seemingly lost in thought. "Well. That makes you an honored guest," he recovered with a grin. "Please. Stay as long as you like."

"Actually... I was hoping I could talk to you."

He did not want to talk to her.

"Uh, okay. Daniel, when's our first meeting?"

"Soon, but I can handle it," Daniel replied. Even though he

knew what the reply would be.

"Well, if it's all the same to you I'd rather not miss it." Then he gestured to Celeste with his hand.

"Miss Davies? Come with me, I think we can make this quick."

"I can come back," Celeste again offered. The last thing she wanted was to make things quick.

"Of course you can. As much as you like, but I'll try to answer what I can today," Mr. Hargrove insisted. "You came all this way, I can't bear to disappoint you."

She followed the elder Mr. Hargrove down the hall to a very large office. He was tall and deceptively spry. Following behind him he just seemed like a young man in stage makeup.

He fought the spinning of the room on the way to his office chair. He gestured for her to take the seat across from him.

"If I thought I was imposing I wouldn't have come," she offered again as she sat down.

"Nonsense," he said, taking the large leather chair behind the desk. "Your accent is delightful, were you born in Guyana?"

"I was," she smiled, her eyes wide with unexpected excitement. "My mother told you about Guyana?"

Mr. Hargrove fought off a web of confusion in his mind, one that had started weaving since the young woman's revelation. He chose his questions carefully. "Is she there now?"

"No, no. She's in L.A."

"I thought so. She loves L.A."

"She does," she answered, nodding. Mr. Hargrove tilted his head with a charming nod of his own that made her laugh.

What the hell is going on right now, he wondered. Why would Camille have an adult child, and why was she coming to him? Time had flown by but not by that much, he was sure of it.

Ten years of virtual silence. Had she adopted a kid? Was

motherhood the only thing left she'd yet to accomplish?

"So what brings you to your mother's old stomping grounds?"

"When I told her that I see this place on my way to work she suggested I stop by."

"Does she still have that brownstone in Brooklyn?"

"She does," she answered astonished.

Celeste realized she'd hit the jackpot with Mr. Hargrove. Camille told her he'd been her mentor, but she had no idea she was sitting with a possible treasure trove of even more memories, presumably of her father as well.

"I was the one that told her not to sell," he bragged.

"I'm glad you did, because I'll be using it in the near future."

"If you ever need to work on that resume, you're welcome here, of course, as well. In whatever capacity you like."

"That's unusually generous, Mr. Hargrove," Celeste blushed.

"Is it?" he smiled. She even talked like her.

"Absolutely. The way she mentioned your... falling out, I wasn't sure that you'd even be willing to see me."

"She... called it a 'falling out'?"

"Yes. One that could not, unfortunately, be reconciled."

Mr. Hargrove leaned forward in his chair, a smile fighting its way to the surface of him. "What else did she say?"

"She told me you were upset that she left the company."

"Of course she would put it so lightly as to make me seem unreasonable," he scoffed in amusement. He sat in silence for a bit.

"But the truth is... well. What doesn't seem silly in hindsight?" he asked rhetorically, glancing at his glass-paneled view of the New York skyline.

"Before this was Hargrove and Associates, it was Hargrove, Bower, Chase, and McCain. But then Mr. McCain started his own agency and poached Ms. Winters from me."

A picture of the two of them in his office flashed before him. Breaking the news together. He was certain they were sleeping together. He'd been so enraged that he still can't remember what he even said in response.

"It was a profound betrayal. Alleviated when I finally was able to sabotage their company well enough that they were forced to sell."

Camille assured him over and over that their relationship was purely professional. Even through her and Mr. Hargrove's continued affair that was not long for the world after that. She hadn't realized how working together had meant just as much to him as sleeping together, and he'd hurt her for not realizing.

Without those eight hours, he couldn't account for her movements. Couldn't see how she was growing, developing. He thought it was all because of McCain's dick. He'd interrogate her the moment her dress hit the floor. And never let up until he was covered in her sweat and saying unforgivable things that left her unable to stay long afterward. It didn't help that she seemed to like that ugly side of him.

"It was a dark time. I nearly brought the company under for the first time in 80 years. I was consumed by the endeavor but thankfully, B&L was able to outbid me when I tried to absorb them. Saved me from myself."

"I see. Well, since your time is limited, I was hoping you could fill in a very specific gap for me."

"I'll do what I can."

"My mother tells me that you were acquainted with my father who lives not that far from here. I was hoping... you could tell me something about him. Perhaps steer me in his direction, if you had any contact information."

Mr. Hargrove did not feel well at all. How on Earth would he know this child's father? Who lived not far from here?

"How old did you say you were?" he asked.

"I didn't. 25."

"25," he repeated, his mind hazy with math and memories.

"Anyway, apparently he was a war veteran. Lived just outside New York in Pennsylvania. Stanley Whitman?"

Silence. Silence he passed off as thinking.

He looked down at his desk, baffled. Was this some kind of code? A lie he was supposed to corroborate?

Why? Why would she do this, of all the bizarre things?

Finally, enough time passed and he shook his head. "Can't say that name rings a bell honestly."

"No?" Celeste confirmed, her voice thick with disappointment.

"No," he faintly repeated with a clearing of his throat. "I'm so sorry. I wish I could help."

Celeste nodded her head, doing a poor job of masking her confusion and emotion as she extended her hand for him to shake. Mr. Hargrove stood and she did the same as their hands met.

"I wish I could be of service, I really do. Perhaps I'll give your mother a ring and see if she can... jog my memory, somehow."

"I think she'd like that," Celeste smiled.

His legs somehow propelled him down the hall behind her as his mouth continued on autopilot, again offering the entire office for her disposal. In fact, the more irritated he got, the more generous his hospitality became until they were finally in the front lobby.

Mr. Hargrove finally sent Celeste Davies off before turning back around, finding his son, and canceling his next meeting on the way back to his office.

24

Chapter 24

"Brooke, get me Camille Winters on the line."

His secretary Brooke looked through her Rolodex with a wrinkled finger until she found the contact. Winters, Camille, VP of marketing at Bausch and Liebowitz.

She dialed the number and learned Camille was out of the office. When Brooke told the woman on the phone she was calling on behalf of Kenneth Hargrove, she was given a home number.

"Brooke," an impatient voice warbled over her intercom. Not unusual.

"She's out of the office, I'm trying her at home," she replied, knowing what he was after.

"Very good."

A second later his phone was ringing, the boxy black phone showing a blinking light indicating Camille on the line. Reality adjusted with ease as he picked up the phone to talk to the woman he loved for the first time in a decade.

"Miss Winters?"

"Mr. Hargrove," Camille replied, equally as adjusted.

He was hunched over his desk, suddenly worried the whole place might be bugged.

"Is this some kind of a joke?"

"I don't know what you mean."

"Some woman calling herself your daughter was just here. Telling fanciful tales that presumably came from you."

"I figured," Camille answered back in a sassy tone. "Lord knows you wouldn't pick up the phone for any other reason."

"Who was it?" he accused before he could properly restrain himself. "McCain? I can't think of anyone else you would've spread your legs for."

The silence reminded him of why their correspondence had dried up.

"She's yours, Stan."

He rolled his misty eyes, shaking his head. It was the kind of thought that simply wasn't his to entertain. "That's impossible."

"It isn't. Must've been some quack doctor who told you you couldn't produce a child. Because you did. Almost immediately."

He sat back in his chair after a bit of silence, wary to even make sense of the notion.

He had a child? A daughter?

"I don't understand," he whispered. "When were you even pregnant?"

"What happened 25 and a half years ago, Stan?" she quizzed him.

"I know what happened 25 years ago."

"Apparently, you don't."

His heart fluttered dangerously hard. As if it were birthing the faith to believe this was real.

"I told you the truth," he said. "At the farmhouse. I told you everything."

"I *found out* the truth, you mean."

"Semantics."

"Right after I figured out that I was pregnant."

Mr. Hargrove was stunned.

Camille was telling him that she actually knew that she was pregnant when she arrived at the farmhouse. He thought about their hysterical lovemaking. For fuck's sake, that woman could keep her mouth shut.

Hold on. Twenty-five and *a half* years ago would've been...

The Christmas party? No. Absolutely no way.

The apartment?

"Impossible," Mr. Hargrove replied.

"If I hadn't found the letters that day I would've had to turn in my resignation anyway. At some point."

It could've only been one of those two. Jesus. The moment was actually pinpointed.

"Camille..."

"I went home to Guyana. She was born in December and I left her there. And it was damned hard," she declared before she started to sob.

Mr. Hargrove just sat on the phone listening. Dazed.

The apartment.

He saw his own feet following Camille in her robe down the hallway. The naturally lit room with the brick wall view. Pink curlers.

The memories flashed so fresh that he was nearly back there, as if this version of his life were a dream.

She was going to live there. And likely sleep in the same room she was conceived in.

"I don't believe this," he sighed.

"Have her tested. I've no reason to lie."

"No, Camille, sweetheart it's not that it's just... I appreciate what you must've went through and all. It certainly makes all this... whatever this is between us make a lot more sense. But still. I can't believe you would keep something like this from me."

"I'm telling you now. It's past time you knew, obviously," Camille said, pulling herself together on the other line. "I was just... waiting for her. Took her seven more years after she turned 18 to even have the courage to find me."

Mr. Hargrove swiveled in his chair a bit as the news continued to have its way with his emotions. Joy seeped out through his pores mournfully. His face and neck grew hot and he covered his trembling mouth with his hand.

"I have a baby?" he marveled.

"You do," Camille smiled.

But the joy was short-lived. The baby was grown up. The love was spent and worthless. The moments were gone.

"How could you keep her from me?" he accused her again in a bitter whisper.

"Oh, what were you gonna do!" she spat forcefully. "What was I gonna do? Tell me!"

Kenneth just held the phone, weeping to his bones as Camille finally spoke the unspoken. He never knew what it was, but he just knew that it was heavy and that he'd been afraid to unravel it.

Every move she had made was a sacrifice, even those made out of self-preservation. Even the parts that had been personal weren't personal in the way he'd imagined.

Camille stayed silent on the other line, holding the receiver to her ear, listening. She shed a tear with him.

She'd told him over and over she could never be a mother. But he never even entertained the thought of being a father. Flesh and blood of his very own.

Was this the first time she'd ever known him to cry, she wondered? For the first time in years, she wished she was there for him.

"She's so beautiful," he finally managed to say.

Camille laughed in agreement. "She's got your eyes."

"When can I see you?" he sniffed.

"You know I hate New York," teased Camille.

"I can't imagine why. It's your home."

"Encino's home, now."

"I'll come to you."

"No need. I'm headed to LaGuardia after my meeting."

His heartbeat doubled. He seemed more imprisoned by her now than ever.

"Why?"

"Why do you think?" she chuckled. "I'm having trouble leaving her. She's going to show me around Pace. I told her it might be a good idea to stop by the office and I was right. As usual."

"So she truly doesn't know that Stanley is me?"

"No. I thought you'd get a kick out of doing a second big reveal."

He loved her. "Surely, she must suspect."

"We'll see about that. Have dinner with us."

Dinner seemed like it was a month away. He smiled. "Where?"

"I'm staying at the Four Seasons, we can eat there."

"You've come a long way, haven't you, Miss Winters?"

"Thank you for noticing," Camille couldn't help but flirt. "Just so you know," she added, "if you're expecting me to put out, I

284

hate to disappoint you."

He let out an amused chuckle, letting her know he was pleased with her presumption.

"I wouldn't dream of it, Miss Winters. I just want to catch up."

Camille grinned, writing spirals on a pad of paper to keep her hands busy while they spoke.

"Well, that's good. Because I'm no spring chicken," she broke the news. "Neither are you, I suppose."

"I'm sorry," he replied.

"About what? Getting old?"

"No. About everything else."

"I know that, Stan," she answered quietly, tenderly. "Me too."

* * *

Camille marveled at how far air travel had come as she landed smoothly on the runway in LaGuardia.

She hadn't been in New York since she was made VP of marketing and didn't have to go anywhere she didn't want to. That made nearly seven years. She hadn't spoken to Stan in ten.

It wasn't because she hated him, or because they were fighting. They simply drifted apart. Though their last conversation had indeed been an argument. The nail in a pre-existing coffin.

As colleagues with an extensive web of mutuals they could never be completely out of each other's lives. The occasional congratulations passed on by a business associate. They always managed to just miss each other and leave messages with secretaries.

But he was never going to be with her. And he was never going to let Hargrove and Associates evolve.

She had to jump ship, the place was a time bomb. He would be sore about it, but he would understand eventually, she told herself.

Turned out she was wrong, on both counts. Which was unusual for her. Hargrove and Associates soldiered on and while Mr. Hargrove may have forgiven her, he never seemed to understand.

But she didn't regret her decision. She went on to be the first black everything. With several award-winning campaigns under her belt within her first years at B&L.

Turns out she *could* write copy. And she even had a hand in a few jingles. Accomplishments she would've never conceived of under her previous employer, riddled with baggage.

There was at least one thing Mr. Hargrove had been wrong about. The success did help. It helped a lot.

As she made her way towards the airport gate, she unconsciously began preening her short haircut. She didn't know if Stan would be there waiting at the airport, and she didn't know if she was hoping he would be.

But she understood what he meant, all those years ago. The second she landed in New York she could feel him. Much like the last time she'd seen him, when they were both accepting an award and she'd flown in, mostly to see him. It was the last time they had ever made love.

She hadn't thought about her vagina in a while and was scared to have to. She couldn't help it.

Even though he'd turned 62 this year, she was still expecting the same tall drink of water from her dreams to come walking up to her. With those same crystal blue eyes full of unspoken demands as if she wasn't a 57-year-old woman.

As she emerged from the United Airlines gate in the timeless LaGuardia terminal, she didn't know what to expect. And she didn't have to walk too far past the gate exit to find out.

There he was, still tall and trim as ever. With a full head of hair, more salt now than pepper. It'd started to thin the last time she saw him. Either it had stopped and never went further, or he'd joined the Rogaine club.

His light eyes were fixed on her already and there were no demands in them at all, only love. Bright, warm, and unguarded.

As she smiled, she realized that she had never seen him give her a look like that before.

And as he enveloped her right there in the airport, untold dozens of travelers whizzing by on either side of them, she realized why.

It was because it was the first time they had ever been together like this. Not at night, or on the weekend, or after everyone had gone, but in public.

It wasn't 1955. It wasn't even 1965.

It was 1982 and they were two old people. Two old people, but nothing more. Random. Insignificant. Finally free.

They held on to each other there for a long time, hugging and touching each other's faces, melting into the transitive scenery of loved ones reuniting or coming home, or starting their official stint as tourists.

They held hands on the way to the baggage claim. They canoodled in the cab all the way to the hotel.

They reminisced in the lounge, not planning to be there until dinner time, but it couldn't be helped.

Celeste met them both at the hotel after her lecture. She spotted them hand in hand and they spotted her, walking towards them.

Mr. Hargrove stood, watching her wordlessly as she ran toward him, nearly collapsing.

"I knew it," she finally said, once her sobs had subsided, her father's long arms enveloping her.

"I didn't. Not even a little," Mr. Hargrove admitted.

"I'm sorry," Camille dabbed her eye as she looked on.

"No, no. You did the right thing, my love. You've always done the right thing," he said, offering her a space in the hug. She took it.

Celeste had inadvertently reunited her real parents. And as much as she loved her adopted parents, she had to admit that her real parents were super hot. She was obsessed with them.

"We're waiting for one more. Daniel will be joining us soon."

"Oh my goodness, of course," Celeste smiled through her tears.

"She'll be meeting her grandmother tomorrow," Camille divulged.

"May I also come?" Mr. Hargrove asked.

Camille bit the inside of her cheek as she grinned, not wanting to hog any of Celeste's moments. But she couldn't help the wave of emotion that clearly wasn't through with her.

"Of course," she politely agreed, trying not to lose it when Celeste squeezed her hand.

"Wait until she finds out that Stan's still alive," Celeste added with gleeful mischief, clearly caught up on all the drama. The elderly couple laughed.

25

2002 (Epilogue)

Kenneth Hargrove drove his 1995 Cadillac from the country club back to his home in Encino after playing a round of golf with his friend Newhouse and a couple of others.

Insipid company, but at his age the bar was low. He just needed an excuse to go outside and get out of Camille's hair.

After their reunion, Ken and Camille were back to being pen pals. When the letters took too long to arrive, they spoke on the phone. Mr. Hargrove sent flowers and the two continued to live on opposite coasts for three years.

He slowly sauntered through the door in his khakis and sneakers and put his car keys in the bowl next to the front door. He walked through the house, past the kitchen where the patio door was half-open.

"Camille?"

"Back here, Ken," he heard faintly.

Camille had a crisis of identity once they reunited. She was still calling him Stan in letters and on the phone and it felt strange suddenly. But calling him anything else felt even more so.

She decided to make the transition official when he flew her in to watch him receive a lifetime achievement award for excellence in advertising. The event was bittersweet and emotional, as much of the old clan was in attendance, each from their respective positions at other firms.

She was a star in her own right and so he asked her to give a speech, which she graciously accepted. Of all the glowing things he'd heard, nothing touched his heart as much as hearing her call him Ken for the first time.

He felt so small in that moment. The only thing he had achieved was getting a woman like Camille to glance at him.

She still called him Stan, every so often. When she was feeling particularly dutiful and affectionate.

"I'm back," he needlessly announced to Camille, knelt down in the dirt of the backyard. She was dressed in one of her many colorful ponchos and large dangling triangular earrings to match. Her graying hair was pulled back in a low, meticulous bun.

"I see that. How was the green?"

"Oh, fine."

"I got a late start on the garden, do you need anything?"

"No, dear."

"There's food on the stove."

"Mm," Ken grunted.

Ken was still married to his wife Trish when his daughter Celeste entered his life all those years ago.

He'd told her the truth without any hesitation, explaining that he would always take care of her, but he was committed to spending as much time with his family now as he still could. She died three years after that, suddenly and horribly of pancreatic cancer.

Camille was hit hard with looming guilt. She remembered the bitterness she aired aloud to him before they parted ways, as well as the private prayers she prayed for her to simply wither and die. She didn't anticipate the delay on them.

Yet she refused to flinch as Ken called her every day from New York with an update on her worsening condition, as well as vestiges of Trish's lifelong resentment over their affair. Telling him that she was glad she had succeeded in keeping them apart for so long and how she hoped she stayed sick for a hundred years.

He even found out that she'd gotten her tubes tied so that they wouldn't conceive, in case he'd been wrong about his condition. Her bitter deathbed was brutal, especially for her children.

After the funeral, Camille convinced him to retire, as well as to quit smoking for good. He was convinced it wouldn't buy him any time. "I didn't take up the habit for my health," he told her. She offered to do it with him.

He told her if she married him, he would quit smoking. She told him if he moved to California, she would say yes when he asked.

Now he was 82. Still lanky and tall with his remaining nest of hair now frothy and white. He was a bit slower, however. They both were.

Camille was 77. So far they had fifteen years of marriage under their belt.

Ken heard the cordless phone hanging on the wall warbling and on the third ring picked up.

"Hello?"

"Dad."

"Danny boy, how are you? Is everything okay?"

"Fine, Dad. I was looking for Camille. I'm supposed to be

helping her with the computer."

"I can't imagine why, she doesn't need any help with that thing," Ken asserted, walking over to Camille's sleek-looking laptop taking up half the space of the kitchen table. She had an office, but she argued that if she wanted to be tied to an office chair she would've bought a desktop.

"For the money I spent, it should do everything you need it to do without a tutorial," he said, perched in front of the machine.

"Are you getting her, Dad?"

"She just went out to the garden, son."

"Well, we sort of have a surprise for her. For both of you, actually."

Ken's adopted son Daniel had fallen in love with the young Celeste, technically his sister. Though they'd kept it secret until they realized it wasn't simply the result of some strange unresolved childhood issue that wouldn't go away.

Obviously, it was a bit taboo. On several levels. Not only were they quasi-related, she was 17 years younger. "Unsettling," was Ken's reaction.

Camille just hated that her daughter was living a bit of the life she had known. She was determined to accept them.

They waited to announce their relationship so as to not steal the shine of their parents and then quickly got engaged. They'd been married a year less than Camille and Ken and celebrated their anniversaries together.

Ken's daughter Katie didn't care, as she hated them all for how her mother died, though it couldn't really be blamed on anyone. She was convinced that the revelation of Camille's daughter had hastened the entire process.

Once her brother fell in love with Celeste, Katie felt she was truly alone in the world.

"A surprise, eh? Are you sure I can't handle this for you?"

"Positive, Dad. Besides, Camille has a Mac."

"So that's it? I should shrivel up and die? You're old too, you know."

"I know. Which is why I know I don't have time to walk you through this."

"We were one of the first agencies to install that MacIntosh," Ken bragged.

"I remember, it was as big as my living room."

"No, you're thinking of the IBM. I'm talking about the personal computers."

"Ah, yes. And you ditched them for Windows."

"'Ditched' them. They were dead in the water."

"Until they weren't."

"They're exactly the same only now they're different colors. Who knew people would fall all over themselves over *that*?"

"It's a little different now than in '87. You have to use a mouse."

"What's the psychology behind making them more and more tiny, you think?"

"What psychology, Dad? The technology gets better, things become more compact."

"Compact," Ken scoffed. "At this rate, they'll make it so tiny all you have to do is swallow it."

"Is that Daniel?" Camille asked, wiping her hands on a dishtowel on her way through the kitchen.

"It is. Did you have an appointment?"

"He's supposed to be emailing me something."

"Okay, she's here," Ken announced, getting up from the table so that she could sit. He still held the cordless phone.

"Tell her it's a zip file."

"He says you have to 'download' it," Ken said, proud of his lingo.

"Got it."

"Put me on speaker, Dad."

"Daniel?" Camille projected. "How are my babies?"

"Grounded."

"Oh no," she lilted in horror. "Well, surely they'll be Scott-free by this weekend."

"Funny, they said the same thing."

Just like their father, Celeste and Daniel had a boy and a girl, aged 12 and 14. Ken and Camille were planning to move to Europe, but the grandchildren put a stop to it.

"Grandma's is a grounding-free zone," Camille commanded, watching Daniel's files finish loading.

"I know, I know," he playfully whined.

When the first window opened, Camille's jaw dropped. "Oh my goodness!"

"What's that?" Ken dipped down to see.

"She really did it."

"Did what?"

"Celeste put all of our letters in the scanner and scanned them. Don't you remember when we gave her all our letters?"

"No," he admitted.

"That memory of yours is sharp as ever I see," she ribbed him.

"It's very sharp, I'll have you know."

"Celeste just got in, hold on..." Daniel announced. There was a shuffle before they heard Celeste quietly reprimand Daniel for starting without her.

"Mom!"

"Celeste, honey."

"Am I on speaker?"

"You are, sweetie. Dad's here too."

"I'm right here, sweetheart."

"Did Danny tell you?" Celeste excitedly asked.

"Tell us what?"

"My agent loved the pitch. We're going to publish them."

Camille looked up at Ken standing behind her, and into the phone's receiver.

"Publish what, dear?"

"The letters. You and Dad's story. Isn't that wonderful?"

"Does that mean we'll have to sit through more interviews?" Ken asked.

"Not too many more."

"You're going publish... *all* the letters?" asked an apprehensive Camille.

Celeste tread carefully. "Well... I know they're personal, Mom but they're priceless. We'll leave out a few if you really want, but you know. I'd rather not."

"Can't this wait until we're dead, Celeste?" Camille pleaded with distaste.

"Absolutely not."

"You can leave all my spicy ones in, sweetheart."

"I will, Dad," Celeste giggled.

"Ask if they got to the pictures yet," Daniel asked in the background.

"Mom, click on the file that says 'pictures.'"

Ken and Camille chuckled with delight when they went through the treasure trove of memories, the cracked, yellow remains of their vivid youth, each from their respective families. Clearly, Celeste had done some digging.

Camille scrolled down further and let out a gasp of shock, her jaw instantly to the floor again. She covered her hand with her mouth.

There was silence on Celeste and Daniel's end of the phone as well, assuming the pair had gotten to the pictures of Carl. Some from his childhood, unseen by either of them. There was even a picture of him in his uniform.

Finally, there was a picture of him overseas, with the caption "eating time with U.S. Marines." A dozen or so colored soldiers carrying tin cups and saucers, mugging for the camera. One solitary white face in the far right, the youngest version of her husband she'd ever seen.

"How on Earth, Celeste..."

"Hundreds of hours looking through microfiche. Possibly thousands."

"Dad?"

Camille looked behind her but Ken was gone, the phone left on the buffet table next to her. Camille was quiet.

"Your dad had to step away from the computer, sweetheart," she explained.

"Oh no, I've upset him."

"No honey, he's touched, that's all. I'm sure of it. It's just emotional. We're both a little... astounded, honestly. You've done an amazing job."

Camille finished up with Celeste on the phone before making her way to the back porch, where her husband was alone on the porch swing silently weeping. She sat down next to him with a hand rubbing his back.

"I'm sorry," he cried. "But it's still so fresh. It's uncanny."

"We can tell her if it's too much," Camille suggested. "She'll be disappointed, but she'll understand."

"No. No, it's beautiful," he said, straightening his back.

Camille laid her head on his shoulder. "Everyone's gonna

know our business."

"Everyone you're worried about is already dead," Ken sniffed.

"That's true."

"Ol' Drew's gonna shit a brick."

Andrew McCain was Camille's age and lived in an upscale nursing home not far from them. He was still sharp but a little less mobile than the two of them. He was doing a lot better in a home than he was with his family, who wasn't exactly running his fan club.

"You should send him a copy. Be a good excuse to give him one last thrill."

"He won't read it."

"He'll have someone else read it."

Ken laid his head on hers still resting on his shoulder. "Life is wild, sweetheart."

"It is."

"People are going to actually know they were here. And what they did. And all because of you Camille, dear."

Camille raised up her head. "Me? It'll be because of you."

"Because of us. Because of that little sleuth you made."

"We made," she laid her head back down. Promptly his returned on top of hers. The porch swing slowly swayed as they overlooked the secluded woodsy property.

"I think I finally understand what it was all about."

"I don't think we'll ever get to that. But time has a way about it, doesn't it?"

"Indeed."

"Mm."

They swayed a little longer before Camille got up to resume her task with the rose bushes.

"What do you want for dinner, Stan?"

"Don't worry about me, you finish up out here."

"Let's order something."

"Sounds good. Italian?"

"I was thinking seafood."

"Who's going to bring us seafood, sweetie?"

"I don't know," she relented, replacing her work gloves. "Maybe it's just the baked potato I want."

"I'm a very old man, Camille," Ken whined. "Show me some mercy."

"Just order anything, I'm not that hungry anyway," she shrugged.

Ken just hung his head with a sigh, feeling doomed from the start. It was some kind of Art of War tactic, he was certain.

"Here goes nothin'," Ken said to himself, venturing back into the empty house.

Join the C.L. Donley Mailing List!

Let me keep in touch with you and let you know about my latest releases, works in progress and other fun exclusives! Sign up now at https://www.subscribepage.com/CLDMLLanding

About the Author

You can connect with me on:

- https://cldonley.com
- https://twitter.com/C_L_Donley
- https://facebook.com/amarascalling
- https://www.bookbub.com/profile/c-l-donley

Subscribe to my newsletter:

- https://www.subscribepage.com/CLDMLLanding

Also by C. L. Donley

Check out more of these fan favorites!

Perfect Harmony
When billionaire mogul Gerald Hawthorne dies, he leaves behind an ultimatum for his son Ethan: in order to get the portion of his allotted inheritance, he must marry the woman who had taken care of him in his final days, Nurse Harmony Rhoades. Chaos ensues as Harmony finds herself playing the role of wife when Ethan loses his memory in an accident.

The King's Vizier
King Khoury of Manaf relies on his trusted vizier, Mazigh, to convince Princess Asha of Ashwari to leave the only home she's ever known, and take her place as Queen of both her country and his. But the burgeoning relationship between the Princess and the King's vizier complicates things even further.

Leftovers With Benefits

When Kenya's husband Cecil unexpectedly leaves her for a white woman, she finds solace with the most unlikely new ally: Kevin Hayes, the other woman's ex.

The Billionaire's Club Series

Spend all day in la la land jet setting with this "plane Jane meets billionaire" trilogy about three couples that are as different as the individuals are from each other. Exotic locales, destination weddings, sex contracts, secret babies, and all the "happily ever afters" you could ever want!